Sean P

From the Little the Much is Known

Dedicated to my lovely wife, Dixie.

Part One

Àite nan Con

The Place of Dogs

Jennifer MacGregor found herself ascending the gentle slope of High Rock Avenue as she made her way to the western entrance of Cairn Park – a small rocky hilltop that surveyed the sleepy township of Esquimalt, British Columbia. The steep rolling slopes of the hill, with the deep scars of its ancient glacial past – ragged, violent cuts now covered in a thick carpet of soft verdant mosses, stone crop, lichens, and all beneath a weathered crown thick with Douglas fir, arbutus, and Garry oak – was one of the rare green spaces in the township located on the western border of Victoria.

Jennifer found it a secret pleasure to cut through the peaceful sylvan green on her way home from school.

Today it was an unusually quiet solitude, with only a few passing children and dog owners who let their animals off leash to roam the thick undergrowth of daphne, Oregon grape, Indian plum, and invasive English holly and Himalayan blackberry. Jennifer ascended the forty-three steps up to the narrow walking trail and then stepped to the left onto a narrow, winding dirt path that meandered over rocks and roots worn smooth by decades of foot traffic. The path that ambled with an air of blissful dreaminess over tall rounded rock, skirting loose stones left behind by a long forgotten glacier, and beside Douglas fir and oak long ago fallen in death, was alive with sounds and smells as chestnut-backed chickadees, juncos, robins, and nuthatches flitted amongst the towering trees and dense brush. Even the vague scent of Earle Grey tea from the local daphne plants filled the air, Jennifer noted with a smile.

Jennifer paused as she heard a familiar high pitched chirp, and a moment of examining the brilliant blue sky that leaked through the thick canopy above allowed her a rare glimpse of a diving hummingbird – an Anna's hummingbird, if she was correct. The chirp and the aggressive movements were territorial; there was a nest somewhere close by. A smile formed when she spied a Bewick's wren flitting amongst the shiny pointed leaves of an Oregon grape. It moved from branch to branch in sharp nervous leaps. Crouching onto the warm earth, Jennifer got a better look, and the small smile on her face grew. The wren plucked at the air with its beak and with a "*spzzz pit*" squeak, disappeared into the shadows.

"Where are you going?" Jennifer whispered as the wren reappeared. The tiny bird darted into a pile of dried oak leaves, rustled for a few noisy moments and then re-emerged. "Back again are you?"

A dog barked; it appeared on the path before her, and Jennifer stood up with the haste of someone being caught in an embarrassing situation. The wren disappeared, and the dog, a panting Lhasa Apso wrapped in a pink jewelled coat, ran up and sniffed her feet before barking again.

"Clio, stop it!" snapped the owner, a woman in her sixties wearing leggings and a sweatshirt. "Come along."

Jennifer stepped aside and lowered her eyes. The woman and her dog passed by and disappeared around a rock. A peep and buzz sounded and Jennifer crouched down to spy the wren again, rustling in the brush. "Are you back again?" she asked as she squatted to peer into the shadows. The wren pecked at the leaves and grass and then darted to another bush a few meters away. "Have a good day," she said as she stood. Moving north, she climbed over rounded upturned bowls of etched stone thick with moist rock moss. She paused for a few moments, running her hand over the moss to touch the luxurious green shroud. It had the softness of a kitten's fur, a silky carpet alive beneath her fingertips.

Back on the path, the uneven footing over rock and tree root slowed Jennifer – a blessing that gave her time to enjoy the smells of warm earth and stone, and the sounds of the birds that flitted amongst the darkened canopy. Not all was beauty, however, she noted with a slight scowl. There was garbage – candy wrappers and water bottles, and graffiti – taggers had painted the heavily cragged bark of the Douglas firs with incomprehensible markings in blue spray paint. She hated it, but she understood that this was no pristine landscape. Located in the middle of a small township within the city of Victoria, this was a well-used park and she had to find solace in the fact that at least it didn't look too well used.

After picking a long stalk of blue wildrye grass, she proceeded over the rough ground to the cairn. Built in the 1960's, the weathered circular stone cairn with its patinated brass tablet pointing out prominent features – both manmade and natural – and their distances, was situated on the highest point of the hill. It was a bare rocky hilltop – a tonsure of scarred stone, dirt, and worn asphalt surrounded by luxurious grass and groves of stunted and misshapen Garry oak. Tall waving stalks of wildrye, bentgrass, sweetgrass, and orchardgrass, and crooked arbutus thickened the hill below the cairn while narrow strands of glossy Oregon grape with leaves turning scarlet in the fall waved occasionally in the light breeze. The wide open vista before her extended to the towering snow-capped Olympic Mountains in the south and the distant West Coast mountains in the north and allowed for an unhindered view of Victoria and its famous hills, Mount Tolmie and Mount Douglas to the northeast.

The early October sun was brilliant, and as a cool breeze rolled in from the southeast, it still cast a delightfully warm blanket over the hilltop so recently bathed in the long, hot summer of a west coast summer. Jennifer sat on the edge of the cairn, felt the heat of the brass tablet absorb through her leggings, and closed her eyes. The fleeting warmth of the air settled on her, and the burning hate she had felt at school slowly faded to be replaced by the sadness that always seemed to inhabit her. She tried to shake it off – to push past the unsettling feeling and the nebulous notions of guilt that plagued her. As tears rose in her eyes and her lip quivered, the vague imagery lurking so deeply in her soul rose through the depths of unconscious denial and emotional subterfuge to appear in her waking mind – the red plastic ball at rest on the seat, the laughing eyes in the rear view mirror, the truck grill of an eighteen wheeler, the shadowy memory of a hand, and the faint words, "I love you."

Jennifer buried her face in her hands and sobbed. Slowly, the disjointed memories faded back into their distant caliginous holding, and she wiped her eyes and nose with her sleeve. The darkness passed, the sun burned through the pain and misery, and Jennifer breathed a heavy sigh. Yet her face crumpled into tears again and she buried it in her hands. The memories, benign in their individuality, were horrific as a collection.

The accident had happened seven months before. A drive to Duncan to see a friend of her father's; the rain pelting down as an early March gale roared over the southern tip of Vancouver Island. Traffic on the often treacherous Malahat Drive was heavy with the oncoming lights blinding in the pouring rain; chatter from her little brother about a Lego set he wanted for his birthday in April was a distraction.

Then nothing.

Jennifer woke up two days later with her arm in a cast and her mother sobbing beside her.

Her father and little brother were dead.

It had taken months, over the long solitary spring and summer, to even begin to get used to the loneliness – no little brother to look after or to annoy her with his incessant teasing; no father to lavish her with the love and attention that only a doting father could. There was nothing now – just emptiness.

Wiping her nose again, Jennifer stood up and brushed the dust off of her leggings. It was time to leave, time to go home to her mother. The path down the hill was short and wound through the wild grasses that had grown tall and faded to a dry golden hue in the heat of the summer, but were again growing luxurious in the autumn. She crossed the old ball field at the base of the hill; the flat, desiccated field muddy and churned from the wet of first hard rains of autumn was now filled with dogs and their owners and children going home from school. She picked up her pace, for she knew Brian Howard and his toadies would be scouring the area looking for blood.

* * * * *

It happened again: Brian playing the bully and picking at her after a meeting with school councillor.

The tow haired brute with fat lips and a dull look in his brown eyes leaned over slightly and asked with a hiss as she sat down, "How's crazy town today?"

Snickers erupted from the children around her but Jennifer said nothing. "You look like you're going to cry," Brian mocked with the makings of a smile that revealed his missing front teeth. "Your mommy cries like that too," he added with an affected sniffle.

Jennifer felt the rage course through her for only a moment before she leaned over and struck Brian in the face with her workbook. It took the boy by surprise, and a trickle of blood ran from a cut on his nose. His eyes tearing at the pain, he touched the blood on the cut and looked at her in shock.

"Who's crying now?" Jennifer hissed as she sat back in her seat and calmly placed the book on her desk.

The commotion, the sudden chatter, and the giggles wrenched the attention of her teacher, Ms. Burbank, from the chalk board. She looked about the classroom and then focused on Jennifer and Brian. "What's going on back there?" she asked. She spied the blood on Brian's nose and walked towards them with a purpose. "I asked a question, you two. What is going on?"

"Jennifer hit me!" Brian cried as he brushed his hand over the cut. "She cut my nose with her book!"

"Is this true, Jenny?" Ms. Burbank asked as she crossed her arms and took on the stern look of a judge. "Did you hit Brian with a book?"

"Yes."

Ms. Burbank sighed and dropped her arms, "Alright then, time for some reflection with the Principal."

Brian Howard couldn't help himself; he chuckled out loud.

"I wonder if there might be more to your part in this, Brian," Ms. Burbank said after pausing, "but the bloody nose a girl gave you might just make it even. Go see the nurse and she'll clean you up."

The class guffawed, Ms. Burbank blushed, and Jennifer held her books tight to her chest and allowed herself to be led out. In the hallway Ms. Burbank paused and leaned against the lockers. "What did he say?" she asked as she held a hand to her forehead. "Was it about your mother again?"

Jennifer's chin dropped to her chest. "Yes," she breathed.

"I'd like to say ignore him, but I know you can't," Ms. Burbank remonstrated with a hand resting on Jennifer's shoulder. "I'll move you away from him."

"No," Jennifer protested. "I won't let him have the satisfaction."

Ms. Burbank didn't look convinced, however, she nodded. "Okay, but at the same time, I can't have you belting him with a book every time he opens his mouth."

"After a while, maybe he'll stop opening his mouth," Jennifer replied, an angry glint in her eye.

"Violence won't solve your problems, Jenny," Ms. Burbank said. "It's only going to make them worse. Come along."

* * * * *

Jennifer was halfway across the field when she spotted Brian and three other boys entering from the southern entrance of the park. She froze, hoping they would look past her, but Brian's eyes were keen; he pointed and roared. The four of them began running towards her, their clenched fists promising a beating as vicious as their breathless curses.

Jennifer spun like a startled doe and bounded back up the path. She cut left and leapt into the heavy brush, wriggling past a pair of hoary, bent oaks and into a stand of towering firs. There was no trail here and she found herself scrambling over tall bulbous humps of moss-covered stone and long fallen trunks and into the grasping thorns of a blackberry patch. She felt her clothes pulling and tearing, felt the searing pain as the canes wrapped around her legs and the thorns bit deep into her flesh, and then she heard the triumphant shouts of the boys as they caught up to her. Gritting her teeth against the pain, Jennifer pushed and writhed in the clutching canes until she finally fell out of them and into an open rocky basin with a carpet of dried arbutus leaves on its floor. Bleeding, she rose unsteadily to her feet, as if a newborn colt, while the four boys pushed through a thicket of snowberry.

"There she is! Get her!"

With a cry, Jennifer made for another stony rise, but one of the boys got close enough to give her a push. Tottering in her haste, she tripped on a branch and fell on the rock, ripping her leggings and scraping her knee.

"Gotcha now," Brian said as he heaved like a bellows, and the other three – like-minded imbecilic confederates, Jennifer thought fleetingly – clenched their fists and prepared to kick her half supine form. "Nobody gives me a bloody nose, 'specially not a fucking girl!" he said as he pointed to the cut with a fat finger. He gave her a kick on the thigh and guffawed at her yelp of pain. "Stand up!" he shouted. The other three boys laughed, threatened violence, and then froze at the sound of an approaching, barking dog.

It was coming close, and fast.

"What the hell?" Brian shouted at the sudden crashing sound behind him. From a wall of brush exploded a Golden Retriever, its lips drawn back in rage and its eyes fixed on Brian. The animal charged and came to a halt a foot before the boy. Barking and growling, jumping and charging – it bared its gnashing teeth. Brian cried out in fear and aimed a few clumsy kicks as he stumbled backwards while the others boys fled in panic.

As the dog pinned Brian against a wall of rock and Jennifer rose to her feet, a voice could be heard shouting, "Leon! Leon, get back here!"

"Your dog's here!" Brian shrieked in panic. Jennifer felt a grin form as she saw the normally boorish bully was now near tears.

"Leon!" shouted the dog's owner as he ran up the path. He was balding and overweight, his button-down shirt open and damp with sweat. "Leon, stop!" He grabbed the dog's collar and said with disbelief as he wrestled the roaring animal back, "I'm sorry, kids. I've never seen him do this before!"

"Stupid dog!" Brian blubbered as he turned and ran down the path. The man followed him for a moment with his gaze before he turned his attention back to Jennifer. "I'm sorry, Miss, I hope Leon didn't hurt you." He looked at her cuts and torn clothing, worry growing on his sweaty face. "You look hurt. Oh, I hope to God that Leon didn't do that."

"No," Jennifer replied as she tried to straighten out her ripped clothing. The man continued to eye the torn clothing, scratches, and dripping blood.

"Are you okay?" He was petting the dog which was sitting at his feet and panting. The dog had assumed the normal serene kindliness of the breed and Jennifer held out her hand to be sniffed. "I've never heard Leon even growl before," the man said, his eyes still wide with shock. "We were out in the middle of the field when he bolted – right out of the blue, he just bolted. You'd think someone had called him; he took off so abruptly and so fast," he continued with a shake of his head. "You sure you're okay?"

"Yeah," Jennifer said with a nod, "thanks." She reached out and patted the frothy muzzle of the dog. "Thanks, Leon."

The man and his dog left, and Jennifer, with a cautious look around her, found the trail and made her way back to the field. The unusually warm day had brought out more dog owners and a few older teens tossing a Frisbee. It appeared safe, and Jennifer limped out of the brush and onto the field. Brian and his followers were gone and Jennifer heaved a sigh of relief. She was safe, at least until Monday, when this whole painful drama would be repeated.

Hoisting her backpack, Jennifer began plodding towards the southern entrance of the park. The air around her seemed to radiate misery and she brushed her eyes again as tears began to fall. As she continued on, Jennifer felt her hearing begin to dull; the sound of barking dogs and laughing children faded until silence – deep overpowering silence – claimed her awareness. She stopped, wiped her eyes, and then looked around frantically as she placed her hands over her ears and then tapped them. No sound, just the dull thump of her fingers hitting her ears; they were blocked, as if she had a cold.

From the silence, whispers began to fill her mind; high and slight, barely audible words that were unintelligible and strangely foreign. She looked around, her eyes darting to the dogs and children running around on the field and to the trees and rock. Where was it coming from? Was something wrong with her ears? More sounds; talking, deep, croaking giggles, maybe even singing? The sounds were so faint, a mere suggestion yet frighteningly real. Within the penetrating murmur, she discerned a voice – cavernous, old, and soothing as a low murmuring brook.

When the wild flowers were springing
And the woodlands were ringing.
To be listening to her singing
Was rapture to me.

Then a figure caught her eye.

Sitting off to the right upon a low hump of mossy rock amongst a brood of low lying deer fern was a dog. It was no ordinary dog that brought Jennifer up short, however. The dog was a massive creature with greying black wiry hair and a powerful body stooped with age. The dog's enormous teeth were exposed as it panted and it gazed upon her in the warm afternoon with a curious fixation. She recognized the breed – an Irish wolfhound – an imposing and frightening creature that might have terrified her with its prodigious size and intense gaze had a feeling of placidity not come over her as she and the creature regarded each other. The feeling persisted and the burdens of the day began to fall away. An odd tranquility arose within her and the strangulating fears vanished to be replaced with an exceptional euphoria.

Jennifer felt a smile form on her lips.

For a few more moments the curious connection endured and then the animal rose stiffly to its feet, turned, and cast a final glance at her before disappearing into the shadows of the twisted Garry oaks.

Jennifer's hearing slowly returned and the sounds of the park again filled her ears.

"Uh, that was strange," she muttered as she fingered her ears and looked upon the mossy rock for a few more moments.

Jennifer smiled again. The first real smile she had had in many days.

Part Two

Gabhaidh an Connadh Fliuch, ach cha Ghabh a' Chlach

Wet Fuel will Burn but Stones Won't

Jennifer dropped her backpack at the door and limped to the bathroom. After flicking on the light, she rummaged in the cupboard above the toilet until she found a box of Band-Aids and a tube of ointment. Taking both, she placed them on the sink and looked at herself in the mirror. Her short dark curls, falling just below her ears, were matted with grass, a few thorns, and leaves. Her face, a dusky Mediterranean hue from her mother's Greek blood, had a scrape near the chin from the rocks, and a thin slash across her nose from a blackberry thorn. Her eyes, a piercing blue from her father, were red from her earlier tears while the skin around them was puffy. Sighing, she dabbed ointment on the scrape and cut on her face, and then proceeded to wash her arms and hands to remove the dried blood and dirt. After cleaning her legs and applying a few Band-Aids to the crisscross of gashes on her legs and her skinned knee, she changed her clothes and made her way to the kitchen for a snack.

The basement suite was empty – her mother wouldn't be home from her job as a legal assistant until at least 5:30 p.m., so she had an hour and a half to do homework and prepare supper. Listening to music on her iPod, she made short work of her math and science homework, then she started preparations for a pan of spaghetti sauce and a pot of pasta for supper. She set the table for two, then went into her tiny bedroom – barely larger than a closet – which contained her bed and a small dresser. She folded a basket of laundry then sat on the edge of her bed and fought the sudden rush of tears.

Brian Howard and his friends had terrified her. What would he have done had the dog not shown up? She wondered as she wrung her hands. Wiping her eyes with her sleeve, she looked up to the ceiling in an effort to compose herself. Her mother would be home soon and she hardly felt like talking to her about this. Would those boys have hurt her? Would they have done...worse? Brian had been furious, truly out of control. Could she have become another Reena Virk? That girl who had been killed by other teens so many years before under the Craigflower Bridge? She began to shake as fear overwhelmed her. How could she go back to school with those boys there ready to do... what? Hurt her? Kill her?

No, Jennifer shook her head. It couldn't come to that. The boys might have punched and kicked her, but they wouldn't have done anything else – at least not in the park, not in the glare of day. At night though, she mused wretchedly as she reached for a tissue to blow her nose, what about then? She decided she needed to concentrate on avoiding Brian and his friends both within school and without. It would be difficult, however, unless she brought Ms. Burbank into her confidence, but telling on Brian would make a bad situation so much worse. A line had been crossed this time – she knew deep down that the bullying by this boy had been nothing compared to what was to come. She had seen it in his eyes – a real hatred, a real threat of violence that he could no longer control. Yes, she realized as new tears formed, had that dog not come along, she would have been hurt.

Badly.

Wiping her face, Jennifer fought to control her overwhelming emotions. Her shaking hands, her pounding heart, and the sick feeling in her stomach belied her hopeless efforts and she allowed herself to fall back onto her bed and weep. All control disappeared and her shoulders shuddered with great wracking sobs as she pulled herself foetal and hugged herself. The shadowy memories – the red ball, the eyes in the rear view mirror, and the truck grill – all flooded back upon her. A great roiling wave of abject despondency grasped her and enfolded her in a blanket of mournful misery and only great tears and gulping wails could assuage the anguish holding her. Slowly, like the fury of a gale, the wretched torment passed, and Jennifer quieted. Reaching for more tissue, she dabbed her swollen eyes and blew her nose. A glance at the clock said she had less than fifteen minutes before her mother returned and she would need that time to acquit herself of the emotions tearing her apart.

Breathing a huge sigh, Jennifer went back to the kitchen to check on supper. Gritting her teeth, she reaffirmed her plans for dealing with Brian and his friends. She would have to talk to Ms. Burbank even if it meant ratting them out. The consequences of not doing so didn't seem much worse than if she did, for their desire for violent revenge was obvious.

* * * * *

"How was school today?" Jennifer's mother grunted as she entered the door and dropped her purse on the kitchen counter. After hanging her jacket on the hook behind the door, she walked into the diminutive kitchen – a mere afterthought in the design of the basement suite – and flopped into a chair. "Smells good," she added as she unzipped her boots.

Jennifer stirred the pot of pasta sauce and hoped the redness of her eyes had faded. "Alright," she replied in measured tones. "Pretty quiet day really."

Helene MacGregor yawned as she glanced at her daughter. "How was your councillor appointment today?"

"Fine."

"Anything new?"

"No."

"As talkative as ever," Helene said with a sour chuckle. "Come on, Jenny, there must be more to it than that?"

Jennifer noted her mother's accent, a faded Greek that reasserted itself whenever she was aggravated. It was best for both if that was avoided, so she forced herself to open up. "We talked about how school was, about whether I should take soccer camp in the spring or if I should try swimming instead." Jennifer paused. "Then she asked me about the accident again."

Standing up, Helene walked to the cupboard and pulled out a wine glass. After placing it on the table, she eased a bottle of wine from a paper bag she had placed by her boots and then unscrewed the cap. "And?" she asked as she poured herself a generous measure. "Do you remember anything yet?"

"No," Jennifer replied as she lifted the boiling pot of spaghetti off the burner. She poured the pot's contents into a stained colander.

Helene leaned back in her chair and took a long sip. "I wonder when you will remember?" she complained. She suddenly fixed her gaze upon her daughter. "I wonder when you will be able to tell me what happened."

Jennifer could feel it as she rocked the colander to remove the last of the water from the noodles, that penetrating hatred as her mother probed for answers she did not have. Jennifer MacGregor was the last person to see her father alive and her mother had not forgiven her for it. There was an atmosphere of perpetual accusation when they were together, an unspoken question between them that had not been answered. Jennifer wondered what exactly her mother wanted – what simple answer would assuage the crippling grief that even now, seven months after the death of her husband and son, wracked her very soul and tore her apart inside? She paused before pouring the pasta into the sauce. A ball on a seat, eyes in the rear view mirror, and a raised bloody hand; three disjointed images, enigmatic yet compelling, were all she had.

"Well," Helene said with a voice now filled with disinterest as she swirled the diminishing level of wine in her glass, "at least you're predictable, Jenny."

Jennifer felt her shoulders slump for a moment before a flash of anger coursed through her. For a passing moment she felt a near uncontrollable desire to throw the pot of piping hot pasta sauce at her mother, to inflict pain upon her as she had done to her daughter these past seven months. The moment passed; her pounding heart began to slow, her hands ceased to shake, and she relaxed the grip on the pot. She released her breath – a slow sigh that evaporated some of her rage. As quickly though, the sudden emotional void filled with pain. A hurt that would not, could not end, as her mother gazed upon her with eyes glazing over.

"Are you hungry?" Jennifer asked as she placed a bowl beside the colander. Helene nodded once and poured herself another glass.

* * * * *

The dishes were done, drying in the rack with the washcloth placed over the tap. Jennifer glanced at her mother, now bleary-eyed as she gazed upon the empty bottle. Beside it, a small orange container of pills lay on its side. Her mother had taken a pill before supper and it was accentuating the effects of the alcohol.

"Your father didn't want to go to Duncan," Helene slurred as she rested her forehead in her hand. "Did you know that?"

"No," Jennifer replied as she placed the hand towel on the hanger. She took a seat opposite her mother, resting her chin in her hands.

"He had wanted to stay home as we were planning to go out for supper that evening. Our anniversary was on the Tuesday, and we thought, it being a Saturday, that we should go out. My friend Gwen was to look after you and your brother." Helene looked away and smiled – a sickly effort – and then continued, "But he decided to take you and Jacob to Duncan for the day. You wanted to see Melanie, remember?"

It was subtle – the reminder that although her father was seeing his old friend, it had begun with Jennifer wanting to see Melanie. The blame, however, was obvious. The trip up island would never have been made, the accident would not have occurred, and her father and brother would not have died if she had not asked to see her friend. That one simple request had put a series of tragic events in motion; that one simple request was now the foundation of her mother's hatred. Jennifer sat up straight and stared into her mother's reddened eyes now dark, loveless, and angry. The warm laughing mother of her memories was gone, replaced by the cold, vengeful creature before her. The barbs were sharp, meant to be sent deep, and meant to hurt. Her mother could not bring herself to strike her daughter with her hands, but she would punish her with her words.

Helene MacGregor broke the spell of silence between them. She looked away from the fury of her daughter's eyes, slowly rose to her feet, and shuffled towards the bag by the door. From it, she lifted a second bottle of wine. After unscrewing the top, she poured herself a generous measure. "We were to go out to Pagliacci's that night. We had a reservation and we were going to take a cab while Gwen watched you. It was our fifteenth anniversary," she continued after a long sip of wine. "Fifteen years and it had been exactly a year since we had gone out alone. It was to have been a very special evening."

Jennifer clenched her fists to stop the trembling. Anger coursed through her as she listened to her mother's drunken reminiscences. Never before had she felt such hatred for the woman before her. As her mother described the menu, the wine, the conversation, all of the imagined joy that the evening would have held, and all the intense happiness that seven months of delusional rumination had created, Jennifer felt her skin grow cold and her heart beat nearly to bursting. Every word was a stab, another infliction of pain, another cowardly judgement of guilt. Her mother was not so brave as to come out and make her accusations plainly – she was content to attack obliquely.

"What else were you going to do?" Jennifer queried as she stared hard at the wreck of her mother. "Were you going to go dancing? A nice romantic walk along the Causeway? Maybe more drinking and getting wrecked?"

Helene snapped from her inebriated musing. "Don't you dare!" she snarled as she sat forward. Her chin was thrust out and her fists were clenched. "It's my memory! Don't you dare ruin it!"

Jennifer leaned back; she suddenly deflated before the fury of her mother with the hot tears rolling down her cheeks and the furious twitch of her lip.

"Don't you dare speak to my memories. They're all I have left!" her mother seethed. "I have nothing left!"

"There's me," Jennifer whispered.

Helene blinked away the tears. After a long pause she said brokenly. "I have nothing left." Abruptly she stood, picked up her glass of wine and the bottle, and left the kitchen.

Jennifer wiped her eyes. Nothing had been said that Jennifer did not know or at least suspect. The blame and her guilt in her mother's eyes was a fact that she had already gathered. The animosity she had long suspected, and now her mother's words confirmed it; her hatred was complete. Any desperate hope that her mother could ever love her again was gone.

Part Three

An Coinneamh Roghainn

Sunset approached as Jennifer sat quietly in a faded plastic Adirondack chair in the backyard. For an hour she had been motionless as she listened to the world around her – a pair of Stellar's jays making their piercing shrieks in the gathering dusk as they sought each other out, a shockingly loud 'chirp' of a hummingbird challenging a territorial rival, children playing on a trampoline two doors down, and the intermittent roar of an out of tune lawn mower in its efforts to mow the thick grass of an early October lawn. She heard the sounds, but they did not register in her mind. She stared blindly, her tears gone, her heart empty. She had nothing: she was nothing; even her mother still had capacity now for anger and hate. Jennifer was jealous of that, for at least her mother still felt something other than her wretched unhappiness. There were no such emotions now for her. She remembered little of her father and brother; her friends had long abandoned her; and there was no other family on Vancouver Island. She felt no connection to anyone. She could feel no anger; not even regret intruded upon her soundless solitude.

Nothing.

Over the noises of life that enveloped her, Jennifer suddenly became aware of a new sound: weeping. It should have been heartbreaking to hear such an emotional torrent, but Jennifer felt nothing. She glanced at the window of her mother's bedroom. It was cracked open, and from it came the sounds of lamenting, an emotional release that had no boundaries. Jennifer stood and entered the house. It was dark inside as dusk settled. No lights were on in the hallway and she crept towards the wailing in her mother's bedroom. A thin sliver of light marked the end of the darkened hallway for the door to the bedroom was ajar. She crept to the door, settled on one knee and peered inside.

Helene MacGregor rested a photo of her family upon her knee. Tears coursed down her reddened cheeks and her mouth worked brokenly over the keening coming from her lips. Jennifer remembered the picture; it had been taken months before the accident, at the Wal-Mart in Langford. A simple family photo against a cheap sky coloured background with everyone dressed in their inexpensive best. It was their first and only family photo.

Wiping the teardrops from the glass, Helene MacGregor lifted the photo and held it to her heart. Her moans and cries began again, the tears rolled down her cheeks and she fell back on the bed. Such remorse, such complete misery finally pierced Jennifer's hardened and empty heart. She felt tears fill her eyes as she backed away from the door.

Jennifer knew her tears were not for her mother. She walked into the kitchen and sat at the table. Why, she wondered, was she doing this? Why was she even here? There was nothing for her here. Misery overwhelmed her as her tears fell; she mourned the loss of her family, the loss of her childhood, and the loss of her future.

She had nothing; she was nothing.

Like a deluge she was suddenly overwhelmed by guilt, an indescribable feeling that she was somehow to blame. She placed her face in her hands and wept. What could she do? Why was she enduring this? For several minutes she cried softly and then she raised her face and wiped her eyes and nose with her sleeve.

Jennifer noticed the bottle of pills on the table.

Picking up the container, she sniffled as she looked at the label on the container: OxyContin. She wasn't sure where her mother got them – her mother rarely ever went to a doctor – but she knew they were powerful. They were a drug that lulled her mother into deep unconsciousness even without the addition of alcohol. She opened the cap and noted it was half-full. There were no directions on how many to take but her mother never took more than one, and she was an adult. Jennifer tipped the container and four pills rolled into her hand.

That would do, she thought.

Pocketing the pills, Jennifer moved to the table with the telephone and pulled a notepad and pen from the drawer. She wrote a note to her mother – she would stay the night at Karen's, an acquaintance of hers that her mother had met once. She would be away all the day but would be home for supper.

That would buy her time.

Jennifer pulled on her jacket to fight the growing chill of the autumn evening. As she grasped the door handle, she looked for one last time around the darkened house. The sounds from her mother's room had stopped and she had likely passed out. Now silence reined – a deadness of sound that matched the deadness of love that gripped her home.

"Good-bye," she whispered.

Jennifer walked down the road with her hands thrust in her pockets and the hood of her jacket pulled up over her head. The darkness was nearly complete save for a last faint crimson bar across the western sky. Stars shone brightly as did the waxing moon overhead. Before her, the singular darkness of High Rock loomed, and as she crossed Lampson Street and turned onto Rock Heights Avenue, the emerging presence grew. There was an odd comfort about that – a darkness where no street or house lights penetrated – a faint memory of the land two centuries before. The elderly trees and the mosses; there was a simple existence there that beckoned her with soft assuaging words.

A hundred meters on and she came to a narrow set of old, mossy, stone stairs that led to the rolling, folded stone of High Rock's northern face. She scrambled over the rock face, climbing the tortured stone that had been scraped smooth ten thousand years before. High Rock wasn't tall and it only took her a few minutes to climb it in the darkness. She arrived at the top, breathless, and took a seat on the rough stonework of the cairn. The heights overlooked the lights of Esquimalt, and Victoria to the east. The darkness of Gorge Vale golf course and the smaller hill and forest behind the Royal Canadian Navy's hospital were the only blemishes in the glow of illumination. To the west was the naval dockyard marked by tall cranes accented with flashing red lights.

It was quieter here, Jennifer thought, as her hand strayed to her pocket. Street noises were dulled by the height, though a distant ambulance broke the solace. She glanced behind her at the dark, brooding forest. In the soft moonlight, the twisted Garry oaks and arbutus should have taken on a frightening mien, but they did not. She felt a quiet contentment to be with them, as if they were silently watching her with a benevolent regard.

Jennifer's hand closed around the pills. She brought them forth and held them in her open palm. Was this the answer? The nondescript pills meant an end to all things – an end to the pain and suffering, an end to the ceaseless loneliness that held her. Jennifer felt the emotions churn within her, felt her heart pound as she pondered her decision. Her hand began to tremble as her thoughts wrestled for her actions.

It would be an end to the guilt.

Tears rose in her eyes again as she popped the pills into her mouth. It took effort to swallow them, but when she had, relief flooded her washing away the conflicting emotions with the finality of her decision. It was finished.

All of this was finished.

Jennifer stood and walked a short distance to a fold of rock. Between two rounded waves of tortured stone was a soft mossy bed and she lay down upon it. Fresh tears rolled down her cheeks and she cried once again for her father and brother. What had she done to cause the accident?

"I'm sorry," she said brokenly. "I'm so sorry."

Her emotions began to fade, like the soft, paling light of dusk. Jennifer became groggy, and her fading awareness knew the end was near. This was pleasant, she thought dully, just like going to sleep. Her final fleeting thought as her breathing grew soft was that maybe she would wake up and be with her father and brother. Her eyes grew sightless, and her breathing slowed and grew silent.

Jennifer drifted into an enveloping darkness.

* * * * *

The chill of the evening grew as the heat of the early autumn day was wafted away by the soft ocean breeze. The clinging warmth of the rock faded beneath the darkness and grew cold to the touch. A south-easterly wind plucked at the tall grasses as it hummed through the brooding forest bringing with it the faint brine smell of the ocean and the distant sounds of traffic. From a crevasse of stone in the deep shadows of the forest, wary and moving with slow purpose amongst the arbutus and oaks, a creature peered through the brush. It eased aside the leaves and the deer fern, and climbed the low summit to step out onto the open rock and asphalt surrounding the cairn. It glanced skyward at the thin bands of cloud crossing the moon's luminous face and at the canopy of dim stars above the ochre of the city glow. The creature closed its eyes, breathed deeply, and gripped the flower in its hand so much tighter. For a moment it stood motionless, and then with sudden determination it padded across the open rock and moved toward the supine form of Jennifer. The last few meters it moved in a crouch, as if unsure what to expect. Finally, it came to a rest on the hump of bald rock overlooking Jennifer.

She was pale and peaceful in the dim light, the creature noted with a sigh, so very peaceful now as death approached. The pinched sadness was gone – the disconsolate gloom that had marked her living face had been replaced by such lovely composed lines as she lay dying. To wake her was to wrench her from a new somnolence and contentment; it seemed such a hateful crime and yet, how could it allow her to give up so easily? The creature held the flower close to it as it crept forward. No, the compulsion to help was too strong. It must help her, must give her a chance. It could not turn its back on such sorrow.

The creature gently slipped the flower into Jennifer's hands, now cold and clasped over her abdomen. The tiny, bell-shaped petals stood out in the darkness, a faint alabaster luminescence against the shadow she lay in. White heather, the creature mused as it placed a thin weathered hand upon the girl's forehead. The flower had an ancient power even if it had not been grown in the Old World. Closing its eyes, it began to whisper soft words in the darkness. The wind picked up the words, held them close, like a mother's embrace, and then released them into the shadows of the awakening trees.

"Fo sgèith daraig a's guirme blàth.
Is luaith' fas, agus dreach a's buaine,
Bhrùchdas duilleach air anail na frois
'S an raon bhi seargta m'an cuairt dhi."

They were old words in an old language, the language of a far distant land and a far distant time.

The creature ran its fingers through the curled locks of Jennifer's hair. A melancholy mien crossed its face. Memories played across its deep mahogany eyes as it spoke:

"In the shade of the oak of greenest foliage,

Swiftly growing and shapely and long-lasting

Its leaves burst forth in the breath of a rain shower

While the ground is withered all around it."

There seemed to be an answer in the soft shaking of the leaves of the oaks and arbutus and the deep sonorous creak of the limbs of a towering fir. A smile formed on the hoary face of the creature. The leaves rustled more loudly and the sound of creaking increased. He whispered more words:

"Gus an crìon gu luaithre a' chlach,

'S an searg às le aois a' gheug so,

Gus an sguir na sruthan a ruith,

'S an deagh màthair-uisge nan slèibhte."

He placed a hand on the deeply lacerated rock and heard the soft, distant memory of the ice from ten thousand years before.

"Till stone crumbles to ash

And this branch withers away with age

Till streams cease to flow

And the sweet spring water from the mountains."

The grass and deer ferns waved in the breeze as the soft, laboured breathing of the girl faded into quiet, deep inhalations. A smile formed on her face.

"A young girl asleep," the creature muttered. "Wake up," it said as it sat back upon the stone. "Time tae come home."

Part Four

An t-innean Beag

The Little Anvil

The chill breeze abated in the hour after midnight. A rare silence descended upon the hill of High Rock as even the faint traffic noises ceased. The scratching of a shrew, the tenuous steps of a cautious rabbit, the shifting of a Barred owl on the branch of a fir – these were the only sounds to penetrate the darkened saturninity of the hilltop. Within the fold of mossy rock, Jennifer stirred, opened her eyes and looked into the sky. The stars were dimmed by the moon and the ochre of the city glow, yet the Big Dipper still stood out faintly to the north. A distant pinprick of light moved slowly across the darkness, a wavering wraith – burnished and clear then fading to darkness – a satellite no doubt. A fluttering shadow crossed her vision, a bat perhaps or a bird of the night. The twinkling lights of a distant airplane to the west disappeared into the high, thin cloud, then nothing but the moon and the stars.

"I'm alive," were the words that eased her from her murky consciousness. The realization was slow – a penetration of awareness that moved through the random imagery and sound of mere existence.

"Why?" she mouthed in a murmur as tears began to fill her eyes. She had summoned all of her courage and commitment to this. She had no hopes and dreams left – nothing to inspire her to stay. It should have worked; the long sleep should have come.

Instead, she was alive and awake.

Jennifer moved her hands to brush away the tears and it was then that she noticed the flower. For a moment she focused on it, wondered at the portent of the white heather, and then dropped it onto the grass. Jennifer brushed the tears from her eyes and looked upon the darkened hill and forest behind the Navy's diminutive hospital. "Why?" she repeated groggily.

"Why are you here, lass?"

Jennifer jerked her head at the croaking, bass voice and her heart skipped a beat. Had she really heard something? Were the words real? The voice sounded deep – a distant, hollow echo as if in a cave far below. Lifting her head, she looked about in the darkness; her heart was pounding as she eased herself up to sitting. There was nothing. No people, though the words had seemed so real. She lay back and closed her eyes.

"I ask again: why are you here?"

Jennifer struggled against her foggy consciousness. There *was* a voice, she thought. Again, she sat up and peered into the darkness; nothing moved.

"Who are you?" she demanded. "I can't see you."

Silence, then Jennifer noted a slight movement in the deep shadows to her left. It was small, an animal perhaps? She thought. It moved from the Stygian darkness into the dull light of the moon, and Jennifer froze, with eyes wide in shock, and gasped. A creature, hunched and wizened, stood before her. It was man-like, yet no taller than her knee.

"Hello, lass," it said in a slow, croaking voice as it squatted on the rock.

Jennifer's heart was pounding and her breath came short. She eased herself back from the creature until she pushed up against the lip of rock. "I'm dreaming," she replied after a long pause while she stared at the wondrous vision of the creature before her.

"No," the creature replied as it sat down with a rheumatic stiffness that suggested the feebleness of great age. It grunted, muttered, cleared its hoarse throat, and then finally sat still. "No, you're no' dreaming. I'm real."

Jennifer blinked her eyes and then rubbed them roughly. It had to be the pills, she thought. What else could it be?

"I'm hallucinating," she quavered without much conviction. Her voice broke with emotion and she coughed.

The creature nodded slowly, allowing a wane smile beneath its massive white moustache. It had a braided white beard that rested on its crossed legs. The hands were thin, almost skeletal, and they held a slender wooden staff with a single fluttering feather tied to the top. The face was old and wrinkled – a vision of something ancient – with eyebrows white as hoarfrost and jutting like cedar boughs.

The nose was Roman, a projecting beak beyond two dark eyes that glinted with merriment. A single braid of snowy hair fell below a peculiar woven hat that smelled of old cedar, and looked much like a woven Salish hat that she'd seen in her Humanities class. The creature wore a homespun plaid blanket belted at the waist that fell to its knees – black and white plaid with small brass buttons sewn on for ostentation. The legs were thin, covered in threadbare woven cedar bark trousers, while two booted feet emerged from the bottom. The voice was vaguely accented – a mere dream of its former thickness.

"You're no' hallucinating," it replied.

Jennifer closed her eyes and cupped her face in her hands. She had taken powerful prescription drugs that should have killed her, yet she had woken up almost clear headed. Now, as she sat in the darkness, a curious and impossible creature was keeping her company on a hilltop in Esquimalt outside of Victoria, British Columbia in 2015.

How could it be anything else but the pills? She gripped the skin of her forearm with her right hand and pinched it until her eyes streamed.

"I bet that hurt," the creature said over a deep, crackling chuckle.

Jennifer pointedly looked away. Should she just get up and leave? If she was merely hallucinating, then perhaps that was best. Yes, she thought as she moved with sluggish progress to roll onto her knees, walking away from this would definitely be for the best. On her hands and knees she paused as the ground began to spin; she was dizzy and her balance wavered.

"You should stay," the creature said.

"I should go," she replied automatically, as if the conversation with the creature was real. Jennifer clenched her teeth against the swimming in her head and looked up. She was facing the creature, but it was no longer there.

A colossal dog sat where the small shadowy figure had been.

Jennifer shrieked and fell back, pushing herself away with scrambling feet that dug up the grass and moss.

The muzzle of the dog was grey, the hair wiry and matted. It tilted its massive head slightly and its mouth opened in a pant. Jennifer recognized the breed, an Irish wolfhound – *the* Irish wolfhound that had watched her in the park that very afternoon.

"I know you," she breathed as she stared at the dog in wonder. Her fear faded and the pounding of her heart began to slow.

Licking its lips, the dog lay down on the rock. Its deep soulful eyes never leaving her.

Jennifer was held by the unfathomable, penetrating gaze for a few moments before she felt compelled to look away. When she returned her gaze, the dog was gone and the tiny creature had reappeared.

"Aye," it said as it pulled a long, curved wooden pipe from beneath the blanket, "you do know me." Placing the pipe in his mouth, he puffed – thin tendrils of sweet smelling smoke wafted around him. He had not lit it, she marvelled.

"How did you do that?" she asked as she shifted forward. Every movement was pregnant with caution. "How did you turn into a dog?"

"I am a dog if I so choose tae be," the creature replied with a careful smile. "I am what I desire you tae see."

"That doesn't explain how you do it," Jennifer persisted. She focused closely on the wizened creature. "Tell me," she breathed.

The creature considered her for a long moment as he sucked on his pipe. The aromatic cloud around him thickened and a curious halo settled around his filthy hat and grizzled head. "I can no more explain it, lass, as you can tell me why you breathe the air or why you dream. You just do and you just can. There are no obscure magic words, no wands, and no silly cantrips. If I choose tae be a dog, then I'm a dog," he concluded with a shrug of his shoulders.

Jennifer was dubious for a moment as the realization formed that she was discussing conjury with a mythical creature. "What's your name?" she asked.

"My name is Aeonghus[1], and I am a *ghille dubh*[2]," he said at length. The words were deep and nasal.

---

[1] Aeonghus – pronounced 'Angus'

[2] Ghille dubh – pronounced 'Yeela doo'

"What is that?" Jennifer held her hand across her mouth. "Are you some kind of," she paused as she fumbled for a word before finally whispering, "faerie or something?"

"A faerie?" Aeonghus replied as he cocked his head in surprise. He considered the question, puffing on his pipe and looking distracted for a time. "No," he replied primly, "no that's no' quite right."

Jennifer shook her head, incredulous at the thought – a faerie, in 2015? It was beyond imagining; it was foolishness that sounded like some badly written fantasy story. Talking to a faerie on a hilltop in Esquimalt, it was laughable in the extent of its ridiculousness.

"There's no such thing as faeries anyway," she concluded with a certain hollow vehemence.

"Is there no'?" the creature named Aeonghus brightened. He puffed on his pipe and then pointed the long, glistening stem at her. "I'm a squirrel then?" he replied, his words a deep plodding amble. "Maybe, I'm a talking racoon? Or perhaps," he said with the beginnings of a smile again, "I'm still that dream you think you're having? Go ahead, pinch yourself again and tell me what kind o' dream I am."

Jennifer gulped, felt the pace of her heart begin to quicken as she fought against the absurd reality that was trying so desperately to intrude. It was not possible. In a world of iPhones, Facebook, electric cars, and Netflix, there was no room for the possibility of a faerie.

"What are you then?" she asked. She would toy with that impossible notion for a moment, if only to gather enough information to finally banish it. Or perhaps, she would simply wake up.

The creature puffed on his pipe for a few more moments, "I've already said. I'm what was once called," he paused for a certain effect, "a *ghille dubh*."

"And what's that?" Jennifer's asked again in a voice beginning to quiver.

Aeonghus pointed his pipe stem towards the shadowy trees behind her. "Your folk many, many years ago would have seen me as a forest spirit." A wide, knowing smile crossed his weathered face.

Jennifer put her hand to her head. She felt faint. This couldn't be happening. She closed her eyes tightly and then opened them. The creature named Aeonghus was still there. "You're still here."

"Aye," Aeonghus replied slowly after puffing on his pipe. "I would imagine that it's no' every day you come face tae face with a *ghille dubh*. I'm no' sure what you could have done tae prepare for it."

There was a subtle scoffing timbre in Aeonghus' voice that penetrated the fear and wonder of the meeting. Jennifer found her eyes narrowing and the beat of her heart charged again, not from fear now, but from anger. Her fists clenched and she murmured, "There's no need to mock me."

"Ahh," Aeonghus replied as he moistened the stem of his pipe with his lips. "*Is fheàrr teine beag a gharas na teine mòr a loisgeas.*"

"What does that mean?"

Aeonghus gave her a long searching eye before replying, "The wee fire that warms is better than the great fire that burns."

Jennifer leaned back against the stone. She brought her hand to her mouth and held it there for a few moments. The air was cool and the soft breeze penetrated her thin clothing. She found herself shivering, a shocking sensation that suddenly drove home the fact that she couldn't be asleep. She glanced at the night lights of Victoria, and the distant headlights and brake lights from the sparse traffic. She looked up into the heavens and saw another aircraft high above. Tomorrow it would be Saturday, with five more days of school until the Thanksgiving Day long weekend in early October. She had a math test on Tuesday and a spelling test on Thursday. Wednesday was supposed to be soccer for gym and they would be beginning to study local mushrooms in science now that autumn had come and the fungi were becoming plentiful. She looked back upon Aeonghus who sat gazing upon her expectedly.

"Are you going to hurt me?"

Aeonghus pulled the pipe from his mouth. He tilted his head, gave her a quizzical look and asked, "Now, why would I do that?"

"I don't know," Jennifer replied as she pulled her knees to her chin. "I've never met a *ghille dubh* before."

Pointing the pipe stem at her again, Aeonghus replied, "You had the death look about you, lass. Why would I bring you back from that only tae hurt you?"

"You brought me back?" Jennifer asked as she unclasped her knees. "Why did you do that? Why didn't you just leave me be?"

A brittle silence followed, and Aeonghus placed the pipe back in his mouth. More smoke rose around him and then he said. "You are far too young tae begin the next journey."

Jennifer leaned against the rough stone. She was feeling faint again. A murky torpor rose around her, a thunder sounded in her ears, and her comprehension faded away from her.

Aeonghus slipped the pipe into the blanket belted around him, then rested his chin on his hand. For several minutes he focused on the lovely, youthful face before him, now once again serene in the pale light.

Peace.

If only she could find it in her waking. Like distant pounding surf, Aeonghus' voice poured forth the soft words in song:

> *'S do chaidreamh fada uam*
> *Gur tric mi ort a' smaointinn*
> *As d'aogais tha mi truagh*
> *'S mar a dèan mi d'fhaotainn*
> *Cha bhi mo shaoghal buan."*

A racoon appeared, curious at the words lifted by the breeze and pulled through the trees. It sat on its haunches and rubbed its paws together. Aeonghus smiled at the creature.

> *"When far from thee I sleep,*
> *But back to thee, my maiden,*
> *My restless thoughts shall sweep,*
> *And few shall be my years*
> *If without thee I must weep."*

Aeonghus closed his eyes and remembered.

Part Five

Sid Mar 'thaghadh Fionn a Chù.

Thus Would Fionn Choose his Hound.

The sounds of battle, an insinuating disquietude that on occasion, if the wind was right, brought the resonance of the horror of combat to the very doorstep of Aeonghus' modest home. He peered through the rolling mists that flowed like an ashen tide around the bare heights of *Sgor na Ciche*. He had been trying to ignore the sounds, to put aside the desire to look upon the events at the forested base of the mountain. The humans always fought, always killed each other, though it had been many years since he had heard a din such as this. He moved slowly to the entrance of the cave, a mere crack in the stone on the eastern shoulder of the mountain nicknamed the *Pap of Gleann Coe*, and peered at the forest not so far below. The sounds were louder, fading in and out with the cool wind. A tendril of mist moved by, obscuring the forest and the river Coe further below. When it cleared, he could see humans, hundreds of them, fair haired and carrying round shields and axes moving from the loch towards the trees lining the river.

Aeonghus crouched at the entrance and watched. To the west in Loch Levan, beyond the river Coe, lay dozens of longships – some beached on the mud at the mouth of the river while others rode gently at anchor. Tall and horrific figureheads dominated the single masted ships – dragons and monsters that caused Aeonghus to catch his breath in fear. There were more of the foreign humans – *Lochlannach* he had heard them called – than he had ever seen before and they were close to the river and moving quickly to the growing lines of their brethren. They were in the village west of the river, a collection of small dry stone houses roofed with sod, and it burned as the invaders moved about it. The people of Gleann Coe had fled deeper into their glen, leaving their men folk to fight off the ferocious *Lochlannach*. There were others here to help, he knew, for he had seen them the evening before – *Eireannach* – from the large island of Eire far to the west. There were a few hundred of them, powerful looking warriors in gleaming armour and earthy plaid with long moustaches and curling hair. They joined the men of Gleann Coe in the fight to keep the invaders away.

As the women and children had fled west up the Coe the night before, he had heard the wails and cries, the lamentations and sadness mixed with fear, and the heartbreaking sound of the crying children. He had wanted to help – had felt that primal compulsion that was so difficult to resist when he heard the voices of children. Their laughter was irresistible enough, but their fear was so much harder to ignore. Moving deep within the cave, Aeonghus had fought the siren call of the terrified children, his fear of being caught and killed by the humans winning out against the children he cared so much for.

One voice had stood out though, a haunting cry in the night by a young boy. Sounds of his crying voice, lost and frightened, had carried to the heights pleading for help. It had taken all of Aeonghus' resolve to leave the safety of his cave, yet he had only travelled a short while down the slope and into the darkness of the forest before he lost his nerve and returned. The voice haunted him all that night, well after it was silenced. A young boy had needed help and Aeonghus had been too terrified to provide it.

The *Lochlannach* were forming a long line before the river Coe that snaked around the gentle slope of forest at the foot of *Sgor na Ciche* to its east. They stood close, linking their shields to form a powerful wall of defence while opposite them, barring their way deeper into the valley, were the Gaels of Gleann Coe and the *Eireannach* beside them. The voices of *Lochlannach* rose in a clamour of fury as they began to walk forward and Aeonghus cringed at their hatred. Arrows from the Gaels and the *Eireannach* dropped amongst them and a few fell. The wall closed the gaps and it continued to move forward until it entered the tree line following the river.

The Gaels and the *Eireannach* threw themselves into the tree line on the river.

For a few moments, Aeonghus closed his eyes to the horrific din - the clang of steel and the 'thunks' of axe and sword biting deeply into shield and flesh - as it rose from the forest below. Cries, both in fury and in agony of the men as they fell, ascended in the cool air to assail him on the heights above.

32

There was nothing to be seen for several minutes, yet Aeonghus could not bring himself to leave his perch. As the noise ebbed and flowed, he fought the need to flee back into the depths of the cave. He needed to watch, needed to know the fate of his home in the glen and of the people he had watched every day for this last age. As if in answer, the *Lochlannach* poured out from the forest, their lines in disarray and their shield wall collapsed. The men of the glen and of Eire followed, and the battle raged until the *Lochlannach* fled west out of the burning village to their waiting longships. Aeonghus felt his heart flutter in joy as the *Lochlannach* were chased into the frigid waters of the loch and slaughtered to the last man.

The Gleann Coe was safe; the children could return.

* * * * *

In the later afternoon, Aeonghus flitted amongst the trees between the rising slopes of the *Sgor na Ciche* and the river Coe. Around him lay the dead and dying – many of the *Lochlannach* but too many of them Gaels and even the impressive *Eireannach*. Sadness rolled upon him like a frigid tide as he viewed the dead, the many familiar faces and the sweet voices now forever silenced. Then he scurried to the river where he had heard that lone cry for help. Pushing aside the brush he came upon a small clearing by the bank, and as he peered into the sluggish brown waters, he saw the boy face down and tangled in a submerged snag. He knelt down, touched the flowing waters, and felt hot tears roll down his cheeks. The boy was named Molloch and he had once played hide and seek amongst the oaks with the child.

"Could you not have saved him?" asked a deep voice behind him.

Aeonghus spun in panic. A human, tall and fierce, dressed in mail and plaid stood a short distance away – one of the *Eireannach*. The man held a length of bandage, likely for the gash on his arm, and his drawn, bloodied sword in the other. The sword he replaced in its jewelled scabbard though his eyes, a piercing green beneath a mane of lank, blonde hair, never left Aeonghus. The desire to flee was intense, yet Aeonghus found himself bound to that spot as the tall human walked towards him. Never had he felt so compelled by a human – so utterly helpless to escape. The human towered above him then slowly dropped to one knee.

"Could you not have saved him?" he repeated.

"I," Aeonghus stuttered, "I do not know."

"Bind my wound," the human commanded as he handed the damp length of bandage to Aeonghus.

It was the kingly mien that held Aeonghus so, and he wrapped the bandage over the gash on the arm with the greatest of care. Here was a leader of men, a powerful leader of men, with something much more about him. The eyes were piercing, otherworldly orbs that seemed to penetrate Aeonghus to his very soul. After the bandage was wrapped tight, and Aeonghus had shrunk back to the edge of the Coe, the human took a weary seat before him.

"You are a *ghille dubh*, I believe," the human said as he stretched his tired muscles.

Aeonghus nodded once, too terrified to speak.

"The tales I have heard about the *ghille dubh* tell me that they are especially fond of children." He glanced at the body caught in the snag. "Yet you allowed this one to die. Why is that?"

Aeonghus could not speak; he sank to his knees and began to cry.

A troubled look crossed the human's face. "Never have I seen such cowardice in one of the faerie folk," he said softly. "What is your name?"

"Aeonghus," was the soft, nearly silent reply.

"Aeonghus," said the human as he reached into a pouch. "I am called Fionn mac Cumhail[3], leader of the Fianna from Eire." He peered at the *ghille dubh* for several silent minutes, contemplating the wretched creature before him. He placed his chin in his hands and considered him until Aeonghus shied away in fear and shame.

"What is to become of you?" Fionn asked as he arched his back and stretched. "You, protector of the young who allows a child to die." He placed his hands on his crossed knees and stared with a frown. "You are a pitiable creature, and one that I am not sure is worthy of your long life."

"I'm sorry," Aeonghus mouthed.

---

[3] Fionn mac Cumhail – pronounced 'Fee-on mac Cool', leader of the Fianna of Ireland

"And yet," Fionn said with a sigh, "who can tell the fate of others? Perhaps there is more to it than fear? Is there indeed a destiny?" The warrior placed a thumb in his mouth and closed his eyes.

Aeonghus shifted uncomfortably before the placid figure of Fionn. For nearly a minute all was still and silent, then his eyes popped open and he pulled his thumb from his mouth.

"The images are confusing," he said as he placed his hands upon his knees. "I looked for your destiny and saw a small hilltop within a great city by the sea. The buildings were tall; perhaps a place far to the east? There was a young girl asleep and a faithful wolfhound looking upon her. Yes, very curious. There were others," he added as he looked upon the slow waters of the Coe, "other creatures and great danger. Perhaps a great battle on a hilltop as well." Fionn paused and closed his eyes. "I saw a great rage; the forest would fight back." He opened them and added, "There seems to be more than this," as he looked upon the submerged boy. "More than this failure."

Fionn again considered Aeonghus for many moments before he abruptly pulled out an object from a pouch and handed it to the *ghille dubh*. In the human's hands it was little more than a small knife, but in Aeonghus', it was a fearsome sword. "Of all the creatures in this land," he whispered, "fear in you has the most terrible outcome for those you should protect." His eyes strayed back to the submerged boy. "He should have lived and you should have helped him." There was no anger in the voice, only sadness and regret. "You must never turn your back upon a child, Aeonghus the *ghille dubh*, never again. It appears you have a destiny to fulfill, one that you cannot fail." Deliberately Fionn laid a finger on Aeonghus' arm. "I place a *Geis*[4] upon you, Aeonghus. Doom if you again turn your back upon a child under your protection. The sword I give you, is called *MacMeanmna*[5] – Courage. It will help you to fulfill your promise."

Aeonghus held the sword and looked upon it; the small weapon held craftsmanship that awed him. Inscribed with waving lines and designs and a handle

---

[4] Geis – pronounced 'Geesh'

[5] MacMeanmna – pronounced 'Mac Me-an-mna', Son of the Spirit or courage

of steel wrapped in leather, the weight and grip was perfect. "How?" Aeonghus asked as he gazed upon the beautiful weapon.

Fionn looked back towards the trees and the pinnacle of the *Sgor na Ciche* that towered above. "It was seen in a dream that I would meet a protector of children and that I should make a gift of this tiny sword," he said after a long silence. "I had the weapon forged even though it made no sense to me. Such a little trinket. I have been carrying it ever since in anticipation of that day. I did not know at the time what the portent of the dream was. I do now, however." He gazed upon Aeonghus with his deep penetrating eyes. "We all must be saved at some point in our lives."

* * * * *

Jennifer opened her eyes.

Dawn was near, a soft iridescent glow in the east that highlighted the distant radiant snow covered peak of Mount Baker. The far mountain stood like a sentry that glowered down upon the world around it and beheld the lands and waters surrounding Victoria like a vast, ominous Titan. Being volcanic, it was a symbol of inevitable catastrophe and yet its familiarity was like a family member. It was always there, had always been there, and would always greet Jennifer if she so happened to glance its way. On this morning, as she lay shivering against the stone and moss at the top of High Rock, that far removed mountain was a meaningful greeting to her eyes that simply said, "Welcome back."

Her stomach growled, and Jennifer dropped her hand to it. The cool morning breeze pushed aside the cobwebs of the night before, and for a moment she enjoyed the silence and the sounds of an early autumn morning: the juncos, nuthatches, and sparrows chirping in the fading darkness, the rustle of a squirrel, and the flapping wings of an owl. She closed her eyes to the placidity of the moment, suddenly feeling the softness of the moss, and scratching lichens and the fragrant grass beneath her. The stone she rested against was hard and cool to the touch, its scars a telling story that she allowed her fingertips to read.

The birdsong faded, the fresh cloying smells of moss and grass, stonecrop and fir dulled, and her consciousness, so keenly aware of her place on High Rock at that very moment in time, receded. The tactile feeling of the deep lacerations gave way to darkness followed by a dawning awareness of ice and snow, and a grey prosaic landscape of tumbled boulders and gravel, and biting cold. For a moment her mind's eye was gripped with the vision; the low oppressive gloom of gun metal cloud over the vast rocky terrain was more like a wasted moonscape than her home of Esquimalt. No green at all, not a single blade of grass penetrated the ashen countenance of the land. The Salish Sea was gone, replaced by a low wasteland of stone, mud, and winding rivers. The distant Olympic Mountains were snow covered but the land below the snowline was nothing more than glistening grey – not a shade of green could be seen. Thin tendrils of cloud, drizzle, and sleet filled the air.

If the land wasn't dead, it sure seemed very close.

"The stone speaks," said a deep, croaking voice beside her.

Jennifer snapped back to the dawn. Her eyes scanned the dim rock and grass, but she saw nothing.

"Where are you?" she breathed.

"I'm here," cackled the voice. From the shadows Aeonghus sat up. He gripped his staff in one hand while looking beyond her towards the distant mountain and sunrise. He closed his eyes and breathed deeply. "*Biodh aoibhneas ort-fhèin, a Ghrian, a thriath 'ad òige neartmhor tha.*"

"What does that mean?" Jennifer asked as she stared at the diminutive creature before her.

Aeonghus rubbed his beak-like nose with a thin filthy finger. After a moment he muttered beneath his dropping moustache, "Be happy yourself, O Sun, O lord, in your powerful youth."

In the growing light, Jennifer found Aeonghus to be a far more curious looking creature. He was filthy, his beard and hair full of bits of moss and lichen. The plaid blanket belted around him was slovenly and well patched, his woven trousers thinning in spots, and his boots, falling apart. His grimy woven cedar hat was perched on the back of his head and as she watched him with a mixture of growing curiosity and fear, he once again pulled out his long wooden pipe.

Aeonghus closed his eyes and breathed in the pure morning air. His chest puffed and he let the breath out in a long even sigh. When he slipped the stem of his pipe beneath his monstrous grey moustache, it immediately started to smoke.

Jennifer said nothing as she stared in awe and disbelief, for she still could not bring herself to accept such a preposterous reality: this faerie on a hill top in Esquimalt in 2015. It defied credence even with the physical proof sitting before her.

There was movement in the corner of her eye and a small brown rabbit appeared from the brush. It loped along cautiously, pausing to glance at her with deep, fearful eyes.

"Don't be afraid, friend," Aeonghus said in his soft, plodding brogue. "

"'S a' mhaduinn chiùin-ghil, an àm dhomh dùsgadh, aig bun na stùic, b'e 'n sùgradh leam, a chearc le sgiùcan a gabhail tùchain,'s an coileach cùrteil a dùrdail crom," he added as he reached out and laid a cadaverous hand on the rabbit. He cast a quizzical eye at Jennifer and said, "In the serene, bright morning at the time I wake at the foot of a little hill, it was my pleasure to hear the moorhen's hoarse prattling and the courtly moorcock's cooing with his head bending over." He petted the rabbit who sat beside him, its whiskers twitching. "It is a fine morning," he added, "a very fine morning." He fixed his gaze upon Jennifer. "Don't you think?"

"I guess," Jennifer replied. There was something terrifying about the creature named Aeonghus. His deep soulful eyes, full of mischief and impudence, held something very much darker in the deepest recesses.

Jennifer found it unnerving.

"Aye," Aeonghus continued. "The dawn coming after the darkest of nights. It is a great blessing."

Jennifer gulped as the memories of the night washed over her.

"I should be dead," she said as she wrung her hands.

"Aye," Aeonghus replied as he puffed his pipe, "so you should."

"Why?"

"I told you last night," he replied, waving the question aside with his pipe. "You are far too young tae decide tae take the next journey. I wished tae see if I might change your mind." He pointed the pipe stem at her. "What did the stone say tae you?"

"What?" Jennifer was oddly embarrassed by the question, as if he'd been reading her thoughts.

"What did the stone say?" he asked as he rubbed his grimy hand over the rough scores in the rock. "There is a story in the stone," he said with a passing wistful look. "Sometimes, if we listen, the stone will tell us." He focused his eyes on her. "What did the stone tell you?"

"Stones don't talk," Jennifer interrupted. She desperately wanted to feel in control of the situation. Faeries and talking stone, she couldn't take it anymore. "I'm not sure what you are or why I'm having these hallucinations," she said with sudden irritation. "I must be having some mental health issues. Stress or some drug induced psychosis," she concluded as she crossed her arms in a fit of petulance. She closed her eyes, as if banishing the image of Aeonghus would disrupt this new reality. When she reopened them and Aeonghus was still sitting there petting the rabbit, she sighed and placed her face in her hands.

"They're going to lock me up," she said.

"Aye," Aeonghus replied after he considered her words for a moment. "They might do that, but no' for seeing me."

Jennifer looked up. The insinuation was clear – a reference to her actions of the night before. She pursed her lips in annoyance and sat up. She crossed her arms again and looked crossly at the creature before her.

"Why?"

"Are you daft, girl?" Aeonghus said with a hint of annoyance. "I've told you why." He ceased petting the rabbit and pointed a thin finger at her. "Now, answer my question. Did the stone speak tae you?"

"Rocks don't talk," Jennifer spat back.

"Och, o' course the stone doesnae speak literally," he replied in some exasperation and a thickening of his brogue. "It no' has a mouth or lips or a tongue, lass. It does, though, have a voice. What did you see?"

Jennifer paused and a thin knowing smile crossed Aeonghus' face. "Aye, now you've ceased your blether. No, stones don't talk like you or I, hen, but they have stories tae tell if you're willing tae listen. They are witnesses, lass, tae the world around them. You and I are the stories o' the world that the stones and trees watch go by."

"I saw rocks and ice under a grey sky," Jennifer said with halting words. She couldn't believe she was even having this conversation. "There was no grass or even moss. The whole world was grey."

"Aye," Aeonghus said as he patted the rock. "This is auld stone, and it gave you a glimpse o' the auld world so very long ago." He closed his eyes as his fingers rested on the rock, "it reminds me o' home."

"I don't understand," said Jennifer peevishly.

"Long ago," Aeonghus said. "What you saw was this hill so very long ago. *An t-innean Beag,*[6] The Little Anvil, I call this hill; my home now."

"Your home?" Jennifer rubbed her arms against the chill as she watched the sun crack the distant horizon. The deep blue sky began to lighten and she closed her eyes to the sudden brightness. "Where do you live?"

"Around," Aeonghus replied, his tone noncommittal. He puffed on his pipe as he continued to stroke the rabbit. "The Little Anvil has been my home for many years now."

Jennifer again placed her hand on the stone and closed her eyes. The visions had come by accident, but would they come when she sought them? She concentrated on the stone, the scratches and indentations, the serrated cuts and withering gouges.

Nothing.

Jennifer opened her eyes.

"The stone, the trees, and the water," Aeonghus said in a slow croak, "speak most clearly when you are ready tae listen, no' when you want tae listen."

"I am ready," Jennifer replied, her brows knitting in irritation.

Aeonghus smiled as he fondled one of the rabbit's ears. "I hear their voices best when I'm no' looking for them."

"That makes no sense," Jennifer snapped. Wait a minute, she thought, how does any of this make sense? She looked upon the rabbit, its eyes closed in blissful somnolence. "May I?"

---

[6] An t-innean Beag – pronounced An chee-nen bek

"Aye," Aeonghus said as he pulled his hand away, "if she'll let you."

Jennifer eased herself towards the creature and watched it open its eyes in alarm as she reached out to touch it. She halted her hand in mid-air, then lowered it. The rabbit didn't hop away, and she slowly raised an extended finger to touch the laid back ear of the rabbit. It was soft and warm.

It was alive.

The rabbit was alive. The rabbit was real, Jennifer thought as her breathing quickened; that meant that she was alive as well. This wasn't a dream or some strange existence after death, nor some psychological breakdown. This was real.

The faerie was real.

"Aye," Aeonghus said as if reading her thoughts, "it's all real."

Jennifer hid her face and began to cry. None of this made any sense.

"*Is ann air a' bheagan a dh'aithnichear am móran*, lass," continued Aeonghus in deep sage tones as he ran his fingers around the base of the rabbit's ears. "From the little the much is known."

Jennifer tried to wipe the tears from her eyes but fresh ones fell as she was consumed by misery. "Why did you have to save me?"

"You needed saving," Aeonghus replied. He plucked at his beard and said softly, "We all must be saved at some point in our lives."

For several moments, Jennifer cried into her hands. When the wracking sobs had eased and she had regained a modicum of control of her raw emotions, Aeonghus leaned on his staff to stand.

"It's time tae go for a walk; it'll get rid o' the evils in you," he said as he brushed some dirt from his trousers. "I have something tae show you which might make you feel a wee bit better." He leaned on his staff, tucked his pipe into his belted blanket, then asked, "Care tae come wi' me?"

"Where are we going?" Jennifer asked as she wiped her eyes and nose with her sleeve as she stood up. She'd only closed her eyes for a heartbeat, but where Aeonghus had stood leaning against his staff, sat the massive Irish wolfhound panting in the cool morning breeze.

"The *Beinn nam Fiadh*[7]," Aeonghus' voice said in Jennifer's head. "The Hill of the Deer."

"Where?" Jennifer asked.

The monstrous wolfhound stood and stretched, and then shook itself. "Across the dale," Aeonghus said as the dog pointed with its massive head to a small hill crowned with trees and grass a few hundred meters from them. There was a playing field before it and a small Navy hospital at its base. "Will you come?"

Jennifer didn't even think before she replied, "I will."

"Good," Aeonghus replied as the dog licked its nose. "Try tae keep up."

---

[7] Beinn nam Fiadh – pronounced 'Bean nam feeag'

Part Six

Beinn nam Fiadh

The Hill of the Deer

The wolfhound walked to the edge of the hill top and cairn, and closed its eyes to the gentle morning breeze. Jennifer followed, curious about the sudden rapture of the moment that seemed to be gripping the creature. A shiver came over her, running from her shoulders to her spine as she suddenly perceived an intense awareness of the world. It was as if the very air was an intoxicating liquid that numbed her consciousness yet heightened her senses, amplifying them to a dizzying intimacy of her surroundings. The noisome smells of the sea air – rotting seaweed and kelp, cedar logs, and shellfish; the sweet aroma of the forest behind her – drying arbutus twigs, deer fern, snowberry, moss, and lichens; the sounds of the juncos, starlings, house finches, nuthatches, and a dozen other birds; and the movement of rabbits, ants, beetles, martens, and a host of other creatures. Everything around her in nature was suddenly, briefly, in perfect focus. Her breathing quickened and she felt unsteady.

"Hold ontae it, lass," Aeonghus breathed. The words were trance-like, unobtrusive yet penetrating. "Hold ontae the moment."

Jennifer saw the wolfhound pawing the ground, its breathing increasing and the lips drawn back to reveal its teeth. "Breathe deeply, lass. Live in this moment, this one moment. Right now.

The hardness of the ground seemed to fade and Jennifer suddenly felt as if she stood atop a great height. The sun was brilliant, and colours played in vivacious clarity upon the hilltop.

"Run!" Aeonghus roared.

The wolfhound exploded into a mighty baying as it leapt down the hillside. Before the thought had even crossed her mind to follow, Jennifer threw herself down the hill behind it, leaping from the rolls of scarred stone, banks of moss and lichen, and the tiny patches of dirt and broken glass from years of teenage drinking. The barking from the wolfhound was intense, a voluminous excitement that elicited a like response from Jennifer.

She howled in delight as she leapt down the hill.

The thrill that gripped her was electric, and it fed energy to her legs, air to her lungs, and elicited a broad smile upon her face. Jennifer had never felt more alive than at this very moment.

The wolfhound reached the base of High Rock and shot out onto the street. It paused, its tongue lolling as it panted from the exertion. Jennifer found herself there moments later, her knee skinned and elbow bloody from a fall.

"Keep up," the voice said. The wolfhound loped down the street.

"This is crazy," Jennifer replied with a toothy grin. She sprinted after the wolfhound, puffing like a bellows and with legs slowly turning to jelly. She was tired and hungry yet the spirit within her was powerful. Jennifer caught up to the wolfhound and together they jogged down towards Colville Road and the ballpark on the opposite side of it. The forested hill of *Beinn nam Fiadh* rose beyond and as they paused, with Jennifer gasping, Aeonghus' voice sounded in her head.

"Keep up, lass." Again the wolfhound seemed to burst with an explosion of energy as it crossed the road and entered the ballpark through an open gate. Jennifer waited for a car to pass, then ran across the road and followed through the gate. The wolfhound was well ahead and running for another open gate on the far side of the field. Jennifer's energy was almost depleted and she slowed to a walk as she reached the gate.

The wolfhound was gone.

"Come along, lass," Aeonghus urged. The wolfhound appeared from the brush for a moment, then turned and disappeared. Jennifer pushed the supple snowberry bushes aside and stepped around the tea-scented daphne. There was a narrow deer trail that wound with animal purpose through the Garry oaks and Douglas fir. She stepped over the mass of broken and rotting branches, pushed through the brush that grasped at her clothing and hair, and leapt across the narrow clefts in the rolling rock. The sounds of traffic faded and the birdsong grew in volume. Movement to her left caught her eye and she spied a small brown deer – a black-tailed doe – smaller than the wolfhound before her.

The forest thickened, and Jennifer marvelled at the ancient nobility of the trees. The moody forest towered into the thick canopy above; a hundred years old and more, the trees existed in a tiny forest in the middle of her hometown. She'd never noticed them before and her obliviousness at the obvious, embarrassed her with nearly as much emotion as the joy of finding such a wondrous Eden in her midst.

"Come, lass."

The wolfhound led her deeper into the Lilliputian forest and her marvel grew. The moss and fern, so thick in their lush, verdant hues, beckoned her to lie down upon their fragrant beds. The trees grew larger, the thickened bark of the firs like the gnarled brows and craggy faces of the elderly. They were wizened and kindly, colossal guardians long forgotten by the people of this world. They stood there, silent and imposing witnesses to life – all life – be it human or animal. They watched over their little world around them, their stillness a contrast to the march of time. Jennifer paused to touch one of the gigantic trees; the tiny sylvan grove gave off an acute feeling of peace.

"We're almost there," Aeonghus said.

The forest became denser with brush that tangled her clothes and hair. It took much more effort to force her way through the grasping foliage of snowberry bushes, Indian plum, and blackberry. As she skirted around the clawing canes that tore her skin and ripped her clothing, and dodged the narrow twisted trunks of Garry oak and the long fallen limbs of firs now covered with a thick leafy blanket of English ivy, she heard a distinctive 'ping'.

They were near the golf course.

"You wanted to show me a golf course?" Jennifer asked as she came to stand beside the dog. A few meters away, through the thinning overhang of the forest, lay an open fairway of the Gorge Vale Golf Course. She watched a cart speed by with a pair of elderly golfers holding coffee mugs.

"No," Aeonghus replied as the wolfhound sat down. "Feel the ground; smell the air."

Jennifer knelt beside the mighty wolfhound and allowed her hands to rest upon the damp soil and moss. She closed her eyes and slowly drew a breath of the moist air of the thick, frowzy forest.

"Aye, breath it in; breath it in deeply," Aeonghus intoned. "The forest is dying a slow death, but the air was once always like this here."

Jennifer took another breath. Her hand seemed to move on its own to rest upon the broad shaggy back of the wolfhound. The dog smell – unwashed hair and fetid breath – faded as did the sounds of golf carts and distant curses.

The forest sounds crept in.

"How is it dying?"

"The ivy," Aeonghus replied. Jennifer was suddenly aware of the strangling plant that obscured the ground and festered on the trunks of the trees. The tendrils rose up the trees, choking the branches until starved of nutrients, they withered and died. Some trees wore a thick mane of ivy halfway up their height giving them a bizarre if not sinister appearance. The alien plant was slowly killing them.

"Can it be stopped?" Jennifer asked as she tried to pull a handful of ivy away from the ground. It was extremely difficult.

"No," Aeonghus said, "it's too late. There would no' be enough interest tae save it." The wolfhound looked about the forest. "It's no' dead yet though," he added. "We'll enjoy what we have left. Breathe in the air. Sometimes you can smell the breath of the elder woods from before my time here."

Jennifer closed her eyes and again inhaled the dank air. The birdsong faded, an argument over golf scores waned, and suddenly a profound silence intruded.

When Jennifer opened her eyes, the golf course and its manicured fairways had vanished. A forest, thick and ancient, much older than the one she had just walked through, was spread out before her. The cloudless sky had been obliterated by a massive canopy of intertwining fir, red cedar, big leaf maple, and oak limbs leaving only thin beams of light to pierce the Cimmerian gloom. There was no ivy strangling the life of the trees, only an open wood beneath the deep shadows.

"Oh my," she said and her eyes widened in pleasure as she slowly stood. "It's beautiful."

"*Gleann nan Darach*[8]," Aeonghus breathed as the wolfhound loped forward into the dream. "The Valley of the Oaks I called this." He walked a few more meters and then sat on his haunches. "I loved this wee glen. The trees were very auld and they told such wonderful stories."

"Now it's a golf course," Jennifer replied.

"Aye," Aeonghus sighed. "At least it's no' under a parking lot or a row o' houses. Most o' the auld trees are gone," he said in wistful tones, "but there are a few that remain," he added, "beside the 13th fairway here. You can still hear the voice o' the auld land if you listen. "

Jennifer knelt on the ground, felt the tree roots and moss, and breathed in the earthy fragrance of damp soil, fallen leaves, and rotting pine cones; it was an intoxicating infusion of the rot of death and the scent of birth. She stared at a nurse tree, a fir long fallen, its root ball a fan of weathered limbs and dried soil. From its rotted length grew saplings and bushes – new lives emerging from the decay of death. The circle of life, thought Jennifer, as she mused over the cliché; death is merely a step forward in the ever emergence of new life.

What would have come from my death? She wondered as she plucked a piece of moss. Misery, she knew. Her mother would be upset, maybe at the loss of her daughter, but more likely at the loss of her target of blame. Without her, her mother would have nothing left to lay the burden of her misery on, and that would be a terrible thing to inflict upon her, Jennifer thought sardonically. Yet, not much else would change, she reflected with a sigh. No friends would mourn her, nor would her family really. She would become a blip in the lives of those she touched, one that would swiftly fade to obscurity in the weeks and months to come.

A giggle sounded amongst the trees and a pair of young native children, long hair tied in loose braids and naked save for a pair of rough looking, shredded cedar bark skirts, appeared from behind the broad craggy girth of a fir tree. They were young girls, maybe seven or eight, carrying empty cedar baskets and they were clearly neglecting their chores as they played tag amongst the trees. The giggling brought a smile to Jennifer's face, a brightening on her dour facade that caught the wolfhound's

---

[8] Gleann nan Darach – pronounced 'Glee-owwn nan Darachk'

attention. She even chuckled at the hijinks; the two nearly naked children were chasing and singing, and laughing in a gaiety that Jennifer had not heard in years.

For a moment, she recalled a distant afternoon. After a trip to see the baby goats at the Beacon Hill Park petting zoo and an ice cream cone from the Beacon Drive-In, she and her brother had played tag amongst the Garry oaks, her brother guffawing as he tripped and Jennifer pouncing on him with tickles. Her parents sat on the grass nearby, holding each other as they watched the antics of their children. They were smiling, laughing, and deeply in love with each other and their offspring.

It had been a bucolic summer day in Victoria, Jennifer thought with a sigh. "Wonderful," she breathed.

"*Thiyass* and *Twanas*," Aeonghus said.

Jennifer glanced at the wolfhound as it gazed upon the playing children. In the depths of its chestnut coloured eyes she could see both great joy and terrible sadness.

The children continued their game, chasing each other amongst the deer ferns and Oregon grape now pregnant with purple fruit. The two children paused, giggling as they wiped sweat from their brows; the air beneath the canopy was heavy with humidity and flies buzzed from some nearby mephitic bog. The two began picking the tiny purple berries from the Oregon grape, filling their baskets as they chattered. The wolfhound looked upon them for a moment then lowered its head.

The canopy faded to black, and Jennifer suddenly found herself in a tiny, stuffy lodge, dark save for the orange embers of a low burning fire and a beam of light from the opening in the roof above. The two children, *Thiyass* and *Twanas*, lay beneath a small pile of blankets woven from cedar bark and dog hair. They were sweating profusely and their skin was pock-marked with angry red sores. Jennifer gripped her hands together and swallowed.

It was smallpox.

An elderly woman held a shallow wooden bowl whose contents emitted thin tendrils of aromatic smoke. Her eyes were closed as she muttered low guttural words while waving the bowl over the two children. Another woman, the mother, sat quietly, her hands held together, her eyes closed, and her lips moving in silent appeal. Jennifer became aware of other figures beneath blankets and skins. Some lay sweating with eyes open, a few moaned piteously, and others were still and likely dead.

Tears welled in her eyes; it was 1862. The smallpox epidemic in Victoria, she realized – another lesson from her Humanities class.

The horrible scene faded to darkness.

"I'm sorry," Jennifer said brokenly.

They were back on the golf course.

Aeonghus said nothing. The wolfhound rose, stiff and tired, its massive head low; it walked for a few steps and then stood still while gazing upon the empty fairway.

Jennifer felt her heart welling at the sight of such pure sadness.

"They did love playing here," Aeonghus whispered. "Right over there," he said with a nod of the wolfhound's massive head, "they would chase each other through the trees. Once, I saw them play wi' a wee red squirrel." The wolfhound turned to look at her. "Have you ever seen a red squirrel?"

Jennifer shook her head.

"Och," she could hear the smile in Aeonghus' voice, "they are the cutest wee things. You look upon them, lass, and you understand the meaning o' joy. There's no' many about now because the braw grey squirrels have come from the east and pushed them out, but still, once in a while you do come across them."

Jennifer gazed upon the wolfhound.

"They played wi' that squirrel for hours. Chased it amongst the trees, intae the ferns, and when they were exhausted and had tae rest the wee squirrel sat at their feet and drank the water they gave him." The wolfhound lowered its head until its nose was nearly touching the close cropped grass of the fairway. "I do love that memory."

"I wish you had more," Jennifer blurted. The wolfhound swung its head to look at her and then looked away.

"Aye, so do I."

For a few moments they were silent as the 'ping' of tee offs and the noise of traffic intruded. Jennifer grasped her hands as she stood in repose. What could she say? What should she say? She wondered. She felt such acute empathy for the creature standing before her.

Jennifer was about to speak but a twig snapped behind her. She spun, and beneath the overhang of limbs, she could make out a standing shape in the dimness.

The wolfhound raised its head.

"*'S ann an siud tha buidheann fhiadh,*
Buidheann fhiadh, buidheann fhiadh,
'S ann an siud tha buidheann fhiadh,
Seachad an Sliabh Dubh ud thall."

Jennifer peered into the murk. From behind the blackberry brambles and Indian plum emerged a magnificent stag.

"*But yonder is the flock of deer.*
Flock of deer, flock of deer,
But yonder is the flock of deer,
Beyond the mountain you may see."

The stag, a powerful creature by the standards of the small breed of urban black-tailed deer that lived by the score in Esquimalt, stepped from the shadows and out onto the fairway.

"I bid you a good morning, Quelatikan," Aeonghus said with a nod towards the stag.

The stag strode forward, and Jennifer was struck by the arrogance and boldness of the creature. It was gallant and confident as it stopped before the seated wolfhound, its noble set of antlers thrust out. It bobbed its head while its small black tail twitched. The wolfhound turned its head towards Jennifer.

"This is Quelatikan," Aeonghus said. "He is the *ty-ee* of the Esquimalt *tillicum* o' the *mow-itsh*." Jennifer's face was a blank and Aeonghus added, "He is the chief of the herd of deer that live in Esquimalt."

"I see," Jennifer replied as she gazed upon the striking creature. With its head held high and its antlers jutting up, there was an arresting nobility to the creature. Pride, something she would never have imagined in a deer, suddenly struck her as she looked upon the creature's countenance. There was pride, she thought. What a wondrous thing to see.

"Och, lass," Aeonghus said with an edge to his voice, "you are addressing a chieftain. You could say a wee bit more than, 'I see', no?"

"Sorry," Jennifer replied as she made an inelegant curtsey. "Pleased to meet you," she said to the stag. It took an effort not to allow the smile she was fighting to escape.

She had just curtsied to a deer. It was ludicrous.

From the depths of the forest more shapes appeared, and a dozen lithe deer, most of them smaller than the wolfhound, appeared on the fairway.

"A wee part o' the herd," Aeonghus said in a conversational timbre as he scratched his ear with his hind leg. The wolfhound stood, shook its enormous body, and then pawed the ground. "Tis a lovely morning, Quelatikan," Aeonghus said. "I could surely go for a wee run if you're willing?"

The stag bobbed its head and glanced back at the herd of does, fawns, and young bucks behind him. It grunted.

"Aye," Aeonghus said as the wolfhound took a few steps forward. "You know the humans will be unhappy wi' you though?"

The stag made no motion, but Jennifer could have sworn there was a look of profound disdain in the creature's prideful eyes.

"I understand," Aeonghus said with a hint of supplication in his voice. "I'm just saying, though..."

The stag huffed, shook its antlered head, and looked squarely upon Jennifer. The wolfhound walked stiffly to Jennifer and nudged her with his nose. "Quelatikan is curious tae know if you're coming for a run."

"A run?" Jennifer repeated. She looked from the wolfhound to the deer, blinked her eyes a couple of times to register her astonishment at the situation and then asked, "What do you mean?"

"Och," Aeonghus replied tersely. "He wants tae know if you'll come for a run wi' us? A run will get the rest o' the ill humours out o' you," Aeonghus added as the wolfhound nudged her again. "And the *Tighearna*[9], himself, knows that you have ill humours tae be gotten rid o'."

---

[9] Tighearna – pronounced 'chee-airna'

"The *Tighearna?*" Jennifer asked stumbling over the foreign word.

"Aye," Aeonghus explained, suddenly evasive. "The *Tighearna* is the Laird of the woods."

"Who's that?"

Aeonghus changed the subject. "Will you come?"

Jennifer considered the situation. Each moment seemed to present her with a new event designed to defy both logic and reality. Deer, she mused, now it's deer; urban deer in Esquimalt, the bane of the gardener and considered a pest by many, wanting her to go for a run and on a golf course at that. As if on cue, she heard another 'ping' from a tee off. It was laughable, another ridiculous prospect on what was turning out to be a most ridiculous day.

"Sure," she said, "why not."

"Come along then," Aeonghus said. The wolfhound broke into a slow trot and Jennifer began a light jog to keep abreast of it. "Breathe deep, lass," Aeonghus said. "*Cho sunndach ris an fhiadh*. Be as happy as the deer." The wolfhound spared her a glance. "Put aside the hurt. Breathe in the air and for just this moment, remember what it was like to love life."

Jennifer closed her eyes and breathed in the fragrant autumn air – the cut grass, the perfume of the leaves beginning to fall, and the cedar needles browning in the cool autumn air. It was an intoxicating brew, an amalgam made from the living scents of the world. It was a reminder that everything around her was indeed alive.

A smile crossed her face as she picked up the pace. She jogged past a pair of elderly golfers and one of them shook his club at her.

"Hey, get your dog off the course!"

> "*MacGriogair nan gaisgeach,*
> *Nam bratach, 's nam pìob,*
> *Dha 'm bu shuaicheantas giubhas,*
> *Ri buadhach ga dhìreadh.*"

"What did you say?" Jennifer asked, a little breathlessly. The wolfhound loped beside her, its long tongue lolling in the air.

> "MacGregor of the warriors,

the banners, and the pipes,

Whose badge was the fir,

When going to victory."

Jennifer stumbled to a halt. "How do you know my name?"

"*Dha 'm bu shuaicheantas giubhas*," Aeonghus said as he came to a halt and looked back. "Whose badge was the fir. You've the look of someone touched by the fir."

It was meaningless, Jennifer thought as she puffed. Touched by a fir? What could that possibly signify?

"Come on," Aeonghus growled as the wolfhound broke out into a trot again. "From the little the much is known."

Jennifer found herself jogging again, her feet pounding over the clipped fairway. It was a glorious morning, cool and fresh. The ill humours were indeed melting away and the horrible events of the night before faded. A smile formed, widened, and Jennifer found herself laughing as a sudden joy filled her heart. For the moment all she could think of was running with the wolfhound over the grass of a golf course on a beautiful autumn morning.

It was incredible.

Like an arrow a doe bounded beside her, hopping comically as it easily outpaced her and the loping wolfhound. More appeared on either side of her; then the magnificent stag named Quelatikan, kept pace with her. The thrill she felt grew, if that were possible, and her reality blurred. Voices sounded in her mind, chattering and chirpy, a sing-song of capricious joy as the deer bounded and hopped.

It was the deer! She realized. She could hear the deer!

Jennifer's legs were infused with sudden power; her heart pounded and her lungs inflated to near bursting. Never had she felt so alive as she sprinted over the fairway with the wolfhound by her side and the deer bounding around her. Never had she felt such unmitigated joy at the mere touch of grass, the very breath of air, and the smell of morning. She was aware of the world like never before.

"Come on!" she yelled as she ran faster. The wolfhound loped stiffly beside her, its tongue hanging. He bayed a long growling howl before exploding in a brief sprint. The two ran beside each other, oblivious to the golfers, the deer, and the world around them. As they began to slow, puffing and coughing, Jennifer noted that they had come full circle and were near where they had entered the golf course only minutes before.

Jennifer stumbled to a halt and then fell to her knees winded. She rolled over and lay on her back, gasping and laughing in the clean morning air. The wolfhound sat beside her, then dropped down leaning its heavy weight on her side. It was panting, its mouth open wide and tongue lolling. Its eyes were half closed in the brilliant morning light.

Jennifer smiled.

"*Nì cridhe subhach gnùis shuilbhir*," Aeonghus gasped.

"What does that mean," Jennifer gasped.

Silence ensued for a moment before Aeonghus huffed, "A glad heart makes a cheerful face."

"Yes it does," Jennifer agreed. She felt tears prickle her eyes, but her smile remained. "Thank you."

Part Seven

Is Ann air Gnùis a Bheirear Breith

It is by the Face we Judge

Jennifer drew a blade of grass and placed it between her lips. Her legs ached, her chest was stiff from the heavy breathing, was drowsy from the morning's exertions and the drugs of the night before. She sat on a soft shelf of grass and moss just below the rocky summit of the *Beinn nam Fiadh*, the diminutive hillock above the Navy's hospital. As she leaned against a roll of glacier etched rock, she looked across to the small boxy 1940's houses on the street below and out towards High Rock a few hundred meters to the southeast. A sudden flush of embarrassment and guilt filled her; she had nearly died there last night.

She could hardly believe she had done it.

Aeonghus also leaned against the etched stone, his eyes closed and his filthy woven cedar hat tipped forward and resting on the beak of his nose. His blackened pipe stuck out from beneath the hat's brim and a thin tendril of sweet, aromatic smoke rose into the morning sunshine. His filthy fingers were intertwined across his belly and his scrawny legs were crossed as he indulged in a brief nap.

"Are you alone?" Jennifer asked. She glanced up into the cloudless sky and squinted at a highflying airplane.

Aeonghus snorted and shifted his legs. He raised his hat and peered at Jennifer with a single piercing eye.

"Why?"

"You must be lonely."

Lowering the hat back over his face, Aeonghus replied with a grunt, "No."

"Lonely or alone?" Jennifer pestered.

"Both," Aeonghus muttered.

"There are more of you?" Jennifer queried with some surprise. "More faeries?"

"Och," Aeonghus' weathered face looked sour. "Don't use that name; it's what you big folk call us. I'm a *ghille dubh*, no' a faerie."

"Sorry." Jennifer was uncowed. "So there are more of you?"

55

Aeonghus was silent for several moments. "No' o' *ghille dubhs*. There are others, mind."

Jennifer brightened. "What kinds?" she asked. The thought of more creatures was making her giddy with excitement. "Could I meet them?"

"Meet them?" Aeonghus spared her a withering glance. "You must be daft." He raised his hat again and pulled the pipe from beneath his moustache. He pointed the tip at her and said, "There are creatures living amongst your kind you'd no' like tae meet in the darkness o' night, and that's the truth."

"Oh." Jennifer watched as he lowered his hat over his face. For a few minutes the sounds of Saturday morning crept in – a few cars, a barking dog, and a lawn trimmer. Then she asked, "How old are you?"

"Auld," Aeonghus returned with a grunt as he again shifted his legs.

"Like how old?" Jennifer persisted as she plucked a piece of clover and sniffed it.

"Bah," Aeonghus grumbled. "I don't know," he said as he again lifted the brim of his hat, "but auld, that's what I do know."

"What's your first memory?" Jennifer pestered with a growing smile. Q and A was clearly bothering the creature.

"My first what?" Aeonghus repeated with some disbelief. "Gae boil yer head and make daft soup! I'm trying tae rest."

Jennifer giggled. There was no real bite in the thickening brogue of his bark. "Come on, what was it?"

Aeonghus sighed. "If I tell ye, you'll leave me be?"

"Of course."

Aeonghus was silent for a moment. "My first memory," he began in his deep, plodding, and nasal voice, "was waking up in the cold and the dark. Like waking up tae nothing," he added. "Awake from darkness tae darkness. The only difference was that I was awake."

Jennifer dropped the piece of clover and plucked another blade of grass. "Where were you?"

Aeonghus ignored her. His eyes closed and his voice grew wistful in his reverie. "I'm no' sure how long I was there," he resumed, "a long time, I think. I remember the cold and the darkness being for a long time. For some reason that I don't remember now, I started to pick my way through the gloom. That cold, rocky darkness grew colder and wetter until one day I spied a sliver o' light. It was a crack in the rock, and when I crawled from it, I stood upon a stony hill. There was no' a tree nor a blade o' grass nor a flower in the world then, nothing but bald rock and piles o' rounded stone and gravel. I wandered that world until I found a single patch of moss and there I stayed until the forest grew around me."

Jennifer felt mesmerized by the image: to remain in a place long enough for a forest to grow around her. She tried to visualize it – the grass growing at her feet, the saplings sprouting one by one in the hostile landscape, the trees growing tall in the empty cold and introducing shadow back to a land that had long forgotten it.

What an inconceivable yet tantalizing image.

"One day," Aeonghus continued as he pulled a small leather bag from beneath the woven blanket wrapped around his shoulders, "I felt the need tae move on. I don't know how long I'd been there, but I knew it was long. I wanted tae see more o' the forest, so I wandered about until one day I came tae the sea. I was helped across by a *selchidh*[10]."

Jennifer, her eyes closed as she listened to the quiet, soothing words, suddenly perked up. "What's a *selchidh*?"

Aeonghus tapped some tobacco into his pipe, then puffed on it. He pulled the stem from beneath his moustache and said, "It is a very auld soul. Very auld," he repeated with the ghost of a smile, "auld enough tae make me feel young." He fixed his wizened gaze upon Jennifer. "It's a creature that looks like a seal," he said with the slightest smile, "but it can remove its skin and become a human."

"Eww, I've never heard of that," Jennifer replied, her eyes wide with pleasure at the thought.

"I should think you have not," Aeonghus said with a chuckle. "They no wish tae tell the world that they are here."

---

[10] Selchidh – pronounced 'shel-chkie'

"Are they here?" Jennifer asked in a voice pregnant with excitement.

"Aye," Aeonghus replied with a nod. "There are a few."

"Wow," Jennifer breathed. She clapped her hands in excitement. "I want to see one!"

Shaking his head in bewilderment, Aeonghus looked away. "You likely already have seen one. You just didn't know it."

Jennifer closed her eyes as she imagined the creature. A seal, like the harbour seals she occasionally saw at Macaulay Point or on the West Bay Walkway, that could come ashore, shed its skin, and become a beautiful woman. "Kinda like a mermaid," she murmured as her smile grew more foolish.

"No," Aeonghus replied. "No' like a mermaid, hen."

"Where did the *selchidh* take you?" Jennifer asked as she clasped her hands in front of her. It took every effort not to nag the creature before her to take her to see a *selchidh* that very moment.

"Tae the mouth of the river Coe in Alba. There I found a home on the *Sgor na Ciche*."

"Where is *Alba*?" Jennifer asked.

"It is an auld name for Scotland, lass."

"How long were you there?"

Aeonghus scratched his beard. "I don't know really," he murmured in puzzled contemplation. "Well before the children came to the *gleann* o' the Coe." He mused for a few more moments and added, "Aye, well before that."

Jennifer again looked towards the low hill of High Rock. She pieced together what little of the story she could understand. The creature was old, she concluded, so old as to have perhaps come into the world in the years after the retreat of the glaciers from the last ice age judging by his descriptions of an empty world of grey stone.

The same world she had briefly witnessed in her vision.

Aeonghus was so old that he had perhaps crossed the Irish or North Sea to come to Scotland before people had even come to the lands. Now this creature was living on a small hill in Esquimalt, British Columbia in 2015. The level of improbability was almost too hard to fathom, until of course she looked at the *ghille dubh* beside her.

Jennifer gazed upon Aeonghus who had again lowered his hat over his eyes. He was silent and still, resting in the morning sunlight.

"How long have you been here?" she blurted out.

Aeonghus raised his hat and sighed. "It seems I'll no' get a moment o' peace from ye until I answer more o' your questions."

"I'm not sure what you expected," Jennifer groused as she crossed her arms. A certain tartness entered her voice as she added, "As you said, it's not every day I come face to face with a *ghille dubh*."

"Aye," Aeonghus nodded, showing defeat. "I suppose that is true." He plucked a small stem of moss and sniffed it. "*Ged 'tha mi 'n diugh 'am chù-baile, bha mi roimh 'am chù-mòintich*, I once heard a man say."

Jennifer pursed her lips and Aeonghus added with a wink, "Though today a farm-dog, I was once a moor-dog."

"What is that supposed to mean?" Jennifer asked.

"It means I may have changed over the years, but I'm still a *ghille dubh*."

Rubbing her temples, Jennifer allowed a sudden yawn. "I don't quite understand."

"You look tired, lass," Aeonghus said as he lay back against the warm stone. "Lie down before you fall down."

Nodding, Jennifer lay on the soft fragrant moss. She propped her head up with an elbow and looked upon Aeonghus with a growing and curious affection as she asked, "How long have you been here?"

Aeonghus cleared his throat and adjusted himself as if preparing to tell a long story. "I came to this land in the year 1848 onboard a British warship named *HMS Constance*," Aeonghus answered as he slipped his pipe back into his mouth, "and there have been more that have come here since. I came as the loyal companion o' the ship's commander, one Captain George William Courtenay." Aeonghus thumbed towards the harbour to the west. "We dropped anchor in the harbour one lovely morning. Mind, it was much different than it is now, all trees and bog and no' a single building. The natives who live here now lived in Victoria Harbour back then.

No," he said, his face growing contemplative as the memories flowed over him, "it was one massive forest; it was a beautiful world to see."

"I can't imagine that," Jennifer said after another yawn. She stretched out her arm and rested her head on it. "I can't imagine this place just covered in trees."

"These wee hills were here," Aeonghus said with a sigh as he rubbed an aged hand over the stone. His eyes twinkled in the brilliant morning light. "*An t-innean Beag* was bare like today, well, maybe a few more trees. Same with *Beinn nam Fiadh*. Lovely rock and moss. A lovely home."

Jennifer's eye lids were low and she was barely awake. "Did they have deer back then?"

"Aye, lass," Aeonghus said after a pause. He sighed again and a small smile formed. "The *mow-itsh*, as they are known in the auld trade language of Chinook Jargon, were quite friendly to me. Made me most welcome, they did."

Jennifer's eyes closed. "It's nice to have friends."

Aeonghus looked upon the girl now asleep. "Aye, lass," he whispered, "so it is." He closed his eyes and allowed the memories to rise over him.

25 July, 1848

"Let go!"

The anchor hanging near the waterline of *HMS Constance*, now stripped of its coat of glossy black paint from the battering off Cape Horne, glided over the mirrored waters of Esquimalt Harbour for several minutes before it dropped with a terrific splash and sank into the cold depths. The anchor's cable writhed with clouds of tiny fibres wafting from the friction through the hawse pipe and then it stopped as the anchor hit the mud below.

"Pay out, Mr. Forester," Captain George William Courtenay ordered as he rested a hand on the broad back of the dog standing beside him. The hand plucked lovingly at the dog's wiry hair, twirling it thoughtlessly in his fingers as he noted the slow but inexorable process of laying out the frigate's thick anchor cable. He glanced down at the dog and a smile crossed his windblown face. "You will have your chance to stretch your legs soon enough, Jupiter."

The dog, an Irish wolfhound, panted in the warm summer morning.

"We seem to have some company, Mr. Forester." Courtney nodded towards the native canoe floating near a trio of small islands a few hundred yards to the north.

"Indians," Lieutenant Forester said as he spared them a glance from working the ship. "Real live Indians to greet us."

"Indeed," Courtney replied. He noted the sailors peering over the hammock nettings and crowding between the ship's massive, burnished black cannon. Their curiosity was keen as they looked upon the forested harbour and its single canoe of Red Indians. "Mr. Forester, let's not turn the gun deck into a circus, please."

"Aye, sir," Forester said as he gritted his teeth. "Mr. Fallings, put those men to work!"

"Aye, sir!" replied the *Constance's* Bos'n. He plucked at his cheek whiskers as he waded into the idle sailors with curses and orders. "At it lads, or you'll feel my bloody wrath!"

Moments later, the sailors were tidying up the deck, cheesing ropes into coils, prettying the hammocks, and generally keeping themselves busy enough to avoid the ire of the First Lieutenant and the Bos'n while still conniving to steal a glance at the distant canoe. Courtney hid a smile; he could not blame his sailors for their inquisitiveness after so many months at sea to round the Horn; then the long journey from the Sandwich Islands, and now the vista of this mysterious and very foreign land before them. Courtney moved to the rail as he stared north and deeper into the harbour. He closed his eyes and breathed in the land smells – deep fragrant smells of fir, cedar, and the cloying hint of rot. A rainforest, he reminded himself, one nearly untouched by Europeans.

The wolfhound nosed his hip and Courtney placed his hand on the creature's massive head. "Aye, it has been a long voyage, friend." He looked upon the wolfhound with his greying muzzle and his movement growing more rheumatic in the months since leaving England. The wolfhound had been his steady companion this past year, ever since he had spied him on the docks in Portsmouth. Courtney scratched behind the wolfhound's ear and then finished with a light ruffle of his head. "I think a run ashore will do us well." He turned to his First Lieutenant, still busy with securing the *Constance's* anchor cable. "Mr. Forester, have my barge, the cutter, and the gig swung out. I could use a walk ashore."

"Aye, sir."

Twenty minutes later, as the shrill squeal of bos'nmates piping the side faded, Courtney lowered himself down the ladder on the frigate's side and into his waiting barge. The wolfhound was there already, panting and sitting between the thwarts, put in place by a pair of burly seaman before the barge was swung out and over the water. The barge bobbed against the towering black side of the *Constance*, held off by a pair of sailors with boathooks while Courtney made himself comfortable. He cast a wary eye towards the canoe which had moved little in the last thirty minutes, then nodded to his Cox'n.

"You may proceed, Mr. Atwell."

"Aye, sir," Atwell grunted. "Toss yer oars! Fend off! Oars! Give way together!"

The barge thrust away from the *Constance* and Courtney had a rare opportunity to view his command. As he scratched behind the ear of the dog, he viewed his frigate and its well-worn hull, battered after these many months at sea. They would have time to repaint and refit he reflected as he looked fondly upon the dog. For now, though, they would stretch their legs.

The barge swerved to the east, the oars rising and falling in a gentle rhythm that drove the boat towards a nearby cove. Courtney glanced at the lone canoe and noted that it was now paddling slowly towards the entrance of the harbour.

"Off to inform the locals, I believe." The Cox'n nodded once and Courtney continued, "They will see Roderick Finlayson soon enough. I am sure he will come to visit."

"Aye, sir."

Courtney hid a smile with his hand. His Cox'n was a reliable fellow but a man of very few words. He put the man out of his mind as the shore loomed. A glance over the gunwale saw the muddy bottom quickly approaching the surface as the cove shallowed out. Suddenly the keel slid into the muck and his Cox'n roared, "Boat your oars!"

Courtney stood and motioned to the wolfhound. "Off you go, Jupiter, but stay close."

With a sudden baying, the wolfhound leapt over the gunwale and into the muddy shallows before sloshing onto the shore.

"Hold up, Jupiter," Courtney called out as he hopped over the side and onto the sucking mire. A handful of sailors joined him quickly enough and all trudged through the mud and onto the boggy shoreline of clinging salal bushes and sedge grass.

"Not much room to run," said Atwell as he and three sailors ran a line from the barge onto the shore securing it to a massive pine.

"No," Courtney replied as he kicked the mephitic mud from his boots, pulled off his bicorn hat, and dabbed the sweat off of his brow. Protected from the harbour breeze, the shore was much warmer. He would leave his heavy broadcloth coat behind. "Still, stretching legs is stretching legs."

Atwell pulled out a musket as did the other sailors.

"Hopefully we won't need those," Courtney said as he pushed through the salal. It was waist height and a hindrance but easy enough to brush aside. "Jupiter!" Courtney called out as a sailor moved in front of him and began hacking at the vegetation with a cutlass. "Stay close!"

The wolfhound barked a deep baying of joy at the sudden freedom. Courtney smiled despite the heat and the sweat rolling down his nose. "Yes, Jupiter," he said as he followed the seaman before him, "it is indeed glorious to be ashore."

The salal thinned and Courtney soon found himself in the rainforest proper. Fir trees, towering in height and momentous in their breadth, soared above him, darkening the day with their spreading canopies while ferns and curious bushes with leaves almost like holly and festooned with tiny purple berries dotted a forest floor that was a labyrinth of fallen, rotting trees; moss covered stones; and branches. Trunks lay like matchsticks – some old and sunken into the soft earth and noisome bog, and covered in brush and saplings, while others were fresh and still attached to their towering root balls. Beside one such fallen giant stood the wolfhound.

"Here, Jupiter!" Courtney called out. The wolfhound was a massive beast, but he was old. There was no knowing what kind of creatures inhabited the deep shadows of this forest.

The wolfhound ignored Courtney as he looked deep into the gloom. To Courtney, it almost seemed as if the animal was considering his new world, a deep philosophical musing about this mysterious place. Courtney found himself doing the same.

The deep murk of the forest and the massive moss covered trees offered a pleasing silence barely punctuated by birdsong. Courtney could pick out a half dozen different voices that spoke of the peaceful nature of this world. He closed his eyes and breathed deeply. When he opened them, the wolfhound was gone.

"Jupiter!" He called out as he strode towards the fallen tree and its massive root ball. "Here, boy! Jupiter!"

There was nothing.

Frantic, Courtney continued to call out, but only silence returned. He sent the sailors off to search the surrounding area but they found nothing.

The wolfhound was gone.

* * * * *

He had rather liked Courtney, Aeonghus mused, as he bathed in the morning sunlight; he had been a patient and fair man. It had hurt to abandon him, yet he had accompanied him for only one reason and that was to journey to the new world. As he had sat upon the low crown of the *An t-innean Beag* and listened to the distant cries of the sailors seeking to find him, he could see the *Constance* as it bobbed in the warm summer sunshine. Eventually, he watched as Courtney returned to the ship in his barge. In the days that followed, he had seen Courtney examining the shore with a telescope, ever eager to find his lost companion. Not long after, the *Constance* sailed and he never saw Courtney again.

Yes, Aeonghus found it hurt very much to have left the man behind, even now.

The sun rose higher in the sky, its heat radiating upon the moist grass and moss of the rock. Neighborhood and street intruded upon the birdsong of chickadees, juncos, and wrens. Aeonghus looked upon the familiar panorama, one that had changed slowly during the last one hundred and sixty-seven years since his arrival. The forest below had been slowly replaced by narrow dirt roads, then streets and houses. The people had changed as well; the narrow glen had once been the purview of natives, and then farmers as they built the Admirals Road from the Craigflower farm to the Admirals House on Esquimalt Harbour. Settlers had come along and then residents of the township. The forest was gone, and Aeonghus found himself asking that most familiar question he posed to himself.

Why are am I still here?

Why indeed, he wondered as he tipped his hat back. He loved the forest with its leafy cathedral whose birdsong rose like prayers of joy to the heavens. There was so little left here now, and he knew that the lands to the north were still thick with forest, some even had fragments of the old forests from the time of his arrival. Yet, something compelled him to remain here, to continue his quiet, solitary existence living on a small rocky knob of a hill in this sleepy township. As much as he wondered why, he always returned to the inevitable answer.

It was the children.

Jennifer stirred for a moment but slipped back into her somnolence. Aeonghus' withered countenance softened as he gazed upon the girl with the curls. She was the first person he'd talked to in more than a century, and he wasn't quite sure why.

No, that wasn't true at all. He knew exactly why.

"*I looked for your destiny and saw a small hilltop within a great city by the sea. The buildings were tall; perhaps a place far to the east? There was a young girl asleep and a faithful wolfhound looking upon her,*" Fionn mac Cumhaill had said so many centuries before.

"A young girl asleep," Aeonghus muttered as he looked upon the girl.

For the first few years Aeonghus had hidden away atop High Rock before he had befriended the two native children, *Thiyass* and *Twanas*. The smallpox claimed them in 1862 and he had banished himself for many years in wretched misery until one day he befriended another child, a young boy name Charlie.

Aeonghus' lip quivered at the memory of the precocious young lad; the boy had been so very fond of hide and seek and yet had been so terrible at it. A child whose very nature was happiness and giggles could never remain hidden. Aeonghus placed the pipe stem in his mouth as a tear rolled down the crags of his cheek.

* * * * *

The 26th of May, 1896 was a glorious day; the warmth of the aromatic sea air enfolded the families walking along the dusty length of Bay Street away from Point Ellice and the Selkirk Waterway of the upper harbour of Victoria. Earlier in the morning, there had been a splendid regatta in the deeper Gorge Inlet with rowboats, cutters, and steam pinnaces whose jaunty whistles had filled the air with commemorative delight. The regatta had been a joy, a yearly event of boat races, bands, and even a few daring swimmers celebrating the birthday of Queen Victoria, the namesake for the capital of British Columbia. Today was not her birthday, however, mused the wolfhound that sat unobtrusively panting in the shade of a Douglas fir. He'd listened to the excited chatter as a streetcar full of soldiers had passed him in the morning; the birthday had fallen on a Sunday and the celebrations had been delayed for two days. Today, the Royal Navy had a special treat for the citizens of Victoria, a massive sham bombardment of the Macaulay Point gun battery and a storming of the beaches by the blue jackets. The soldiers were excited at the opportunity to rub the noses of the senior service on the beach, the wolfhound had heard more than once. It was going to be quite a show.

The heat was oppressive, and Aeonghus hoped desperately that the streetcar would arrive soon. That morning, the young boy he had befriended many months before, a tow haired six-year-old named Charlie Rose who lived in a small house on Admirals Road, had whispered in barely contained excitement that he and his family were going to watch the regatta on the Victoria side of the harbour and then hop the streetcar to bring them back to Esquimalt.

"Would you please wait for me on Esquimalt Road, Hector," Charlie had said with an impish grin and a handless pat on the head. "Father said we're going to watch the battle from McLoughlin Point today! It'll be so much fun to the see the ships firing their guns!"

Aeonghus lay upon the packed dirt of the street. It was early afternoon, and he knew the boy was coming soon.

"Remember, wait for me please, Hector," Charlie had again squealed in growing excitement as he clapped his hands. "Father said we'll catch either the 6 or the 16 streetcar and be there in the afternoon!"

Hector; it was more pleasing to the ear than his previous name, Jupiter, Aeonghus thought as his tongue lagged in the heat.

The familiar bell of a streetcar sounded, and Aeonghus sat up in anticipation. Around the corner a diminutive streetcar appeared packed with revellers. It was the

Number 6, a smaller and older vehicle that he'd seen running for years on Esquimalt's narrow gauge tracks. It paused to unload a handful of chattering families carrying picnic boxes and parasols before carrying on in a cloud of dust and reverberating noise as it clacked over the rails. Aeonghus saw that little Charlie and his family were not amongst the animated merrymakers, so he lay back down and panted in the oppressive afternoon. The walk to the ocean and its much cooler air would not come soon enough. For several minutes he dozed in warm lethargy, lying now on his side in the shade and gleaning what coolness he could from the grass before the sudden hustle of people penetrated his drowsy musing.

It was peculiar, the frantic movements of men, women, and children walking with alacrity up Bay Street and back towards the Selkirk Waterway in the upper harbour. Was not the celebration on the beach? Aeonghus wondered. A few were running now, which was even more puzzling. The enthusiasm to go to the gun battery and watch the ships of the Royal Navy had been palpable, but now, people were moving away – they were running back up towards the waters of the upper harbour. There was something new here, Aeonghus believed; there was panic and fear. The wolfhound stood up and stretched, and then shook his massive frame. He cocked his head as a pair of young boys dressed in navy blue sailor suits ran past him.

"The street car!" a young boy shouted as he ran down the dirt road. "The street car is in the water!"

The streetcar? Aeonghus puzzled. In the water? That made no sense.

"Oh Lord," a young woman wailed as she trotted by in her tight boots and confining dress, "the bridge collapsed!"

"Hurry," said her husband with an outstretched hand, "the Parkers were supposed to be on the 16!"

The 16? Aeonghus thought as his eyes widened in panic. The streetcar named the 16?

Charlie was on the 16.

The wolfhound exploded in a burst of speed as it raced across the dirt road and ran up Bay Street towards the Point Ellice Bridge. His powerful frame devoured the distance as he galloped and his deep baying filled the air as he pushed past the growing crowd. Charlie had to be safe! He thought as his legs propelled him beside the empty streetcar tracks and towards a growing throng of people near the bridge. He could no longer see ahead for the tumult of humanity that packed the road. The chatter was loud and panicked, and there were wails of anguish and tears everywhere. Aeonghus came to a halt in the jostling mass; he skipped from side to side in growing panic, his deep voice barking as he tried to find a way forward before he used his powerful size to simply push his way through. Men, woman, and children recoiled from his baying and barking, and they split a path before his terrible size and roaring voice, allowing him a path to lope forward. He could see the bridge now and the still waters of the Selkirk Waterway. The missing span on the Victoria side of the waters made him pause.

Charlie, he thought, as his heart beat near to bursting. Oh, Charlie.

The rowboats, yachts, and steam pinnaces of the morning regatta filled the waters as the men searched the floating debris for survivors. Aeonghus could see a few huddled passengers in the boats and a handful already on the shore weeping and covered in blankets.

Then Aeonghus saw the bodies.

On the deep, lush lawn of a house on the water's edge lay the dead: men, women, and most terrible to behold, children, laid out in horrible rows. The children's tiny bodies were covered in curtains and tablecloths, jackets and vests, while adults keened and wailed at the dreadful loss.

Aeonghus pushed his way towards the house and then through the open gate into the yard. It was chaos and panic, misery and heartbreak. There was at least a score of dead on the grass already, most covered, some not, and their cold, grey faces pinched in death were more than he could bear. More men came into the yard, their clothes wet and filthy, and they were carrying more of the dead. New cries and tears and Aeonghus was in agony at the sight of a small boy in the brawny arms of a weeping fisherman.

It was Charlie.

The fisherman laid the limp form of the boy on the lawn with exaggerated tenderness as the tragedy of the limp and tiny form wrenched tears and great sobs from him, then he spun in surprise at the roar from the wolfhound behind him.

Several people stepped back as the formidable creature loped forward and lowered its muzzle to the pale face of the child. He sniffed the child's grey face, touched noses, and then raised his massive head to look upon the watching crowd. The wolfhound seemed horrified; it looked around with wide, distraught eyes and a lolling, panting, tongue before it collapsed beside the child. The howling and crying, the baying and the abject misery of the animal wrestled new tears from the people around it, and they cried openly as a man lay a jacket over the child's tiny body.

The bodies continued to arrive as the afternoon progressed, and the crowd grew from hundreds to thousands lining both sides of the waterway. The balmy May weather couldn't warm the penetrating chill that hung over the host as they stood in horror amongst the carnage. The sodden dead, pulled from the waterway beneath the collapsed bridge, represented the growing city's youth; whole families, young families with children, were laid out and covered to preserve what little dignity remained.

A young woman, shocked and devastated at the loss of her friend, looked upon the wolfhound as it lay its great grizzled head upon the cold, upturned hand of the boy, and wept openly as she sank to the grass.

* * * * *

Aeonghus pulled the pipe from his mouth and brushed a filthy hand across his eyes. He'd stayed away from the children ever since – one hundred and nineteen long and lonely years. Now, without so much as a thought, he found himself once again on the verge of becoming a friend and protector of a child. It was what he was – his seeming purpose in this world, and yet it could only end in tragedy. It had been foreseen, however, he reminded himself as he gazed upon the still form of Jennifer; Fionn had described it in his divination.

"No," Aeonghus growled as he gritted his teeth. He fought the need, the absolute desire within him, to befriend the child. It would end in heartbreak, he told himself as he clenched his fists. It must end in heartbreak with long nights of bitter tears.

He could not go through that again.

The wolfhound rose upon stiffened limbs, his greying muzzle low to the carpet of moss as he looked upon the girl's tranquil form. For a moment it seemed as if he would change his mind and resume his place beside the sleeping girl – protector and friend.

Turning away, the wolfhound padded off down the hill towards High Rock.

Part Eight

Is Treasa Dithis a' dol Thar àn àtha na Fad' a Chèile

Two Are Stronger Going Over a Ford Than Far Apart

Jennifer MacGregor stirred the pot of beef barely soup as it warmed on the stovetop. Her mother was on her iPad looking at her bank account as she sipped from a half-filled glass of wine. They had not spoken since Jennifer's return just before lunch, but her mother had given her an odd look when she pulled some dry moss and seeds from her hair.

"Where were you?' she had asked as she dropped the moss into the sink.

"Cairn Park," Jennifer had replied. Her mother said nothing, but she was clearly sceptical.

Jennifer ladled soup into two bowls and placed them on the table. Her mother continued to scan her bank records while Jennifer sipped the scalding liquid and ruminated in silence on the events of last night and this morning.

When she had awoken, Aeonghus was gone, and the surety that everything that had happened over the previous few hours was merely a dream or hallucination suddenly reasserted itself. That she had found herself on the small hill across from High Rock was inconsequential; she may have wandered there in a drug induced daze sometime in the night, she told herself. Upon returning home and seeing her mother, the reality of life intruded upon what had been a thoroughly puzzling though somewhat pleasant fantasy. The fantastic creature of her imagination was gone, the curious events had not happened, and she had somehow survived her suicide attempt. Her mother's chilly reception upon her return home merely solidified the resumption of her misery.

Jennifer was back to where she had begun.

It was a new reality, however, Jennifer realized, and one she could not ignore. The difference between the misery of yesterday and the misery of today was the suicide attempt. The failed effort to end her suffering was something impossible to ignore. That she had failed was irrelevant; the acknowledgement that she had tried to kill herself was both frightening and revolting.

Revolting, she thought as she sipped her soup; now that was a curious response. What did that mean? Did it mean she would not try it again? Did it mean that she had somehow found some subterranean strength of character buried deep within her that refused the finality of that solution? She was unsure what to think as she shook pepper onto her soup. The misery was still there, the abject self-pity still consumed her, yet the thought of ending it all was now suddenly abhorrent.

"What are you doing with yourself today?" Helene asked evenly as she flipped through Facebook.

"Homework at the library," Jennifer returned with little emotion. "I have a project on Victoria history I'm working on."

Helene said nothing; she merely nodded.

* * * * *

An hour later, Jennifer was seated in a corner of Esquimalt's small public library. She had before her several open books on Victoria's early history detailing the arrival of James Douglas and the *SS Beaver* in the early 1840's and the building of Fort Camosun, which became Fort Victoria soon after. In one book she found a watercolour painting of *HMS Constance* anchored in Esquimalt Harbour. The harbour today looked nothing like the painting in the book which was a panorama of deep brooding forest and small rocky islets with the frigate at its centre. She leaned against the wall, the book on her lap as she imagined the creature named Aeonghus in the forests, dark and foreboding, as he made his way through them to High Rock.

Jennifer flipped a few pages and found an early map of Esquimalt. It was from the 1860's and the township had been divided into three sprawling farms. The village of Esquimalt was tucked close beside the dockyard near the harbour mouth, and the vast majority of the land was still lush with ancient forest; those three farms were farms in name only. Only near the shore had the land been cleared; near Macaulay Point and Saxe Point crops were grown for the burgeoning colony and the small Royal Navy base while cows, sheep, and goats roamed on small pastures of rough grass and exposed stone.

What would that have been like for the imaginary creature? Imaginary, she thought with a thrill. Yes, what else could it have been?

An imaginary creature.

So what would that have been like?

It was easier to imagine the land as the creature had seen it while aboard the Royal Navy ship than as it was as the years and decades went by and township was logged and turned to farmland and then residential land. Now, in 2015, Esquimalt had a healthy urban forest with plenty of trees. Stand on most streets and the urban forest intruded far more so than it did in other parts of the City of Victoria. Musing on the slow encroachment of humanity upon the ancient forests was difficult, and Jennifer wondered why such a creature would have stayed?

It was a forest being, a tree spirit, she mused. To inhabit High Rock surrounded by the shrinking ancient forests would have seemed an anathema. Yet, the creature had stayed.

Why?

Jennifer continued to read through the history book replete with its black and white photos of houses, people, and ships. One photo in particular caught her eye – a young boy dressed in knee length trousers and socks and a white collared shirt while dwarfed by an aged Irish wolfhound sitting beside him. There was no caption save for the fact that it was taken in April 1896 on the front lawn of an Esquimalt home.

Could that dog actually be the creature named Aeonghus?

Jennifer shook the idea off as a coincidence and closed the book. The image of the wizened creature haunted her. After waking up from her nap and finding herself alone on the mossy hilltop, she had wondered if everything had been a drug fuelled dream. She had puzzled it out as she went home, rolling every impossibility around her mind as she considered whether the events of the night and morning had really occurred. Now, hours later, she was still reeling from the effort of trying to decide if it had all been real.

Of course not, a reasoned voice said in her mind. Think about what you are suggesting.

"Yes," Jennifer said out loud. "It cannot be true. It was a dream."

Jennifer thumbed through another history book on Esquimalt, but nothing caught her eye. She returned the books to their shelves, hoisted her backpack over one shoulder, and exited the quiet solitude of the library. In the warm autumn sunshine, she ambled through Esquimalt's Memorial Park with its mown green grass and leafy chestnut trees now turning orange as the season changed. She paused to sit on one of the wooden benches that was scarred with some recent graffiti and then found her gaze drawn to the northeast towards High Rock. The low height was obscured by trees and houses, but there was a gentle tug towards the park. Perhaps it was only to confirm what she had already decided: there was no creature or a wolfhound named Aeonghus.

Minutes later Jennifer was walking towards the hill, her eyes focused on the bald summit and its thinning crown of oaks and firs. She came to the forty-three steps that led up to the park's western entrance and after climbing those, she found herself beneath the shadow of the forest canopy. She could hear children playing, dogs barking, and even some teens dressed in a mishmash of medieval and fantasy clothing and armour chasing each other through the brush calling out silly nonsense in mock English accents. The park held the normal and peaceful air of an urban forest.

As she moved through the trees and brush, Jennifer felt her heart begin to pound, her breathing quicken, and her legs shake. She was approaching the cairn and just beyond it, the small fold in the rock where last night she had laid down to die. In the warm glare of the afternoon sun, the mossy fold of rock no longer held the sinister aura of a place of death. It was simply a fold of rock covered in grass and moss. She examined it for some sign that would prove or disprove the dream; footprints of the massive wolfhound were the most obvious yet there was nothing to see. She examined the moss for tobacco, for string, for anything that could have fallen off the creature – the slightest hint that there was a possibility for its existence.

There was nothing.

"It was just a dream," Jennifer admitted with a sigh as she sat on the grass and leaned against the warm rock. She was disappointed, she had to acknowledge. There was something so alluring about the idea that she had been saved by a faerie last night. "A *ghille dubh*," she corrected herself with a small sad smile, "no' a faerie." And yet, she had to admit there was something equally frightening if everything that had happened was actually true. Everything she thought she knew about this world would be mistaken.

That was a truly alarming thought.

Jennifer cupped her chin in her hands and stared off into the distance. A single tear rolled down her cheek. The events of the morning had given her a strange feeling of euphoria; there was a brief sense of belonging and a certain sentiment of friendship that she hadn't experienced in months. The sensation of empathy and caring that she had felt, even if it was an illusion, was a welcome one, and she was thankful for it. It was a dream, she remonstrated while staring towards the faint outline of Mount Baker. But the dream of the creature and the wolfhound had given her a new strength to carry on, even if only for a little while.

"Thank you," she mouthed as she brushed the tear away.

* * * * *

The wolfhound sat in the tall grass, its head cocked as it looked upon the girl sitting in the fold of rock. It was well hidden between a pair of Garry oaks, giving it the opportunity to watch the girl with certain impunity of being discovered. Even with eyes dimmed by age, it could see the shuddering shoulders as the girl cried. Aeonghus felt pain in his heart and the almost irresistible compulsion to lope out and comfort her; the wolfhound lowered its massive, grizzled head in shame.

After a moment, Aeonghus pushed his way closer, moving silently through the grass and pausing within the leafy branches of an Oregon grape. The girl was still crying softly with her hands covering her face, but her sobs were distinguishable enough. He placed his tiny withered hand over his heart, a heart that was pounding in remorse and sadness as he watched her. To go running out and comfort her would be an elixir of joy that would satiate the desires and compulsions of his soul, yet he fought it.

The girl stopped crying. Aeonghus watched as she brushed the tears from her cheeks and breathed deeply, looking into the brilliant blue sky to compose herself. Standing, she seemed for a moment uncertain what to do, and then she lowered her head in sadness and walked down the hill.

Aeonghus felt his own tears form – great weepy tears – and he closed his eyes and gave in to the memories.

"Hello, Aeonghus!"

The girl was named Catriona, and she darted quietly beneath the beryl gloom of oaks, her homespun dress ragged beneath the folds of her colourful *arisaid*[11] plaid of weathered blue and purple. Her hair was a glorious copper mane that hung down her back in a single braid, and it framed a face that was more handsome than beautiful and one that was peppered with freckles. When she smiled, and it was often, her blue eyes nearly disappeared in the crow's feet that belied her very young age.

Aeonghus adored her.

"Aeonghus," she called out as she padded through the forest on a pair of feet nearly black with grim. "I have a present for you." She held a package wrapped in burlap and tied with cord. "I think you will be pleased by it," she said; the Gaelic words she spoke were a light and lilting sound that meandered joyfully through the forest of pines and oaks.

It brought a smile to Aeonghus' face.

Catriona moved through the woods, advancing deeper into the moody atmosphere. Above, a whispering breeze tumbled along the floor of the glen, charming a soft chorus from the leaves of the oaks. They rustled, singing the simple joys of summer in *Gleann Coe*.

"I will leave it here, beneath the Seat of Fionn," she shouted as she stooped to place the package on the mossy ground at the foot of a large round stone the size of a throne. "Open it up and tell me if it pleases you," she added in an undertone, her smile returning as she searched the shadows.

From behind a majestic oak, the head of the wolfhound appeared, and Catriona's smile widened.

"There you are, Aeonghus," she said with a pretty wave. "I've missed you."

The wolfhound emerged from the brush, a powerful creature, lean and muscular, its grey coat matted and its eyes a piercing brown.

---

[11] Arisaid – pronounced 'air-ee-saitch'

76

"It is there," she said pointing to the package. She took several steps back and sat beneath a towering pine. "Don't be shy," she said with a giggle. "I've been working on it all winter."

The wolfhound moved with some caution, then nosed the package on the ground.

"Go on," Catriona urged. Her hands were clasped in anticipation. "I cannot wait and you are teasing me."

"Fine, lass," Aeonghus' deep voice sounded in her mind. The wolfhound picked up the package in its jaws and loped into the shadows of the deeper forest.

"Do not be long!" Catriona called out as she clapped her hands. "I cannot wait!"

* * * * *

Aeonghus ran a filthy hand over the rough burlap and touched the thin leather cord with a hand shaking in anticipation. He was loathe to unwrap it, for he was deeply uncomfortable with the idea of a gift. Catriona was his dearest friend, but he had been very careful not to tie himself to her with any spiritual bonds. Gifts had the ability to do this for him and acceptance would force him to honour the *geis* he had been put under so many centuries before by the legendary man who had once sat upon the stone where the package had been placed. Yet, he felt a sudden rush of curiosity and adoration for the wrapped bundle before him; one that was as beguiling a nectar as human whisky. The package, brown and unlovely and smelling of horse, dazzled him with its prospects, for it was a gift – a token of the very affection he so craved from the children he sought to protect. As much as his logical mind said, "Shun it", his dominant, spiritual side demanded that he open it.

Aeonghus undid the leather cord and slowly pulled aside the burlap. He held his breath as the covering was finally removed and then released it in an exhalation of purest joy.

It was a length of beautiful plaid.

Holding up the soft folds, he brought them to his grimy face and smelled the sharp aroma of the dyed and woven wool. He gathered the folds around him, a lovely chorus of green, brown, and black tartan and then gasped at the tiny round leather targe beneath it. The shield fit him perfectly, the rough leather tooled and studded like the targe of any highlander. The belt beneath the targe was supple and embossed with flowing knot work; the miniature blue woven bonnet brought a tear to his eye.

It was beautiful.

Aeonghus laid the plaid out and pleated it over the belt. He then laid down on top of its width to belt it around him. When he stood, he wrapped the upper half of the plaid across his chest and then picked up the targe and the sheathed sword that had been a gift and a charge from so long ago. Shouldering the weapon and the targe, he pulled the bonnet over the knots of his long russet hair.

He wished he could see himself. He turned towards the hidden form of Catriona beyond the press of trees and ran.

* * * * *

"You look so very handsome," Catriona tittered as she knelt on the ground before Aeonghus. She clasped her hands before her; and Aeonghus, proud in his tartan and bristling weapons, felt his adoration for her grow. This young girl, who was no more than eleven, and who he had watched over her entire life had given him a powerful and spiritual gift. She had made it; she had poured her love into it. This gift he accepted gladly but with a slightly selfish calculation. He was bound to her, more closely than ever because of the *geis* placed upon him so long ago, but only for another year or so. The bond would be broken when she became a woman. His adoration would remain, but it would diminish, and he would then seek a new child to watch.

"Thank you," Aeonghus breathed as he ran his fingers over the plaid. He looked into her limpid blue eyes and smiled beneath his massive brown moustache. "Thank you."

Catriona's eyes disappeared as she smiled in pure joy.

* * * * *

Jennifer shouldered her backpack and left the house without saying goodbye. She should have said goodbye, she mused, as she walked down the pathway from her house to the street and then turned north. She knew instinctively that saying nothing to her mother would not solve anything – demonstrating her anger accomplished the opposite, no matter how right she was. Her mother was simply unable or unwilling to face her mistakes and nothing, no demonstration of hurt or temper by Jennifer, would address that.

And yet, there was a certain smug comfort in holding her mother accountable for her actions. The hurt was deep; the words had penetrated and caused a terrible wound. She would make sure that her mother knew that at some point; they could not turn back the hands of time. Some things, Jennifer thought with growing anger, cannot be unsaid.

Her spirit was boiling with anger and resentment, but it didn't last. It never lasts, Jennifer thought as she turned west towards High Rock Park and her school beyond. The vision beyond it of the small bare hill and the wall of trees behind it brought her to a halt.

"*An t-innean Beag*," she muttered. The unfamiliar words sounded much different from the utterances of the creature in her dream. "The Little Anvil," she whispered. A small smile formed at the sudden thought of Esquimalt's little deer. She had run with deer – springing bucks and does. At least in her dreams, she remembered. Just in her dreams. "It was a nice dream though," she said as she began walking again. Unlike so many of her dreams, however, this one was clear and lingered like a memory. "But it was only a dream," she protested with a sigh. "It was not a memory."

Jennifer entered the park, wandered beneath the tall firs and oaks, breathed in the scents of damp grass and moss, then paused in the shadows. She could hear the sounds of children and the traffic on Lampson Street and Colville Road as it made its way to the Navy's dockyard. She closed her eyes and willed for those sounds to be blotted out. They faded to silence, a silence from which birdsong slowly appeared. A cool south-easterly breeze played with the boughs and leaves, rustling the browning leaves of the arbutus and Garry oaks. There was a fleeting joy there; a faint memory in this modern world that was not quite extinguished. Even here, amidst the city, as she stood in the presence of these trees, the memory of what had once existed lived on in the towering children of that much older world.

"Gonna be late, Jennifer," said her classmate and neighbour, Heather Chong, as she walked by, back bent by her backpack.

"Yeah," Jennifer said as she began a slow, plodding, walk to the school, "wouldn't want that to happen."

* * * * *

The wolfhound followed Jennifer; its pace was cautious. If someone had witnessed the powerful creature skulking through the brush, they might have said that the massive animal almost seemed fearful. He watched the girl, his penetrating eyes a window to the churning emotions deep within. There was adoration, maybe even love. The wolfhound paused to gaze upon Jennifer, his deep, russet eyes following the slow dejected pace of the girl as she followed the winding trail through the woods and onto the stairs that led down towards her school. He wanted to reach out to her, to charge forward and nuzzle her with affection.

Aeonghus watched Jennifer walk down the stairs. He followed her at a distance, flitting from tree to bush while his heart beat near to bursting. The compulsion was powerful, nearly overwhelming, and it took every effort to not rush to her side.

* * * * *

When she walked onto the school grounds, the wolfhound sat behind a car while his eyes followed her agonizing progress. She was stopped by a group of girls who laughed and jeered at her. When she tried to pass, one of them pushed her to the grass.

The wolfhound stood and his hackles rose in swift anger.

Jennifer stood up dejected and shedding tears as she brushed blades of fresh cut grass from her jeans. The children laughed and their malevolent words cut deep into her. Head bowed, she rushed away, grasping her books close to her while her face crumpled in misery. Aeonghus watched as she entered the school and then the wolfhound's greyed head dropped in sorrow.

An hour passed; the children had long disappeared into class and the wolfhound padded across the field, his gaze focused while he loped towards the line of classroom windows. He approached one in particular and after a cautious glance around, rose on his hind legs to a towering height and peered inside.

Jennifer sat at her desk, her head bowed and her shoulders slumped.

The wolfhound dropped to all fours, then sat. It had been an age since he had witnessed such complete desolation. He knew instinctively that the efforts to save her before would be wasted if he turned his back on her now. No human could be subjected to such sorrow and loneliness and survive; she would die. Yet to befriend her, to dedicate his soul once again, was a pain he was not ready to endure. It had been a century since he had done it and even now, the pain was great. Once again the wolfhound rose on his hind legs and looked into the window. A fat boy, the one he had spied days before chasing Jennifer, was whispering malevolent words and tossing balls of paper at Jennifer. She didn't respond, but merely sat there enduring the torture while the children around her tittered. The teacher addressed the class, chastised the fat boy, but when she turned her back, the abuse resumed. Jennifer said nothing.

The wolfhound dropped to his four legs, paused for a long wistful moment before turning away from the window.

* * * * *

Jennifer held the pencil loosely in her fingers before writing a sentence in her workbook.

'I hate my life.'

The words were an admission of failure and defeat. She knew exactly what that admission would bring and as much as she feared death, there was a certain comfort in the acknowledgement of the truth. There was no more avoidance, no more deflection; her battle was over.

She underlined the word 'hate' several times and placed her pencil on the desk.

Jennifer fought back the tears that threatened to overwhelm her. The dream had brought a brief solace into her desolate world, but it was not enough. The fond memories were fading swiftly as she drowned in the rising tide of her bleak reality. She placed her face in her hands and rested them on her desk.

"Class," Ms. Burbank said with a fearful urgency, "class, everyone stay calm."

There was a general muttering, some frightened words, and gasps of surprise. Jennifer looked up and saw that Ms. Burbank had backed towards her desk, a comically small pair of scissors in her hand and her terrified eyes focused on the door. The children around her slowly rose, their eyes wide in fear as they began backing towards the window in alarm.

Jennifer eased herself up, her heart pounding and her breathing in shallow gasps. She took a tentative step towards the door.

"Jennifer," Ms. Burbank whispered in panic as she reached for her smartphone with a shaking hand, "go to the back of the class, now."

Jennifer took another step towards the door. Behind her, the children murmured in growing fear as they lined up at the back of the class.

Ms. Burbank reached out a hand. "Jennifer," she pleaded, "Jennifer, please. Go to the back of the class."

Jennifer took another step towards the door and then knelt on one knee.

Ms. Burbank was near tears as she tried to tap in the numbers for the police. "Jennifer, please go to the back of the class."

The open door to the classroom creaked as it swung wider and a mighty greying wolfhound, a giant, almost otherworldly monster that dominated the narrow opening, stood intently watching Jennifer. Its deep brown eyes were narrowed and penetrating; its large body tensed, and its breathing was slow and measured.

"Jennifer," Ms. Burbank mouthed as tears began to fall and the phone fell from her fingers.

The wolfhound entered the class, his steps cautious as his massive presence moved towards Jennifer. While the children gasped in horror and Ms. Burbank looked as if she'd faint, the monstrous animal stopped before the girl, towering over her kneeling form.

Jennifer said nothing as the wolfhound touched noses with her, allowed the gentlest flick of his tongue on her cheek, and then took another step forward to place his immense head on her shoulder and then lean it against her ear. She heard the creature's deep sigh, felt the weight on her shoulder as the head slumped, and heard the deep, breaking voice in her mind.

"I missed you," he breathed.

Jennifer felt tears rise in her eyes. She grasped the wiry hair of the wolfhound's neck and buried her face in his coat.

It was real; the dream with its salvation was real.

The creature named Aeonghus was real. She was no longer alone.

"I missed you too," she mouthed as her voice broke.

Part Nine

Thig La a' Choin Duibh Fhathast

The Dark Dog's Day Will Yet Come

"You asked me whether there were more of us," Aeonghus said to Jennifer as he puffed on his pipe. The two sat together on the mossy carpet of *Beinn nam Fiadh* above the naval hospital, not far from the forest and the golf course.

Jennifer toyed with a tiny strand of moss she had plucked before sniffing it. "I did." She glanced at the diminutive *ghille dubh* resting against a rounded hump of rock. "Are there?"

"Aye," Aeonghus returned as he drowsed in the late afternoon sun. "There are a few. There was once many, but over time, they've moved off tae follow the forest as it retreats from the city, or they've delved deep underground to sleep in the cool darkness until they awake again."

Jennifer sniffed the moss again. There was little noticeable scent, yet she still found it pleasing. She gazed upon the miniature creature, frowzy and somnolent in the sun. Smoke rose from the blackened bowl of his pipe which he shifted on occasion beneath his massive moustache. She found her hands shaking and her breathing increasing. There were more, she marvelled with incredulity. There were more creatures; how wonderful, Jennifer thought, and how frightening.

The world so familiar to her days before was now a stranger.

"I would like to meet more," she said as she dropped the strand of moss. "Are they close?"

"Some are," Aeonghus replied as he tipped his hat back. He fixed a dark eye on her, and Jennifer felt a thrill of angst. There was the palest hint of warning playing across his craggy face. "There is one very close that I have not seen in many years," he grunted as he placed the pipe back in his mouth. "He arrived no' long before me. I have seen him on occasion, but no' often. I sometimes wonder if he still lingers."

"Is he a *ghille dubh* like you?" Jennifer asked. The solemn timbre of Aeonghus' voice suggested otherwise.

"No," Aeonghus said with a mild shake of his head. "No, he is a much different creature than me." He seemed to muse on that statement and then shook his head again. "No, he is very much a different creature."

"What's his name?" Jennifer asked as she toyed with a patch of lichen splayed across the rock, running a light fingertip over the pale, crusty filaments.

"Fachtna[12]," Aeonghus muttered. "His name is Fachtna, and he is a *púca*[13]."

"What is a *púca*?" Jennifer asked. "Is he bad?"

"Bad is relative," Aeonghus returned with an edge to his voice. "What is bad tae you and I is no' bad tae him. He would likely say that I was bad if he was asked," he grumped as he crossed his arms and feet.

"I don't understand what you mean," Jennifer returned with a frown of confusion.

"Moral judgements are no' absolutes," Aeonghus spat. He pulled the pipe from his mouth. "Fachtna came here aboard the *HMS Pandora* two years before me," Aeonghus said. "He left the auld world like me. We met, and we did not like each other much. I've no' seen him in many years, though I believe he is still close."

Jennifer pulled her legs in and hugged them. "I'm not sure I want to meet him," she gulped.

"Why?" Aeonghus snapped. "What are you afraid o'? Did you no' just say you wished tae meet more o' us?"

Jennifer bit her lip. "I do, just the friendly kind."

"Bah," Aeonghus huffed as he popped the pipe back into his mouth, "stuff and nonsense. You either have the courage tae face the real world, and no' the simple one you've lived in until now, or you don't." He fixed a glaring eye on her. "I'd wager Fachtna has already seen you if you ever went tae the auld Macaulay gun battery."

Jennifer cleared her throat in a nervous cough and stammered, "I have."

"Aye," Aeonghus said as he crossed his arms again, "then he's already seen you. He's a sharp creature with a guid head for faces. He'll likely know you on sight and that's no' a lie."

---

[12] Fachtna – pronounced "Fakcht-na'
[13] Púca – pronounced 'Poo-ka'

"Would he hurt me?"

Aeonghus considered the question. "If he thought he could get away with it, he might. More likely, he'd trick you, or frighten you. Creatures such as ourselves can hide pretty well when we wish, but we don't go out of our way tae attract attention. To hurt a human is to attract some very unwelcome attention. Unless of course," Aeonghus added with a wicked grin, "as I said, he thought he could get away with it. He's done it before, that I know."

Jennifer toyed with a twig before looking at Aeonghus. "Why do you want me to meet him?"

"You said you wished to meet others," Aeonghus sniffed. "You do or you don't. Make up your mind, lass."

"I do," Jennifer protested, though not very strenuously. "I guess I just want to know why you are willing to allow me to meet others."

"Ahh," Aeonghus said as he pulled the pipe out of his mouth. "Now that's a guid question." He considered it for a few moments and then replied, "I guess it's because there's so very few o' us left, and even fewer who know our story." He looked upon Jennifer and allowed a small smile. "Long ago, lass, there were many more o' us. The glens of *Alba* and *Eire* were full of *ghille dubhs, bauchans*[14] and the *cu sith*[15]; the lochs full o' *cailpeachs*[16] and the *each-uisge*[17]; the coves and bays full o' *selchidhs* and the *seonaidh*[18]. We no' met many humans, preferring tae stay wi' ourselves. There was always a risk when you revealed yourself tae a human, whether you were trying tae befriend them or tae kill them."

"Kill them?" Jennifer gasped.

"Aye," Aeonghus said with a nod, "kill them. There are those amongst us who have the compulsion tae kill a human while others have the desire tae help."

"That's awful." Jennifer bit her lip as Aeonghus fixed a frosty gaze upon her.

---

[14] Bauchan – pronounced 'baowch-an', a Scottish or Irish goblin

[15] Cu sith – pronounced 'Coo-she', a faerie dog

[16] Cailpeach – pronounced 'kale-peech', a kelpie

[17] Each-uisge – pronounced 'Echk-ooshka', a water horse

[18] Seonadh – pronounced 'she-on-ag', a water spirit

"You don't know why nor what drives them, lass, so you cannot judge. The *each-uisge* would kill a human in a heartbeat for the murder o' their young so very, very long ago, well before your recorded history. They have no' forgotten, even now, five thousand years later, nor will they ever."

"Oh," Jennifer placed her hands on her lap and looked towards High Rock.

"Even back when there were many o' us, we befriended few humans," Aeonghus repeated, his voice sad and plodding, "but those that we did, we told our stories to."

"Why?"

Aeonghus shrugged and was silent for several moments. "We exist in two worlds, lass, but we truly live in neither. We see the world that you cannot see, yet yours is a wonderful existence that we cannot experience." A small wistful smile crossed his face. "We cannot have children and our life is one no' o' birth and growing up, but one o' waking to an existence. You," he exclaimed as he pointed a skeletal finger at Jennifer, "you grow up. You learn, you fail, and you succeed. You fall in love, you have children, and you grow auld. Your life is a mere flicker tae me, lass, yet you pack so much into it. Beyond that, you're remembered. Your existence is real and remains real. No' mine," Aeonghus sighed, "no' unless I share my existence wi' someone. But it's a dangerous thing tae do though, tae share our existence wi' a human. We are not known in your world and we are no' accepted when we are discovered. Humans are afraid o' us and they will kill what frightens them most." He stared hard at her. "If we die, that's the end. We have no young tae replace us. When we're gone, we're gone. It's final."

"That's why you don't reveal yourself?"

"Aye," Aeonghus nodded. "We live on the very fringe o' your existence. We may spend years, decades, even centuries hidden away from humans only tae succumb one day to the desire tae interact, tae prove tae both worlds that we really do exist. We become a memory, then a legend, and then a myth. Every once in a while, though we truly exist."

Jennifer stretched her hand out and touched Aeonghus' boot.

"You're real," she said with a smile.

"Aye," Aeonghus returned with a smile and a wink, "for now, I exist again. You'll remember me tae your final day," he said with an emphatic nod. "Since I've revealed myself tae you, others may be interested tae meet you, though maybe not. We'll see."

"When will we go?" Jennifer asked. She was decidedly uncomfortable with the idea of meeting this *púca* named Fachtna.

"It must be at night," Aeonghus replied after a moment. "He'll no' show himself in the light o' day. Others might, but no' he."

"What others?" Jennifer prodded.

Aeonghus nodded. "Others," he repeated with a frown. "You may or may not meet them; depends if they're willing. I don't even know if Fachtna will be willing."

"Tonight?" Jennifer asked.

"Aye," Aeonghus replied as he rose to his feet. "Come tae the cairn at sunset."

Jennifer turned for a moment to stand. When she looked at Aeonghus again, the wolfhound stood panting before her. A smile crossed her face. The animal was a colossal yet elegant creature. She reached out and placed a hand behind the wolfhound's ear. She scratched him and he leaned his massive head into her hand.

"Thank you," Jennifer said.

"Tonight," Aeonghus replied. He turned and loped over the grass. "I will see you tonight."

* * * * *

The sunset over Victoria was glorious. A soft, cool breeze blew from the west, a whispering zephyr that brought the moist intoxicating smells of autumn to Jennifer as she sat on the rock of the cairn. She closed her eyes and felt a smile play over her lips. A pair of Stellar's jays were making a racket as they chased each other through the branches of an oak, their piercing shrieks blotting out the traffic sounds below. All sounds faded as she focused on the calls – those sharp piercing resonances that seemed to echo through the trees and penetrate her mind.

"Hear me! Hear me! I will adore you!"

Jennifer opened her eyes. The words were gone, replaced by only the shrieks. She had heard words! Her smile grew wider. She had definitely heard their words.

"What is it that tickles you so?" asked a voice, gritty and chuffed yet hinting at amusement.

Jennifer hopped off the cairn and walked towards the tall grass. "I heard the jays talking," she replied as she scanned the brush for the *ghille dubh*.

"I have no doubt," Aeonghus returned as he parted the grass and shuffled out, his legs stiff and rheumatic. "They carry on so. *Cluinnidh tu air a' chluais a's buidhr' e*," he groused. "You'll hear it with your deafest ear."

Jennifer noted that Aeonghus was carrying a small leather bag over his narrow shoulder. With the pipe jutting from his mouth, one hand holding the staff with the feather, and his woven Salish hat pulled down to his nose, his was a comical appearance that elicited a quiet giggle.

"Bah," Aeonghus grunted as he rested the staff on the cairn and spared Jennifer a withering glance. "*Far an taine 'n abhainn, 's ann as mò a fuaim.*"

"What does that mean?"

"Where the stream is shallowest," Aeonghus said as he began crawling up the rough stones of the cairn, "it is nosiest."

Jennifer hid her mouth with her hand to cover her smile. When Aeonghus reached the top he puffed like a bellows as he placed the small bag on the dark, bronze patina of the cairn's directional dial.

"What's in the bag?" Jennifer asked as she clasped her hands in front of her and took a tentative step forward. A distant dog barked and she cast a furtive look around her. "Aren't you afraid of being seen?" she whispered, her eyes looking east towards the playing field two hundred meters away.

"No," Aeonghus replied as he knelt down and rummaged through the bag. "There will no' be anyone coming to the top for a wee bit."

"How do you know?"

"Because I know," Aeonghus replied, his voice gruff as he opened the bag and pulled out an object. "If I no' want humans to come up here, I have my ways to keep them away for a short period o' time."

Jennifer looked at the object in Aeonghus' hands – a lumpish bag with pipes coming from it. "What is that?"

Aeonghus placed the pipes on his shoulder and the bag under his arm. "My pipes," he said with a look of pleasure on his weathered face. "I've no' played them in many a year; never felt the urge until now." He paused and peered at Jennifer; a brief, affectionate smile crossed his face. "Aye, I've no' felt the urge until now."

Movement caught Jennifer's eye, and she took a step back in surprise as a racoon ambled out of the grass and squatted before the cairn.

"Uhh," she said as she looked around. Her eyes widened as she noted a pair of rabbits hopping from behind a slender, gnarled oak. Within a minute, there were several animals – racoons, rabbits, squirrels, a dozen Norway rats and a sleek black martin – all sitting attentively before the cairn.

Aeonghus looked at each creature with fondness. "I know you've heard the stories o' my pipes," he said as he gazed upon the menagerie. "Though it's been many generations since your kin have heard them."

The racoon clapped its paws, the small brown rabbits sat on their hind legs, and the squirrels, rats, and martin remained unmoved.

"Do they understand you?" Jennifer asked in a whisper. She looked at the creatures that gave her no more attention than they would to a blade of grass. She could not stop the smile that crossed her face.

"Aye, they do," Aeonghus replied.

Aeonghus placed the chanter into his mouth and inflated the bag of his pipes. Jennifer looked at the animals and then gazed at the darkening summit of High Rock.

"Aren't you afraid someone will hear you?" she breathed.

"No," Aeonghus said out of the corner of his mouth. "I'm no' afraid o' anyone hearing me because I know that they will hear me."

"I don't understand." Jennifer saw merriment in the creature's eyes. "Aren't you afraid of being caught?"

Aeonghus shook his head. "No," he said, speaking again from one side of his mouth. He blew more air into the bag. "This is how I remind them that I'm still here."

The drones of the pipes began to sound, a deep penetrating growl that far belied the tiny size of the instrument. Aeonghus' fingers ran over the chanter, and the skirl of the pipes shrieked into the dusk, a powerful war cry from the old world.

Jennifer's eyes widened in alarms as she stepped back and plugged her ears. Then Aeonghus raised a foot and began to stamp. She could feel the slightest vibration of the pounding beat and she smiled again in growing wonder.

"Oh my God," she said as the shuddering grew. The pounding tremors felt like an earthquake.

Jennifer could see a pebble sitting on the brass dial of the cairn shiver and roll as the tremors grew. It stopped, started, rolled, bounced, and then stopped. The trembling at her feet rolled through her legs and body; the piercing shriek of the pipes and the bellowing drone battered her like a hurricane.

Leaves began to fall.

The trees were moving, their limbs shaking as they rocked in unison to the trembling ground and the blasting sound. It was if they were enjoying the resonance that reverberated around the park.

Then the animals began to dance.

As Aeonghus' fingers became a blur and he stamped with clockwork regularity, the racoons, squirrels, rats, rabbits, and the lone martin were pulled into the dance. It was more like comical shuffling or simple bouncing, but they were all enthralled by the sounds of the pipes and pounding of the beat. They bounced and jumped, clapped their paws or stamped their feet as the trembling grew and the noise of the pipes became a dissonance of body shaking droning.

Jennifer, herself, was drawn into the dance.

As much as the sound was overwhelming and the trembling was a frightening distraction, she found herself in a clumsy dance – a sort of awkward highland fling, an ungainly version of what she had seen at the Highland Games once. She twirled, jumped, hopped, and smiled, while the trees rocked and the animals spun. As the sun finally set behind the hills in the west, Aeonghus stopped his stamping and allowed the sound of the pipes to fade. All was suddenly eerily quiet, except for a few distant car alarms and the mad chattering of frightened people from the houses at the base of the hill below.

"I think that woke them up," Aeonghus chuckled with a wink. He slipped the pipes back into the bag.

As the animals disappeared back into the brush, Aeonghus lowered himself from the cairn. "I'll be back in a moment," he said. He chortled as he disappeared into the grass.

"That was an earthquake!" Jennifer heard someone yell from their window at the base of the hill.

"Was that the big one?" another asked.

Jennifer smiled as the pounding of her heart began to slow. Was all of this honestly real? Did she just see and hear what had occurred?

"How can this not be a dream?" she asked herself as she sat on the cairn.

Even now, after everything she had experienced, it was difficult to believe that she was not enduring some incredible waking illusion or some elaborate delusion while she lay atop High Rock, dying in the night as her suicide slowly came to fruition.

Yet, the evening smells of autumn leaves and distant traffic noises were all curious, and normally inconsequential, details in her dream narrative that she could not ignore. How could she note the chill of an evening southeasterly wind, or the intoxicating Earl Grey tea scent of a daphne plant, or the incessant barking of a Pomeranian in someone's backyard? These were the minutia that so quickly undermined any consideration that she was merely dreaming or in a drug induced coma as she lay unconscious on High Rock. There was no logic here, no explanation of how that could happen.

"Is a faerie logical?" she asked herself as she plucked a blade of grass and chewed it. The tart bitterness of the grass brought a smile to her lips. Would she taste that in a dream? Would she feel the foreboding she was experiencing now as she prepared to meet a *Púca*? Would she feel the terrible joy she had experienced as the pipes and the tremors shook High Rock?

"No," she murmured.

"No," Aeonghus croaked. Jennifer glanced at the wolfhound, panting in the gathering darkness. "No you would not. Come along, lass." The wolfhound turned and trotted down one of the shadowy paths. Jennifer gulped away her growing fear and jogged after him.

* * * * *

The light of the waxing moon was intermittent, for clouds often obscured it, bathing the city in a gloom that was battled away by the ochre glow of the streetlamps. The walk to Macaulay Point took thirty ambling minutes until they stood in the vacant parking lot of the park. The wind had died and all was darkness save for the intermittent stars, the distant lights of Port Angeles to the south, and the surrounding lights of Esquimalt.

"I've never been here at night," Jennifer said as she remained fixed at the entrance of the parking lot. "Never really felt like it, I guess," she added with an uncomfortable chuckle.

"I shouldn't think you would," Aeonghus replied as he bounded onto the gravel parking lot leading towards the diminutive beach bordering Fleming Bay. "Come along."

Jennifer willed herself to follow, but her heart was pounding and she found herself a little short of breath. "Breathe," she whispered as her feet scrunched on the gravel. "Just breathe."

She soon found herself on a cement path skirting the tall cliffs of Fleming Bay, a popular place for rock climbers. In the pallid light of the moon and clouds, she could pick out the usual climbing paths by the build-up of chalk. Aeonghus led her deeper into the park, past Buxton Green and onto a gravel trail, until they came to the old Royal Artillery battery, now marked by grassy humps and protective wooden fences.

"Aye," Aeonghus growled as he peered into the darkness, "the auld villain is still here. I can feel him."

The breeze had started again; its voice was, however, now a murmur colder and malevolent. The land smells were replaced by those of rotting seaweed and a more noisome aroma that suggested death rotting on the nearby shore. There were words in the breeze, Jennifer realized with a thrill, meaningless to her, yet the veiled implications were frightening.

"I don't think I want to go any further," Jennifer said. Her voice had a quaver of fear in it, and she took a step back. She'd been to Macaulay Point many times: picnics, walks, even a school field trip once to walk amongst the ruins of the old British gun battery. Now, in the chill darkness, the place had an ominous and pervading feeling of evil. She clenched her hands and fought the need to flee.

"Too late," Aeonghus replied. "Besides, lass, I'm here. He'll no' hurt you."

The dark grassy humps of the batteries took on a sinister mien, like ancient burial mounds over long dead kings. She looked to the north, at the low Observation Tower that rose like a spectral finger against the horizon, then to the east where the path moved into a shadowy cleft between two berms – one held a battery and the other a hill choked with brambles and blackberries. Aeonghus walked forward into the darkened cleft.

"Come along, lass," he murmured.

Jennifer bit her lip and then strode forward. Her eyes darted here and there as Aeonghus led her deeper into the old battery. There was no noise save for the breeze; no sounds of traffic disturbed the breathless hush, nor did the bark of dogs nor the chatter of drinking teens. Not even the sounds of night birdsong could be heard. It was an oppressive silence that seemed to terrify all sound away. Even the sound of her footsteps faded.

"Hold here," Aeonghus whispered.

They had walked past the first open battery where a powerful gun had once resided. Several meters beyond, a low concrete outbuilding emerged from the bank, its barred windows and door open and black like empty eye sockets. She'd seen this building a dozen times – a small guardhouse perhaps or an ammo store? Now, in the darkness, she found it terrifying. She inched closer to the wolfhound and placed a shaking hand upon his head.

"I want to leave," she whispered.

Aeonghus said nothing but nuzzled her hand with his cool wet nose.

The night grew deeper as cloud rolled over the waxing moon. The silence was suffocating and the darkness unusually complete within this park amidst the bright ochre lights of the city. She felt faint as she leaned against the wolfhound.

"He's here," Aeonghus whispered.

Jennifer felt a thrill pierce her heart and she stifled a shriek with her hands when she saw movement in the barred doorway. A deeper shadow moved in the gloom, a small sloth-like blackness that oozed through the rusted bars to emerge on the grass before the entrance. The shadow seemed to coalesce, and when clouds obscuring the moon thinned, the form solidified. The creature stood no taller than her waist; it was wizened and bent, its long arms nearly touching the ground, and its curiously shaped head cocked as it stared towards them with a pair of burning amber eyes.

Jennifer gripped the wolfhound's hair even tighter.

"Oh my God," she whispered.

The *púca's* head was that of a goat; the long, twisted horns were worn and chipped, the ears tattered as they twitched. It was the eyes, however, that held Jennifer in thrall. As the creature cocked its head back and forth and sniffed the air, the eyes, a glowing yellow with the thin horizontal bar of the pupils, focused tightly upon her. The *púca* took a tentative step forward, and Jennifer noted the hooves and goat legs so at odds with the spindly human arms and hairless, protruding belly.

"Fachtna," Aeonghus said by way of a business-like greeting, "it's been a long time."

"Aeonghusss," the *púca* said after a long pause. The hissing of his high nasal growl, a gravelly whisper that made Jennifer's skin crawl, was made worse by his slow slinking form. "It hasss indeed been many yearsss." The burning, unblinking eyes never left Jennifer. "Who isss your friend, *Ghille dubh?*"

"One of the *Gríogaraich*," Aeonghus replied with an edge. "I thought she'd like tae meet you."

Fachtna crouched low to the grass, his pale hands and splayed fingers spread out like front legs as he gazed curiously upon Jennifer. She took a step back and the *púca* remarked, "She doesss not look very interesssted in meeting me."

"I've told her a wee bit about you," Aeonghus growled.

The *púca* crawled slowly forward and then like a death flower opening its black petals in the moonlight, it stood upright. The short black hair on his legs and back made it difficult to discern in the night, but the pale belly and most especially the blazing, malevolent eyes – terrible unwinking orbs – could not be missed.

"Yessss," he said as he took another step towards Jennifer, "I'll bet you have."

Jennifer was terrified. Her limbs shook, her breath came in gasps, and she was nearer to running than staying. Aeonghus manoeuvred his massive body between her and the *púca*, but he could not bar the dreadful eyes that held her in their grasp. It was a nightmare, Jennifer thought; this truly bizarre dream had become a terrible nightmare. The creature was hideous, a terrifying vision that should not be, but there it stood with cocked head and glowing eyes. Now, more than ever, did she want this whole experience to be nothing more than a drug induced illusion, but those eyes looked upon her with a curious malice, stripping away her meagre defences and exposing her most primal of childlike terrors.

Jennifer knew this was real.

The *púca* took a step back and squatted on the grass. "Aeonghusss," he hissed, "why a new friend now?" Fachtna ran a long skeletal finger over the dirt, tracing some arcane symbol as he continued to stare at Jennifer. "So many yearsss you have hidden away in your deep, dark hole," he said, "but now you come out, find a friend, and bring her to find me."

"You need tae be remembered as much as anyone," Aeonghus replied as he sat on his haunches. "You can't hide in the shadows of this auld battery forever, Fachtna."

"I can," Fachtna replied, his voice a growling squeak. "I will."

"In between the killings," Aeonghus replied. "At one time, you were known for those killings. You were feared. Now, any death here is a mystery. You are forgotten."

Fachtna continued to trace lines in the dirt. "I am forgotten," he replied. "I do not mind that." He gazed upon Jennifer again. "You did not mind it either," he said. "*Aithníonn ciaróg ciaróg eile*," he added with a horrific chuckle. "One beetle recognizesss another."

Jennifer gripped the scruff of the wolfhound.

Fachtna wiggled the fingers on its hands. "*Bíonn ciúin ciontach*," he said as he again gazed upon Jennifer. "The quiet are guilty."

Jennifer tried to speak. It came out as a gasp, then a squeak. She cleared her throat, and asked in a violent quaver, "What do you mean?"

"She speaksss, Aeonghusss. Not quite like the lassst friend of yoursss, the one who drowned."

"Mind your tongue, Fachtna," Aeonghus growled. The hair rose on his scruff and back. "Do not speak of the dead."

Fachtna ignored him and spoke directly to Jennifer. "You, who comesss here to see me and remember me, why isss it that you wish to be forgotten?" he asked in a whisper. His words were slow, thoughtful, and penetrating. "You have the shadow of death upon you." Fachtna glanced at Aeonghus. "You were almossst too late."

Aeonghus said nothing.

Fachtna raised a hand and pointed a dark, thin finger at Jennifer. "It isss not too late, girl," he croaked. He cocked his head again and considered her for several moments. "It isss never too late."

"For what?" Jennifer mouthed.

"For death," Fachtna replied.

"No' from you, Fachtna," Aeonghus replied as the wolfhound took a step forward. "Mind your manners."

Jennifer blinked and let out a shriek as she took a step back and fell – in place of the hideous visage of the small *púca* stood a massive black horse.

"Does thisss pleassse you more?" Fachtna asked as he pawed the ground with one hoof. He shook his head, and his lustrous, sable mane flowed like water. The sulphurous eyes still glowed brilliantly. "Doesss thisss frighten you lesss?"

"Yes," Jennifer squeaked, "a little."

The horse took a few steps forward and swished his tail. "I misss the daysss when I could asssume thisss form," Fachtna said as he stepped towards Jennifer. The horse stuck his muzzle into her face, making her take a step back. "There were daysss I would take a child like you on such a ride," he whispered.

"And kill them?" Jennifer choked.

Fachtna stepped back, his fiery eyes holding hers. After a long pause he said, "No, not kill. You would not forget me though," he growled.

"Aye, and now look at you," Aeonghus interrupted in a churlish tone. "You hide in the shadows. When was the last time you even collected your *Púca* Share o' the crops?"

"You," Fachtna replied mildly, "are not in a place to lecture me, *Ghille dubh*. You who hidesss in the shade, maudlin and keening over the deathsss of children." Fachtna glanced at Jennifer. "Lie down with the dog, you will rissse with fleasss."

The wolfhound lowered his head and then sat on his haunches. Fachtna turned his head back to Jennifer. "You should come for a ride," he said.

Jennifer felt a sudden longing, an intoxicating desire to ride the horse. The terror was still there; the horror at seeing the previous apparition had not faded. Yet, there was a compulsion to mount the creature and ride into the night, an imagined joy that would overcome the horror.

Jennifer took a step forward.

"No," Aeonghus growled as he stood in front of Jennifer. "You'll no' take her, Fachtna."

The horse swished his tail, and in a heartbeat, the hideous goat-headed creature returned. "Aeonghusss," he grunted, "I wonder why you have brought her here. Why bring her to see me when there are others lesss...frightening?"

"Bah," Aeonghus replied. "You're no worse than some, and less worse than others. There was always Ailpein."

The *púca's* thin shoulders shook and Jennifer recoiled at the hideous cackle.

"Yesss, take her to Ailpein. What a meeting that would be."

"Who's Ailpein?" Jennifer asked in a nervous hush as Fachtna's eyes flared.

"He's a powrie," Aeonghus grunted. "A red cap some call him. Lives in some ruins not too far away. He too came here many years ago, in 1850 on the auld barque, *Norman Morrison*, I believe. I would not have you meet that one," he added as the hair on his back rose. "Fachtna is a risky meeting, but Ailpein, that's a far different matter. I have every hope that he is now asleep deep below the ground, never to wake up again."

"Would he hurt me?" Jennifer asked as she inched closer to the wolfhound.

Fachtna chuckled again and Aeonghus leaned back against the girl. "Aye, he would. Red Caps kill and they use the blood of those they kill tae dye their cap and keep themselves alive. Without the blood, they shrivel and die. They can use animals, but it's no' the same as human blood. I would not have you meet that one," Aeonghus repeated. "Fachtna though," Aeonghus said as he fixed his gaze upon the shrunken figure before them, "he's a risk tae meet, but a worthwhile one."

"Why?" Jennifer asked as she locked eyes with the *púca*. "Why should we meet?"

"Yesss, Aeonghusss, why should we meet," Fachtna growled as he crouched low to the ground. "What isss so important that I mussst meet your new friend?"

"Now, you'll be remembered for a while, Fachtna. You've been forgotten."

"I am not unhappy to be forgotten, Aeonghusss," Fachtna replied.

"Aye, that may be, but I'll wager you'll be that much happier knowing that at least one person in this world knows that a *púca* named Fachtna is living in the old gun battery at Macaulay Point. Maybe you'll even collect your *Púca* Share again."

"What's a *Púca* Share?" Jennifer asked in a whisper.

"In days gone by, this auld villain would roam the town at night and take a small share of vegetables from the garden and eggs from the chickens. At one time, they were left out willingly, then the humans stopped and Fachtna had tae steal. Then they put the dogs out to frighten him away. He eventually came here and now he never leaves."

"I have no need," Fachtna grunted as a long skeletal finger traced patterns in the dirt.

"Someday," Aeonghus growled, "you may find a reason. Time tae go," he muttered. Jennifer found herself staring at the shadowy creature. Her fear was still palpable, but it had faded somewhat. The creature was frightening, of that there was no doubt, but it seemed more nasty than evil, she felt.

"Good bye," she whispered. "It was nice to meet you."

Fachtna cocked his goat head again. "I doubt that," he hissed, "but it isss rather kind of you to say so."

Fachtna took a step back and faded into the darkness of the barred opening to the old building. "Good-bye, Aeonghusss," he rasped. "We may see you again someday."

"Och, I doubt it," Aeonghus replied as he loped out of the cleft and back towards the path leading to the entrance.

"That," Jennifer breathed as she glanced back at the darkness, "scared the crap out of me."

"Aye," Aeonghus replied casting his own glance backwards. "It's a guid thing he liked you."

Jennifer gulped and focused on the trail before her. She didn't want to think about what would have happened if the *púca* had not.

* * * * *

It was no effort to sneak back into the house. Jennifer found the key hidden beneath a rock in the garden by the back door and let herself in. Her mother was asleep, drunk and drugged, most likely, Jennifer thought with a frown. Even though it was a Monday night, her mother would have indulged herself – would have taken what was now her preferred self-medication for the pain that would not dispel. Jennifer felt a passing sorrow for her mother, but the biting words, the deliberate attack meant to inflict such horrific emotional damage, came back to her. Her lips stiffened in anger and she stepped lightly to her darkened room.

What was she to make of all of this? She wondered as she lay in bed an hour later, her mind alert and pondering the events of the last few days. It had the makings of a weird fantasy book, or one of those cheesy, teen fantasy movies with drop dead gorgeous actors save for the fact that Aeonghus was hardly a teenage heartthrob. That brought a smile to her face.

The wizened old creature in the Salish hat and plaid blanket.

It was easier to imagine him more as a talking dog, though no less ridiculous. The towering dog, stiff and old – an analogue to the rheumatic *ghille dubh* – was a palpable link. It all seemed real but it defied logic and reason. No matter how real the images and emotions of the last four days, she could not get beyond the idea that she was dealing with a mythological creature – a faerie, the stuff of fantasy writers and old wives' tales. The creature called the *púca*, however, had changed everything. How could she continue ignoring the growing body of evidence? Aeonghus was one thing, but a second creature? And Aeonghus had said there were more.

100

Unable to sleep, Jennifer rolled out of bed and sat at her computer desk. She powered up her laptop and then typed *'ghille dubh'* into Google; if this was not a series of dreams, delusions, and psychotic episodes then she needed to understand exactly what kind of creatures she was dealing with. She looked at the Wikipedia entry first. The description was basic, *'a Scottish faerie that was a guardian spirit for the trees and was also kind to children.'* She clicked on the images icon and a series of curious caricatures appeared; they were cartoonish or romantic, and none of them resembled the dour, aged creature she had met. She sat back and crossed her arms. She had no idea what all of this meant: the meeting with Aeonghus that saved her life on High Rock, Aeonghus disappearing and then coming as the wolfhound to her school, and the meeting with the *púca*. All she could understand was that it was real and she was alive because a mythical *ghille dubh* had saved her.

Part Ten

Is ioma rud a tha 'n cuan a falach

Many a Thing is Hidden by the Sea

"You seem different this week," remarked Mrs. Fletcher, the school counsellor, as she glanced at a text on her phone. Returning her attention to Jennifer she said with a half-smile, "I'm not sure how to describe it, but certainly I would say it's positive. How do you feel?"

"Alright," Jennifer replied as she sat looking downcast.

"How was your weekend?"

An image of the wolfhound came to her mind and then one of her running across the fairway of the golf course surrounded by bounding deer. She could not fight the small smile that crossed her face. "It was alright."

Mrs. Fletcher pounced on the tiny display of happiness. "It seems like you did have a good weekend because that's the first time I've seen you smile. What did you do?"

"Mostly just walked around," Jennifer confessed. She willed the smile to disappear; she didn't want to share the memories.

"Well," Mrs. Fletcher replied with a hint of disappointment, "exercise is always good for the soul."

Jennifer felt a pang of guilt; Mrs. Fletcher was only trying to help.

"I walked around High Rock a lot. I really enjoy the forest."

"The oak leaves are beginning to turn," Mrs. Fletcher observed, her smile returning. "What's your favourite tree?"

"I like the Douglas fir."

"Me too," said Mrs. Fletcher as she placed her hands on her lap. "I'm rather fond of the arbutus as well. I've seen the arbutus on High Rock – small and twisted little trees with their red peeling bark like paper, very fascinating. Why do you like the Douglas fir, by the way?"

Jennifer considered the question. "It's old and it has seen so much. I think they would have a lot of stories if they could talk."

Mrs. Fletcher nodded and said nothing.

The conversation continued, going back and forth: favourite trees and bushes, birds that could be seen in the branches of the oaks, and whether or not she had seen any deer.

"A couple," Jennifer answered with a small grin as she recalled the regal stag named Quelatikan. "Yes, I saw a couple."

"Some people don't like them," Mrs. Fletcher remarked, "but I think they're kind of cute. Then again, I live in a condo and don't have a garden," she added with a laugh.

It was a pleasant dialogue that was suddenly halted when Mrs. Fletcher inevitably moved onto the usual line of weekly questioning.

"Have you remembered anything from the accident?"

It was as if a roiling, dark cloud had suddenly blotted out the sun. That fleeting brightness – the happiness, the first she'd felt in a long time – suddenly vanished.

"No," Jennifer muttered.

Mrs. Fletcher fidgeted. She realized immediately that she had ended their progress. She asked a few more questions – inconsequential and flighty – and then paused with a frown.

"I'm sorry our conversation went south," she said with a sigh and a drumming of her fingertips on her leg. "We were making good progress."

Jennifer said nothing and continued to look at her feet.

Mrs. Fletcher sniffed as she placed her pen and notepad on the table. "Okay, Jenny. I guess we'll see you next week."

Jennifer slowly stood and gave Mrs. Fletcher a passing glance. "Okay." She turned to leave but Mrs. Fletcher reached out and touched her arm.

"I'm sorry, Jenny, I completely forgot to ask you about the dog."

Jennifer turned back to face her councillor. She had a lopsided grin on her face as she said, "Mr. Larson told me about the dog that snuck into the school and came into your classroom. He told me how it had scared the children and Ms. Burbank, but not you. You must have known the dog?"

"It was a friend's dog," Jennifer lied. "I guess he followed me to school."

"Mr. Larson said it was huge. I would have been terrified," Mrs. Fletcher chortled.

"He's pretty friendly," Jennifer replied. The smile came back and Mrs. Fletcher beamed.

"Well, that's a relief. I heard it was a big dog." She touched her hand. "It's nice to see you smile, Jenny. I'll see you next week."

"Okay."

* * * * *

Jennifer had too many chores to do; it meant she had no time to stop in High Rock as she walked home. She looked for the wolfhound as she walked through the park but saw no sign of it beneath the trees or in the grass. Disappointed, she made her way home and began vacuuming and dusting while she boiled pasta for homemade macaroni and cheese. As the supper hour approached, she watched dark clouds roll in, followed by showers and wind as a storm appeared from the southeast. When her mother arrived home from work, she was wet and cranky.

"Are the chores done?" she groused as she shook off her umbrella outside the front door. Jennifer nodded. "Good."

"What's for supper?" Helene asked as she watched the shower begin to abate. The low scudding cloud continued and the wind was brisk, but it looked like the worst of the rain was over.

"Mac and cheese," Jennifer replied, her voice hushed and noncommittal.

"Okay," Helene returned as she sat down to remove her leather boots.

The silence was pervasive as it had been ever since Friday night. Days after the fight there were no signs that the icy tension would melt any time soon.

Supper was a morose affair with eyes that looked ahead and mouths that chewed silently. No words were exchanged and Jennifer wondered if this was now the new normal. She was twelve years old and would be conceivably living at home for the next six years. Would it be an existence of brittle solemnity where they two shared the same space and nothing else? As angry and hurt as she was, she found that

104

thought difficult to bear. And yet, as fast as the burning anger in her would fade, it would flame again as she thought of those terrible hurtful words.

"I have nothing left."

Each time she thought of that sentence, the pain of that rejection reasserted itself. She was nothing to her mother.

The meal was finished in silence and Helene left the table to watch television.

Once the dishes were done, Jennifer glanced at the sky through the kitchen window and noted that the low cloud was gone to be replaced by lighter, fast-racing cloud carried from the southeast by a brisk but dying wind. She decided a cup of tea out of the house would be a pleasure, so she grabbed her jacket and her iPad mini, and left the house without a word. The walk to Serious Coffee in Esquimalt's outdated plaza was not long, barely twenty minutes by way of Lampson Street to Esquimalt Road. The plaza had all the faded glory of an aging buzzard; an institutional and unlovely commercial space that was seeking to renew itself. Serious Coffee occupied the corner location nearest Esquimalt Road, and she went in and immediately ordered her favourite tea, a London Fog.

It took a few minutes to make, and Jennifer found herself idling away by the counter, looking at the thin crowd on this Tuesday evening. There was an older couple in their sixties sipping lattes as they reminisced over some photos on a laptop; a trio of young and bearded hipsters with swept back fedoras and ridiculously large glasses enjoying wide mugs of black Coal Miner's dark roast; a mother, with her sleeping child in a stroller, sipping an Americano as she swiped away on her smartphone; and two single older women too wrapped up to talk while they typed furiously on their tablets. One other person sat in one of the battered leather chairs by the faulty electric fireplace at the far end of the coffee shop. Jennifer wouldn't have normally noted the young woman, but for a brief moment their eyes had locked, and inexplicably, a curious thrill had swept over her. The woman looked away and resumed sipping from a cup allowing Jennifer to covertly assess her.

She was young, likely in her early twenties, and not much taller than Jennifer. Her hair was a deep chestnut with a hint of curl, though pulled back into a loose tail. She wore nondescript yoga pants with a yellow waistband, a loose fitting University of Victoria hoodie, and running shoes that were surprisingly dirty. It was her face though, or more precisely, Jennifer thought, her eyes that caught her attention. They were somewhat large and an unusually expressive, deep brown; they seemed quite piercing in the brief moment that she had examined Jennifer.

"Here's your London Fog," the girl behind the counter said.

Jennifer thanked her and then looked for a seat. All of the tables were taken; only the other leather chair across from the curious young woman was empty.

"Weird," Jennifer muttered as she picked her way through the tables and chairs to take a seat opposite the woman.

The tea was delicious, and as she stared out the window into the clearing sky now beginning to darken as sunset approached, Jennifer got the distinct impression she was being stared at. She glanced at the young woman and again their eyes met. The young woman looked away, sipped her tea, and pulled out a smartphone. Jennifer was again drawn to the woman's eyes – a deep mahogany brown with flecks of gold, almost soulless in their depths. Like the eyes of a shark.

Creepy, Jennifer thought. She suddenly felt a desire to move away from the woman; she gathered her coat in preparations to leave.

"You're not leaving?" the young woman asked as she lowered her phone and looked up.

"Uh, yeah," Jennifer replied. Her feeling of discomfort grew, for the mien of this young and pretty woman was suddenly foreboding. She couldn't tell what it was, but there was a kind of otherworldly malevolence in those dark eyes.

"I think you should stay," the young woman suggested as she placed her phone in a small backpack. "Maybe we could talk."

Jennifer eased herself back into the deep leather chair, though now she was very much on guard. This was wrong, so very wrong, but she was in a coffee shop surrounded by people. As much as she sensed danger, she had a fleeting feeling of safety in numbers. "Okay," she replied. "What are we talking about?"

"You, of course," the young woman returned as she crossed her legs and sipped her tea. "Aeonghus thought you might be more comfortable talking to a woman than to a dog."

Jennifer nearly dropped her cup. She looked around the coffee shop, as if expecting to see the wolfhound or even the *ghille dubh* himself sitting on the counter. She saw nothing.

"He's not here," the young woman added. "He'll be up in his cave or under a tree or peeing on car tires for all I know," she finished with a smirk.

Leaning forward, Jennifer whispered, "How do you know him?"

The young woman allowed a small smile. "I welcomed him when he came. I've known him for a very long time."

"You were here?" Jennifer gasped. She sipped her tea, looked around again, and asked, "You welcomed him to Victoria?"

The woman's smile grew. "No, in *Alba* first, then Victoria."

The leather creaked as Jennifer sat back in the chair. This was incredible.

"What are you?" Jennifer found herself asking as she again leaned towards the young woman.

The woman looked around and then leaned in towards Jennifer. "I am a *selchidh*," she breathed with a small smile.

"A *selchidh*?" Jennifer returned in her own wide-eyed whisper.

"I am a seal," the woman said with a wink. "When I take my pelt off, I am a woman."

Jennifer's eyes widened. "What?" she whispered. Aeonghus had told her about this very creature day before. Was he really talking about this young woman?

The smiling woman nodded. "Yes. Look it up on Wikipedia if you need to. I'm a seal. Not a mermaid, by the way," she added as she waved her finger. "Sometimes people mix us up."

A brittle silence followed as Jennifer decided if the woman was for real. Everything that had happened so far, her meeting Aeonghus and then the *púca* named Fachtna last night, suggested that what this woman was saying was true. Of course it should have been confirmed in her mind when she mentioned Aeonghus by name, for who could possibly know of him save for another mystical creature. A seal though? It defied every fabric of logic.

"What is your name?" Jennifer asked.

"I'm called Braonán[19]," she replied.

"Where are you from?"

Braonán finished her tea and stood. She shouldered her backpack and picked up her yoga mat. "Let's you and I go for a walk. I can explain things then."

Jennifer hadn't shaken the sense of caution that was still gripping her. Had her experiences over the last few days not occurred, she would have thought this woman a lunatic and avoided her. A *ghille dubh* had saved her life, however, and she had met a *púca*, so meeting a self-professed *selchidh* should hardly be surprising now. However, she felt no real desire to go off with her.

"What are you afraid of?" Braonán asked with a crooked smile. She looked around the coffee shop and then leaned close to Jennifer. "Are you afraid I will take you some place dark and drown you?"

Jennifer was tongue tied for a moment before blurting out with a forced smile, "No, of course not."

"A *selchidh* does not kill like the *each-uisge* does," Braonán said as she tossed her head towards the door. "We kill only when the need is there. With you," she added with a wink, "there is no need. Not when you're prepared to do it yourself."

Jennifer reddened; that was uncalled for. Angry words were on the tip of her tongue as she stood and followed Braonán out the door of the coffee shop and onto the sidewalk outside. "Where are we going?" she asked.

"Down to the water, Saxe Point to be precise," Braonán replied as she turned right and headed south towards the exit of the plaza.

Jennifer hurried along trying to keep up to the fast pace set by Braonán who walked with a smile and a purpose. When she noticed Jennifer struggling, she slowed down.

"Sorry," she said. "I sometimes forget myself when I have legs."

Jennifer was walking beside her as they crossed Lyall Street and headed south towards Saxe Point. They found themselves on Fraser Street, part of a neighborhood of assorted architecture that included stately Victorian and Edwardian houses, small

---

[19] Braonán – pronounced 'Braoo-naan'

wartime houses from the Second World War, and building of modern construction. The street was quiet and early evening traffic thin as they walked towards the lofty firs of the small coastal park.

"There is a small cove to the east of the park entrance," Braonán said as she pointed. "It's called Inspiration Cove; there is a set of steps that go down to the beach."

The tide was out exposing the narrow beach thick with small rounded stones, driftwood, kelp, and beach glass. To the right rose sheer, rocky cliffs topped with stately Douglas firs. To the left, lower cliffs and housing behind trees. The lapping waters, clear and cold, were still as Braonán lowered her backpack to the ground and then laid out her yoga mat. She sat down, crossed her legs yoga fashion, and closed her eyes.

"Even amongst the modern houses, I still find peace in this little cove," she said after a few silent moments. "It's where I first came ashore so long ago."

"How long ago?" Jennifer asked as she took a seat beside the woman. She still felt cautious, but the serene bearing of the woman, as she took in the cool evening breeze and the growing orange of the sky as the sun set, put her at some ease.

"A long time ago," Braonán replied. For a few more moments she said nothing and Jennifer sat in uncomfortable silence as she fingered the small rounded beach stones. Braonán then opened her eyes, reached for her pack, and unzipped it.

"Oh my God," Jennifer gasped as Braonán pulled out a seal pelt and laid it on her lap.

"Go ahead and touch it," Braonán offered.

A glance at Braonán's face saw no obvious trickery, so Jennifer reached out with a tentative hand and touched the soft folds of the pelt. "It's nice," she said.

Braonán chuckled. "I've heard my pelt called many things, but nice is a first."

"Sorry," Jennifer replied. She wasn't sure what to say or even what to think. She was sitting beside a creature that said she could turn into a seal by simply pulling on a pelt. What do you say to a claim such as that? She wondered.

Braonán ran her slender fingers over the soft, mottled, grey hair of the pelt and a small, secret smile crossed her lips. "It was over a seal pelt that I came to these shores so long ago," she remarked, her voice soft as she reminisced over a distant memory.

"Really?" Jennifer asked. Her curiosity was overcoming the fading sense of caution. "When was that?"

Her fingers still caressing the pelt, she replied, "In the summer of 1811."

"1811?" Jennifer whispered with wide eyes. "Have you been here ever since?"

"Ever since," Braonán returned with a nod. She turned to look at Jennifer, her unblinking mahogany eyes holding hers. "I came with many others to rescue one of our own."

"Rescue?" Jennifer knew she must look foolish as she sat gaping with wonder at the *selchidh* who sat beside her, but she didn't care.

"Yes," Braonán said. "A few years before I came here, one of my kin, an innocent named Caoimhe[20], was kidnapped."

"How do you kidnap a seal?" Jennifer interrupted with a cocked eyebrow.

"You don't," said Braonán as she smoothed the folds of the pelt. "You kidnap a *selchidh* in her human form by stealing her pelt."

Jennifer shook her head in confusion and Braonán continued. "You see, a *selchidh* will often shed its pelt to walk amongst humans. We are quite comfortable on land and we find a certain joy with humans," she said with a touch on Jennifer's knee, "but our home of course is the sea. Once we tire of land, we slip our pelt back on, and we return to the ocean. Sometimes, however," Braonán said as her eyes darkened and her jaw hardened, "humans discover that we are a *selchidh* in human form and they steal our pelt to force us into marriage. That is what happened to Caoimhe. A human by the name of Jack Bristow captured her pelt on Islay in the Hebrides and forced her into marriage. He then took her away to New York and being displeased by the unhappy creature he had forced into slavery, he sold her pelt to another human, a sailor in the United States Navy named Jonathan Thorn who took her on as a slave of sorts."

"That's horrible," Jennifer gasped.

---

[20] Caoimhe – pronounced 'Coo-ye'

Braonán nodded. "It was. We knew of it of course; the tale of the marriage spread and when we heard that she had been taken to New York, a most courageous *selchidh* named Rionach[21], gathered many of us to follow and rescue her." She glanced at Jennifer and allowed a small smile. "It's quite a tale if you wish to hear it."

"I do," Jennifer said with a nod. "I do." She leaned back against a log, closed her eyes, and listened to Braonán's soft words as wondrous images filled her mind.

* * * * *

There were thirty-two seals bobbing in the slow, roiling swell offshore of Sandy Hook, New York. They were mottled and grey with deep, black eyes; the placid gaze of the creatures masked the simmering rage within them. A few had oilskin-wrapped bundles hanging from their bodies. Though exhausted after weeks of crossing the Atlantic, an air of purpose emanated from the creatures as they intently surveyed the distant harbour. Ships lay at anchor, some with their yards crossed as they prepared to sail, while others were idle with little activity as they waited their turn to load their cargo or provisions. Between them moved lighters, tenders, and smaller boats – like flies amongst a heard of docile grazing cows – delivering passengers and cargo.

"It has been days," growled Morbhan[22] as she gazed upon a fishing boat now on a closing tack. "What can be keeping Rionach so long?"

"Could she be captured?" asked Alana as her dark eyes widened.

"Much would I pity the human who tried to capture Rionach," answered Fiona with a sniff.

The fishing boat changed tack in a squeal of ropes and squeaking yards, and Morbhan puffed in annoyance. "How long should we wait before one of us goes to find her?"

Seosaimlún[23] cocked her head as she glanced at Morbhan. "I believe we should wait one more day, and then one can go in."

"Who?" asked Morbhan. "Who will take off their pelt and walk amongst the humans?"

"I can," Braonán replied as she swam in a slow, lazy circle. "I can go in."

---

[21] Rionach – pronounced 'Reeo-nachk'

[22] Morbhan – pronounced 'Mor-van'

[23] Seosaimlún – pronounced 'Seeo-saym-luun'

"I would go with you," Athracht said in a soft, resigned voice. "You must not go alone amongst the humans."

"Rionach did," Braonán answered.

"She is as brave as she is foolish though," interrupted Gelis. There was a general nodding and murmur of approval. "It was unwise for her to go alone."

There was a splash and suddenly a new seal bobbed before them. "Aye," puffed Rionach as the remaining seals clamoured in surprise. "Very unwise, Gelis, but we have our answer." The seals gathered closer and the noise fell to a hush.

"And?" Braonán asked as the seals crowded around Rionach. "Have you found Caoimhe?"

Rionach shook head and gazed back towards the long finger of sandy beach. "No," she sighed, "we are too late. She is gone."

There was a gasp from the seals and a few cries of anguish.

"Where?" growled Morbhan. "Where has she been taken? Not inland?" she asked as her dark eyes widened in growing horror.

"No," Rionach replied. "I learned that a man by the name of Jonathan Thorn has her now and that she is aboard a ship named the *Tonquin* and it is sailing for a place called Astoria."

"Where is that?" the seals cried.

"Far," Rionach replied, "it is very far. We will have to swim very far, my friends. We will have to swim south, far to the south, down to the land of ice and swim around a piece of land called 'The Horn'. I have heard many terrible things about that place," Rionach said in a soft voice. "It is a dangerous, deadly place, and many humans perish there in their ships. We must swim around it though and then swim very far to the north. That is where a river named, Columbia, flows. That is where the ship named the *Tonquin* is sailing."

"How far ahead is it?" asked a smaller seal named Muadhnait.

"Far," Rionach breathed. "We must head south now. We cannot wait. I hope you have been fattening yourself as you waited for me these last days."

The seals nodded and Rionach breathed in deeply before remarking, "Good. We swim south to a place the humans call the Falkland Islands. That is where the *Tonquin* sails to provision before it sails around The Horn."

"Was there any word," asked a young seal named Triduana. "Was there any word," she repeated as Rionach spun to stare at her, "on Caoimhe? Is she okay?"

None of the seals spoke, and Rionach seemed to deflate and sink in the low swell. "I spoke to a human woman who said she appeared much beaten, but still alive."

"To beat her as one might beat a common dog!" growled Morbhan in growing rage. "There must be blood for that."

"Aye," Rionach nodded, "there will be blood for that, but only if we catch them."

"Then we must swim," shouted Braonán as she dove into the deep, grey waters.

"Yes," Rionach agreed as she looked at the remaining seals. "We must swim as if Caoimhe's life depends upon us, and it does," she added.

The seals disappeared into the swell.

* * * * *

"They are not here!" wailed Triduana as the gathered seals gazed upon the bleak, open harbour of Port Stanley. The land was low and grassy with the last hints of snow in the treeless hills and mountains beyond. It was a windswept wasteland with a handful of bleached buildings scattered like dice and a pair of whaling ships anchored deep in the harbour.

"The *Tonquin* sailed five days ago!" cried Morbhan, and Braonán who had swum in with her splashed the water with a fin.

"We have missed the ship," she seethed. She looked upon Rionach who bobbed and looked down in disappointment. "We were close," Braonán muttered, "so close. The ship had a mutiny, I was told, by an old, drunk whaler who thought the naked woman standing before him was a vision of his mother."

"What happened?" Rionach asked through clenched teeth.

"Thorn sailed without eight of his crew, and the ship mutinied and forced him to return to the harbour to pick them up. They almost killed him," she added. "We were close, and in more ways than one," Braonán said as she blinked away tears. "We could have ended it here!"

Ríonach stared upon the desolate whaling village and then turned to face the south. "We must not tarry," she barked, "we must move on and try to catch them at The Horn! Swap out who carries the bundles; we must swim until darkness."

The seals breathed deeply and again dove into the depths.

* * * * *

The waters were as warm as milk, beneath a blazing sun that bleached the world into a blanched, shimmering haze. The seals were thin and hungry as they bobbed in the pale blue waters, and they were one less in number as Braonán looked upon the group huddled silently in the gentle swell with their faces downcast and forlorn. They had lost one of their own at The Horn, taken by an orca as they fled into a forest of kelp. Aoibheann[24] had been a joyous creature; a remarkable happiness had filled her soul that even the torment of chasing down the *Tonquin* could not dull.

She was badly missed.

"We must linger here and eat," Ríonach said, her eyes dull and her voice listless through want. "We are always behind the *Tonquin* and we have missed her by two weeks this time."

"What place is this?" Athracht asked as she eyed the distant island and its unusual trees.

"They call it 'The Sandwich Islands'," Ríonach replied as she and a mottled black seal named Muirne slid the oilskin bundles off of themselves and onto the bodies of two other *selchidhean*[25]. "We talked with an English woman, the wife of a chandler. She said the *Tonquin* came in to water and take on stores; they then set sail for the river named Columbia."

"It's been months now," grumbled a seal named Órfhlaith[26] as she watched a pair of fish dart in the waters below her. "Months of swimming, months of chasing,

---

[24] Aoibheann – pronounced 'Iee-vawn'

[25] Selchidhean – pronounced 'shelkieen', plural for selkie

[26] Órfhlaith – pronounced 'Oohr-lay'

114

and months of starving. Every time, we find we are still far behind." She glanced at the others. "How long will we go?"

The seals were downcast, and a few shed tears of sorrow and frustration. Rionach looked at each before speaking in a soft voice, "We shall take a great chance and not pursue them to the river, Columbia."

Morbhan's head jerked from her brooding thoughts. "What is this?" she asked. "Do you mean we are giving up? After coming so far?"

"No," Rionach replied, her voice rose over the protests of the gathered seals. "No, of course not. The woman said the *Tonquin* sails for the river Columbia, but after that, it will head north to trade in sea otter pelts."

"Animals!" spat Thorna as she shouldered an oilskin bundle.

"We will wait for them in a place called Clayoquat Sound, far to the north of the Columbia." Rionach stared into the eyes of each seal. "That is where we will wait for the *Tonquin*; that is where we shall find our beloved Caoimhe!"

The seals nodded in approval, and a few of the more bloodthirsty ones growled in anticipation.

"Eat, my sisters," Rionach instructed. "Eat fish, grow fat, and soon enough we will swim north to this Clayoquat Sound."

With a final nod, the seals slipped beneath the warm blue waters to feast upon the fish below.

* * * * *

Braonán beheld the grey waters and the deep, brooding forest of Clayoquat Sound. Low cloud, pregnant with rain, clung to the crowns of stately spruce, hemlock, fir and red cedar, while a cool breeze from the southwest whipped the waters into a chop. The other seals bobbed amongst the bull kelp watching the *Tonquin*, her sails buffeted as she drifted towards her chosen spot to anchor. The ship's crew climbed her three masts and took in her patched and threadbare sails, gathering them to the yards and slowing her speed; the anchor, hanging loosely below the forepeak, was then let go with a yell. The splash marked the finality of the ship's movements and Rionach turned to the silent seals.

"We have pursued her for many months," she crowed, "and now we have her. Tonight we will rescue our beloved friend."

"It will not be with the first stroke that the tree falls," grunted Morbhan.

"My stroke on the human, Thorn, will be the last," Rionach fumed as she glared upon the ship.

"There will be a chance for many strokes this night," croaked Thorna. There was a general growl from the seals.

"We must wait until the evening," Rionach cautioned as they watched a pair of dugout canoes emerge from the nearby native village of Echachist.

There were many people standing on the shore watching the *Tonquin* and none seemed particularly concerned as the two canoes paddled slowly to close the distance.

"You will wait on the islet over there," Rionach said as she tossed her head, "while Braonán and I swim in closer to watch what happens."

The seals disappeared, and Rionach and Braonán dove beneath the frigid waters, swimming amongst the waving strands of bull kelp until they surfaced a short distance from the towering ship. The men were bearded and filthy as they watched the cautious approach of the canoes, and one swarthy man called out, "They are the *Tla-o-qui-aht* of the *Nuu-chah-nulth*, Lieutenant Thorn; I heard of 'em before!"

The seals started and looked at the tall American standing in the ratlines of the ship's mizzen mast. Jonathan Thorn stared hard at the approaching canoes, nodded, and then dropped to the deck.

"Let the savages onboard and see what they have to offer," he cried.

The two canoes bumped against the rounded hull of the *Tonquin*, and amidst much excited chatter, the natives were allowed onboard. Rionach and Braonán could see and hear little; they drifted closer and positioned themselves so that they could peer into the opening of the tumblehome. A crowd of gesticulating *Tla-o-qui-aht* now filled the waist of the ship. There seemed to be much bartering, but as time passed the general air of cautious enthusiasm seemed to grow tense. The tone of the clamour changed and the *Tla-o-qui-aht* separated themselves from the *Tonquin's* crew as anger seeped into their words. The chief of the *Tla-o-qui-aht*, whom Rionach and Braonán had heard called Wickahissin, was gesturing wildly and his voice rose in anger. Lieutenant Thorn's face reddened as his voice mirrored Wickahissin's rage. As the two yelled at each other, Thorn, who was holding a bundle of sea otter pelts, threw it at Wickahissin who recoiled in rage at being struck.

"Get them off this ship!" Thorn barked, and his crew moved amongst the natives, pushing them to the opening in the tumblehome and down towards their waiting canoes.

"That is not good," Rionach breathed as the natives tumbled into their canoes.

"There will be blood," Braonán replied.

There were many dark looks and angry mutterings as the canoes returned to shore. Thorn turned his back and disappeared below deck.

"We must act this night," Rionach murmured as she sank into the dark depths.

* * * * *

"How did you know?" asked Jennifer as she looked upon Braonán. The *selchidh* stared at Gillingham Island, a small hump of rock at the mouth of the cove. "How did you know the natives would attack?" Jennifer repeated.

Braonán sat back with her arms braced behind her. She looked upon the distant Olympic Peninsular across the Straits of Juan de Fuca. "We were so close," she continued, ignoring the question, "in this strange dark land. The seals and sea lions told us of the *Tla-o-qui-aht*, a proud and noble people who would not allow the insult of Thorn to pass. They would kill the sailors and take their goods. We had to move swiftly and find Caoimhe before the slaughter began."

"It must have been so frightening," Jennifer mused as she thumbed a smooth stone. "I can't imagine being so far from home and in a place so empty."

"It wasn't empty," returned Braonán, "but there were none like us."

Jennifer nodded as she gazed upon an oak leaning near the cliff side. A large fir was beside it, and Jennifer wondered if it had been there when Braonán swam ashore over two centuries before. Beyond the point of land on her left lay the low rocky hump of Gillingham Island; tinged green with low grass and moss, it was the sentinel to the entrance of the cove. Did Braonán spend her time there as a seal? She'd seen them lounging there before, a picture of peaceful lethargy. The image of the sloth-like creatures basking in the noon sun brought a smile to her lips. Braonán also looked upon the tiny island.

"Yes," she sighed, "it is a great place to sleep."

"You were telling me of Caoimhe," Jennifer prompted.

"Yes," Braonán replied as she closed her eyes. "Caoimhe and the last hours of Thorn and the *Tonquin*."

* * * * *

The night was deep, a Stygian shade that descended upon the sound and bathed it in dispiriting shadow. Everything was black, a gloom where only the flickering pinpoints of fires in Echachist and the lights of the slowly rolling *Tonquin* fought against the perfection of the night.

Rionach and Braonán considered the ship as it rocked lazily in the ebbing tide. They saw two sentries, one near the forepeak, the other leaning against the mizzen mast. There was no other movement.

"They must be asleep," Rionach breathed.

"We will have little time," Braonán replied in a hush. "They will come tonight, will they not?"

"Yes," Rionach affirmed. "They will come tonight." She spun and looked upon the seals bobbing close by. "Now is the time, sisters," she spat. "Now is the time for Caoimhe!"

They nodded and growled, and Rionach croaked, "To the bottom."

The seals dove down through the depths until they reached the rocky bottom. There the oilskin packages were dropped and their contents laid out: swords, daggers, and axes. The seals wriggled and squirmed; from the darkness there slowly appeared arms and legs as their full bodies emerged from the pelts. Pale skin flashed in the murk as the *selchidhean* wrapped their pelts around their hips. Their hands reached for weapons while their dark eyes searched the depths, their long hair floating around them. Facing towards the rounded bottom of the ship, their pallid bodies slowly ascended through the darkness. Reaching the surface, the blades of swords and axes broke the calm waters, followed by the pale faces of the *selchidhean*. Their dark eyes beheld the ship and a bestial rage emanated from them as they swam towards the *Tonquin*.

"The *Tla-o-qui-aht* are coming," whispered Morbhan as she glanced back towards the shore. The others looked and all could see the faint movement of many paddlers propelling a line of canoes towards the *Tonquin*.

"Not tonight," Rionach growled as she and the others faced the canoes with their weapons raised, it cannot be tonight!"

The canoes closed the distance, silent in the darkness as they crept upon the anchored ship. A warrior in the bow of the lead canoe grunted in shock when he spied the thirty-two pale women floating in front of them, and a hushed order stopped the progress of the canoes which glided to a halt.

"Go home," Rionach said in a quiet yet commanding voice. "Your business is tomorrow. Ours is tonight."

The warriors, cloaked and grasping their paddles and weapons, looked horrified as they peered at the unlikely creatures before them. They clearly did not understand the words of Rionach but the appearance of so many mysterious, pale women armed with swords, axes, and knives clearly unnerved them. For several moments there was a brittle silence before a croaking sound emanated from above.

"*Ohk, ohk, ohk!*"

There was a sound of fluttering, and then a subtle movement as a raven landed on the gunwale of the lead canoe.

"Tell them," Rionach urged as the raven ruffled its feathers. "Send them home tonight. Bring them back at dawn."

"Ohk!" the raven shrieked. It cackled and babbled, and rose in the air to circle the canoes and lead the way back towards Echachist.

"Go," Rionach repeated as water lapped at the canoes.

One by one the canoes turned and began the slow return to the village. There were many furtive and frightened looks as the *Tla-o-qui-aht* faded into the night.

* * * * *

"Braonán," Rionach whispered as she pulled her gaze from the vanishing canoes, "take half and climb the ship's cable. We will come up the side and board the ship in the middle."

Nodding, Braonán slid her cutlass into the seal pelt tied around her slender waist and grasped the bristly cable that led up through a hawsepipe and into the forepeak. "Follow me," she mouthed to the other *selchidhean* before she began to climb.

The cable was rough, prickly with manila fibers that cut her skin. Braonán ignored the pain as she climbed hand-over-hand until she reached the hawsepipe. She stood on the nip of the cable and pulled herself over the smooth wood and flaking paint of the bulwark. In the darkness she could see a shadowy figure leaning against the foremast smoking a clay pipe and holding a musket in the crook of his elbow. Dropping to the deck, Braonán eased the cutlass from her belt and padded forward. Though her eyes were focused on the figure leaning against the mast, she could hear soft padding as other feet landed lightly on the deck.

"Hey!" shouted a voice near the ship's wheel. "Nathanial, behind you!"

The figure spun and raised his musket. "Jeremiah!" he called out as he raised his head from the musket's sites, "they're women; white women!"

"What?" the far figure named Jeremiah said as he flounced forward. "What dae ye mean?"

"They're bloody women," Nathanial chuckled as he lowered his musket. "Indians must have captured them." He looked at Braonán's nakedness with a critical eye and allowed a smile, "Bloody good lookin' wenches at that. 'Ere," he said as he placed the butt of the musket on the deck, "what's your story?"

"*Is ladarna gach cù air a shitig fhèin*," she murmured as the other *selchidhean* crowded behind her.

"Eh?" said Nathanial with a puzzled grin on his whiskered, leering face. "What does that mean?"

"Every dog is bold on his own midden, you scabrous cur," growled Braonán as she charged towards him with her cutlass.

"What'er you doing?" Nathanial shrieked as he tried to raise his musket. Braonán swung wildly and the blade sliced through his throat.

"Nathanial!" Jeremiah screamed as he raised his musket and fired. A flash and pop and the *selchidhean*, Órfhlaith, was punched backwards with a scarlet hole in her face.

120

"Aireamh na h-Aoine ort!" Braonán wailed as she threw herself at the retreating Jeremiah. The man dropped his musket and shrieked. He turned to run and Braonán hacked at his arm, cutting it deeply. He fell to his knees clutching the terrible wound; his eyes were wide in horror as Braonán raised her cutlass and hacked at his neck.

Nathanial was gripping his throat and choking on the blood. The *selchidh*, Thorna, knelt upon the chest of the dying sailor and pulled out her axe.

"Is fuar gaoth nan coimheach," she whispered as she raised the axe.

"Please!" Nathanial choked.

"Cold is the wind that brings strangers," she spoke as the axe fell.

"Morbhan, take them below!" Rionach ordered as she hopped over the bulwark. Morbhan was behind her, and the screaming *selchidhean* ran towards the open hatch.

"Braonán, Thorna," Rionach said as she pointed aft, "come with me for Thorn!"

From below there were shouts as the crew tumbled from their hammocks and into the horde of furious *selchidhean* who cut them down without remorse. Rionach crept towards the cabin door and pushed it open. A double pair of flashes, two deafening reports, and Thorna was flung backwards.

"Thorn!" Rionach screamed as she threw herself towards him.

Jonathan Thorn stepped back from the arc of the swinging axe and parried a wild stab of a knife with the pair of empty pistols he held.

"What is this?" he cried as he pulled a cutlass from the bulkhead and parried another swing of Rionach's axe. "Who are you?" he roared as he stabbed and hacked at the two half-naked women in his cabin. Neither answered but their dark, soulless eyes caused him much terror.

He saw nothing but hatred.

The *selchidhean* attacked, swinging their weapons, and Thorn deftly side-stepped their attacks. The cabin was small, however, and he was easily pinned into a corner where he could only stab. Rionach parried his sword thrust with her axe and backhanded him in the face with the pommel of her dagger. Stunned, Thorn's cutlass dropped long enough for Braonán to dive in, under his wavering guard, and thrust her cutlass into his ribs. Thorn staggered and fell to one knee, and as he looked up in pain and shock, Rionach's axe fell in swift finality.

Slipping in the pooling blood, Braonán reached for a hanging lantern and called out, "Caoimhe! Caoimhe, where are you?"

There was nothing for a moment, only the fading screams from below as the last of the crew were slaughtered.

"I'm here," whispered a voice from behind a small door in the corner of the cabin. Rionach saw that it was locked and noted the ring of keys lying on a small mahogany writing desk.

"Wait, Caoimhe," she hissed as she fumbled with the keys, trying three before the fourth one opened the door and a frail, thin form fell out from the fetid gloom.

"Oh, Caoimhe," Rionach whispered as tears swelled in her eyes. She knelt and grasped the sickly creature that lay before her, gathering her in her arms. "We're here, my dear friend. We've come for you."

Caoimhe stared at each *selchidhean* and then at the others as they entered the cabin, bloodied and battered, and she began to cry.

"You're going home," Rionach soothed as she held the weeping *selchidh* close. "You are going home."

* * * * *

Rionach held Caoimhe in her arms as they lay upon a rocky islet a short swim from the silent *Tonquin*. It was dawn, and the sound was bathed in the crimson rays of a rising sun that reveled in the deaths of the night. The other *selchidhean* were resting, back in their pelts, and lazing in the cool airs of the fading night as they banished the horrors of the battle. Braonán had not slipped back into her pelt for she stood watch over the still forms of four of their kin; Thorna, Órfhlaith, Beatha[27], and Nóinín[28] had died at the hands of *Tonquin's* crew and they would find their long rest in this strange land so far from home.

There was little noise to break the silence and Braonán's tears were soundless as she looked upon the four friends before her. She glanced back at the *Tonquin*, backlit by the rising sun, and saw movement in her masts.

---

[27] Beatha – pronounced 'Bey-a'

[28] Nóinín – pronounced 'Nooeen-een'

"There are survivors," she muttered. The selkies rose from their somnolence and looked upon the ship.

"Not for long," Rionach replied as she spied the canoes that were paddling towards the *Tonquin*. All of them watched as a small skiff was lowered from the *Tonquin* and four crew members climbed into it.

"They'll escape," growled Morbhan.

"They will not," returned Braonán.

The drama was slow to unfold; the canoes, dozens of them filled with warriors, swarmed the ship. All watched as the men climbed the rounded sides of the *Tonquin* and began looting the vessel. They could hear yelling and shrieks as other canoes pursued the four escaping crewman. The *selchidhean* could see they would be easily captured.

Rionach was smoothing the hair of Caoimhe and whispering soft comforting words in her ear when the *Tonquin* exploded.

Braonán gasped as the ship seemed to bloat and burst amidst a bright flash and, seconds later, a shattering roar. She and the others gazed upon the tumbling forms of warriors as they were thrown high in the air from the exploding ship only to fall amongst the whirling timbers and crashing masts. The screams were horrible, and as the smoke cleared, the shattered *Tonquin* appeared as a smoking and steaming ruin. Moments later it disappeared beneath the still waters of Clayoquat Sound.

Rionach wept.

* * * * *

Jennifer held her hands to her face. The story was gripping, a horrific tale made so much more fascinating as she now recalled hearing something of the loss of the *Tonquin* in her humanities class, except it had been at the hands of natives, of course. She remembered that nearly two hundred had been said to have died that day.

Jennifer felt her stomach leap at the thought of the horrific end of all of those warriors.

"One crewmember supposedly survived, an interpreter," Braonán said as she rested against the log. "He was captured and made a slave, and then he escaped. His story of the *Tla-o-qui-aht*, or the Nootka, attacking the ship is the story that history now knows. I doubt anyone would have believed him had he said thirty-one naked and pale women storming the ship and killing the crew was what brought about the demise of the well-armed expedition," Braonán remarked with a bitter smile. "And as for the *Tla-o-qui-aht*, most who knew the truth died that day on the *Tonquin*. If the few survivors had any stories of what really happened, they never shared them."

"What finally happened?" Jennifer asked. "I mean, how did you come to be here?"

"We swam south," Braonán said as she cupped her chin in her hands. "Some of us rather liked this strange land so we swam down the straights into the Salish Sea and came ashore here in this little cove. About a dozen of us decided to stay, but not Rionach and Caoimhe. They chose to go home. It was a tearful goodbye, but I was tired and I wanted to stay. So here I have been ever since."

Jennifer had so many questions as she watched Braonán brush a tear from her eye.

"There's a point to my telling you this story, though," Braonán said as she again closed her eyes to the deepening hues of dusk. "Caoimhe endured her captivity for years. She existed within a hopeless circumstance where every day was filled with despair – confined in a box on a ship sailing for months and years, denied the light of day, and sold and treated as a slave to a brute of a human."

"I can't even imagine it," Jennifer replied in a hush.

"No," Braonán nodded, "nor can I. But I tell you this: Caoimhe endured. She endured that unimaginable existence of torture and despair. She dug deep for the strength to persevere against the oppressive despondency that should have gripped her." She looked upon Jennifer and reached out to touch her hand. "And so can you."

Jennifer felt a thrill go through her; she looked away, suddenly ashamed that she could have given up so easily. Braonán patted her hand and said nothing.

For long moments, Jennifer could find nothing to say.

Finally, she asked, "How do you live here?" The thought of this apparently immortal creature living in Esquimalt all this time was nearly inconceivable.

"Oh, that's easy," Braonán replied with a laugh. "I only become a human for short periods of time – sometimes a few months; once, it was a year. Then I simply return to the sea for a few years before I come back again." Her eyes glazed as she reminisced. "Once in a while I have an uncomfortable encounter, like I did in the 50's with a human I had known in the 20's." Her smile grew when she added, "I only have to appeal to reason that I could not possibly be the same young woman they had known decades before to end that line of questioning."

"Do you work?"

"I have money from a long time ago," Braonán returned. "It is more than enough for me to live in some comfort when I come ashore." She smiled as she remembered some secret adventure.

"How long have you been a human now?"

"For seven months," Braonán replied as she shook herself from her reverie. "I took up yoga this time," she beamed as she reached out to tap her yoga mat. "I must say I rather enjoyed it, that and a new Imperial Earl Grey tea made by Silk Road. Very enjoyable; I shall miss them."

"Miss them?"

"Yes." Braonán pulled off her running shoes and socks and placed them in her backpack. She stood, stretched, and faced the last of the lingering light of sunset. She pulled off her hoodie and sports bra and then stripped off her Yoga pants. Standing naked in the near darkness, she reached down and touched Jennifer on the shoulder.

"Remember the story of Caoimhe, Jennifer." Braonán picked up the seal pelt and stepped down the beach and into the chill waters. Jennifer was mesmerized as she watched Braonán wade out, until the water lapped at her luminescent hips, and then dive into the ocean. For a minute, Jennifer watched in silence as the ripples moved away in an ever growing circle and the waters smoothed. Finally, in the light of the growing moon, Jennifer saw the head of a seal emerge.

"Goodbye," Jennifer said as she stood and picked up the backpack. "I'll hold onto your things for now."

The seal nodded and Jennifer's eyes widened as other seals appeared. There was at least a dozen, their dark eyes focused on Jennifer. Slowly, one by one, they slid beneath the surface; the seal that was Braonán was last.

Jennifer shouldered the backpack feeling a mixture of joy and sadness. She would never look at a seal the same way again.

Part Eleven

The Pulkwutsang

The Place of the Ghost

It was Thanksgiving weekend and Jennifer was unsure of what to do with herself. Since the meeting with Braonán, she had not seen Aeonghus, neither the wizened *ghille dubh* nor the massive wolfhound. Each afternoon she would leave school, her hopes high as she walked with a purpose towards High Rock. She would wander the silent paths beneath the canopy of firs and hope that she would spy the head of the wolfhound peering around an arbutus tree or perhaps lifted above the growing sedge grass or the deer ferns that were nearing its full emerald height, but he was nowhere to be found. She would leave reluctantly, her gaze always lingering to see if the wolfhound would appear at the last moment, and each time she exited the park with her hopes dashed. The happiness she had felt was fading and the haunting dreams she had thought were gone had suddenly reappeared.

The dreams contained the imagery of the terrible accident: a ball, eyes in the mirror, and a bloody hand. They were the thin filaments of her memory that held the confusing recollections of the accident, but she could not place them in any context. Beyond that, however, there was a truly horrifying feeling that suggested she was at fault for the deaths. There was no proof, of course; the police report said the minivan had crossed the centre line of the Malahat highway before hitting the fully loaded Kenworth. Her brother had died instantly; her father, only a few minutes after. No reason was ever found for the accident save for driver error. Somehow Jennifer felt she had complicity in that, but she could not remember.

Jennifer was ruminating on these thoughts as she sat in the lawn chair outside with a glass of lemonade. She was enjoying the fleeting warmth of an autumn early evening in Victoria, a warmth that was undercut by the offshore breeze blowing through the distant fog bank in the Salish Sea. It meant flashes of warmth and cold that blended into one long amalgam of temperature variations and it required a hoodie, opened and with sleeves rolled up, instead of a t-shirt.

Friday night would soon be upon her, Jennifer mused. One week after her attempt at suicide and she had the vague feeling she was moving back towards that existence of continuous misery. There had been some unusually bright moments during the week involving Aeonghus and Braonán, but with the disappearance of the *ghille dubh*, she now found herself struggling to maintain that thin veneer of emotional composure in the face of her mother's continued indifference.

Her mother's indifference, Jennifer reflected.

Jennifer had been tempted to tell her about the suicide attempt, if only to shatter the icy silence. She felt like yelling and blaming, even threatening to do it again. She wanted an emotional response – sorrow for helping to drive her to it or regret that she had so emotionally abused her surviving child, and acceptance they were all each other had left in this world. Yet, she could not bring herself to do it. It was certainly not out of fear of hurting her mother; it was out of fear that it would not. She was terrified at the thought that her mother might be able to hear such stunning news and take such emotional blows and still maintain the façade of indifference.

Jennifer knew she could not cope with that reality so she said nothing.

In her mind's eye Jennifer could see High Rock in the early evening light. *An t-innean Beag* – The Little Anvil – she thought as she brooded over what to do. Should she go back tonight? Would Aeonghus be there? More frightening to her was the thought that there would be nothing. He had to be there she reasoned as she stood up and walked to the maple tree located in the corner of her front yard. She caressed the smooth bark and touched one of the browning leaves as she contemplated. She would go there tonight and she would look for Aeonghus. There was nothing else for her to do.

Jennifer glanced at the open bedroom window. Her mother was already there watching the small television in her room as she sipped wine to wash down the OxyContin she had taken at supper. Soon enough she would be passed out and Jennifer would be free for the night. She thought about writing a note, but her mother rarely rose before 10 a.m. on the weekend so she didn't bother. She would be back long before her mother crawled out of bed and even if she was not, her mother would simply assume she was out for the day.

Twenty minutes later, Jennifer ambled along the narrow paths of High Rock, disappointed at the number of people occupying the park: dog walkers, lovers, families and their children, noisy teenagers with cheap beer in their backpacks as they sought a spot of quiet seclusion to drink. Aeonghus wouldn't appear unless it was as the wolfhound, and even then she had her doubts. When she came to the cairn, a young family was already there taking pictures of the fantastic vista and the coming sunset. Saddened, Jennifer found a grassy depression just below the summit and sat down. She closed her eyes and breathed in the chill breeze wafting through the distant fog that lined the Straits of Juan de Fuca in the Salish Sea. The smells were fresh in the cool air – the grasses, green and lush in the early autumn after months of summer drought that had turned them brown; the dying leaves of oak and arbutus, the bark of the pines and oaks behind her; and the salty sea air.

"*Ohk, ohk, ohk!*"

Jennifer's eyes snapped open. Standing on a mossy mound of rock a few meters away was a massive raven.

"*Ohk, ohk, ohk!*" it cried as it took two steps to the left. It ruffled its feathers, dipped its obsidian head, and shrieked, "*Cr-r-uck!*"

Jennifer glanced at the family near the cairn, but they were focused on the distant form of Mount Baker. When she looked back at the raven, it had hopped a few steps away before turning back to her. "*Ohk, ohk, ohk!*" it shrieked before hopping a few more steps and emitting its strange knocking sound.

Jennifer felt a small grin form as she again looked around to see if anyone was watching; they were not, or they were oblivious to the show the bird was putting on. She slowly stood, hoping not to startle the bird as it again hopped a few more steps, moving away towards a small grassy knoll in the southwest. Jennifer followed as the raven leapt and flew a few meters before landing on the branch of a nearby Garry oak. Again the bird screeched at her, "*Ohk, ohk, ohk. Cr-r-uck!* Come with me!"

Stumbling to a halt, Jennifer swore she'd heard words. The raven bobbed its head again. "Come with me!" it croaked.

Her steps now cautious, Jennifer followed the bird to the knoll. The raven was on a nearby branch glaring at her with its beady, black eyes. "Sit down!" the bird cackled. Jennifer sat down on the grass, her eyes focused on the bird. There was nothing particularly malevolent about the raven as it perched there staring at her, but she could hardly feel comfortable with the thought that she was being ordered around by a bird. Every time she figured she had a handle on the unusual events of the past week, some new encounter reminded her that hers really was a strange new existence.

The raven spread its capacious wings and dropped lightly down to the grass a few meters in front of Jennifer. It moved towards her in its comical, hopping way, thoughtful yet determined, before it halted nearly within reach. It cocked its head back and forth and Jennifer smiled as she watched its humorous behaviour until it asked, "Why are you here?"

The voice was grating; the high, gravelly words were pointed and biting. There was nothing friendly about this creature. "Why are you here?" it asked again as it bobbed its head.

Jennifer glanced around to ensure she was not being watched. "I'm looking for Aeonghus," she replied.

"He's not here," the raven cackled. "The dog is not here. Why are you looking for the dog?"

"He's my friend."

"*Crooaak*," the raven shrilled with a mocking laugh. "Friends are you?" The bird leered at her with its dusky eyes. "The dog has friends he does, strange friends indeed." The raven chortled again. "The dog is visiting his other friends. Watch out for a girl, the dog said. She will be looking for me, the dog said." The raven paced, with amusing hops and wing flapping as it spoke. *If she comes this night, bring her to me*, the dog told me." The raven paused and bobbed its head. "You have come this night. A long walk it is, a very long walk to see the dog."

"Who are you?" Jennifer asked.

"*Ohk*! Mlá! I am called Mlá!"

"And where am I walking to?" Jennifer continued in a matter-of-fact tone that seemed to bother the raven.

"To the *Pulkwutsang*," the raven croaked, "we will go to the *Pulkwutsang*. The Place of the Ghost. Follow that to find the dog!"

"Where is that?" Jennifer asked. She wasn't prepared to go anywhere, but it would be easy to stop by her house if needed.

"A long walk, *tawk-tawk*! Many hours in the darkness," the raven replied.

"I'm not sure that's a great idea," Jennifer returned. She was feeling uneasy, and it wasn't simply because of the fact that a raven was talking with her.

"Fearful, are you?" the raven chuckled. "You should be. You are going to meet Him."

"Aeonghus?" Jennifer was puzzled.

"No. *Crooaak*! Not the dog! Him!"

"Who is 'Him'?" Jennifer snapped. Her patience was quickly melting in the warm evening. "I don't know who you are talking about when you simply say, 'Him'."

The raven flapped its massive wings. "The *Tighearna*."

"Who is that?" The name was familiar; she'd heard Aeonghus mention the name once.

"He is the Lord of the Forest," the raven snickered as it hopped round. "The dog will take you to Him."

"Why?"

"Why, why, why!" the raven cackled in annoyance. It cocked its head and blinked its dark eyes. "Too many questions!" It hopped around in a rage and then flapped its broad wings again. "The dog will take you to meet Him or not. It depends on you!"

Jennifer slowly rose. "When will we leave?"

"Now," the raven cried as it flapped its wings and rose to a tree branch. "Now."

"All right," Jennifer said. "I need to stop off at my house though if it's going to be a long walk."

"Then go," the raven screeched as it leapt off the branch and rose into the air.

* * * * *

The Esquimalt and Nanaimo Line's railway tracks were poorly lit in most sections and especially within the section that ran through the Songhees Band Indian Reserve. There were few streetlights from the Reserve to illuminate the empty tracks, and the brush on either side was dark and gloomy. The breeze had risen again, cool and piercing now with the hint of coming rain, and Jennifer was glad she had gone home first to grab a jacket and to stuff snacks and a water bottle into her backpack. Throughout that time, as she puttered silently in the kitchen, the raven had sat on the fence of her front yard, shrieking out in general annoyance until Jennifer heard one neighbour shout, "Shut the hell up, bird!"

The raven was overhead now, soaring high above in the darkness. On occasion she would here "*Quark-quark*!" from the night sky and she knew she was on the right course to wherever she was going.

"This is kinda ridiculous," she muttered as she walked past the muted glow of Admiral's Walk plaza on her right and onwards to Craigflower Road. The tracks seemed to be getting darker, and she stumbled over the uneven ties often. "I can't believe I'm doing this," she said under her breath. "I don't know what I'm thinking."

"*Ohk*!" the raven squawked as it flew past her head. Jennifer ducked at the powerful 'whoosh' of its widespread wings. "*Ohk*! Little feet must be picked up! Little feet must walk faster in the darkness!"

Jennifer stumbled to a halt. "It's dark!" she called out into the night. "I'm walking as fast as I can!"

"*Crooaak*! Not too fast! Little feet are slow! Little eyes are blind!"

"Yes," Jennifer seethed. "I can't see the damned tracks!"

"Too much television for little eyes! *Ohk*! Children become fat and lazy!"

"I'm not fat!" Jennifer shot back. "Not even close!"

The raven swopped by again. "*Ohk*! The fat children are slow with tired little legs! Come, *stṁa*, time to walk faster!"

"What's a *stṁa*?"

The raven cackled. "A milk cow!"

"Not funny!" Jennifer said as she crouched down, grasped a stone, and threw it into the darkness.

"*Crooaak*! Come *st'ma*, the night is growing old and we have the darkness to travel." The raven swooped low and sang out,

"Okoak Pish-pish,
Yaka memaloose tenas mowitch,
Yaka muck-a-muck la-reh,
Midlight copa house
Jack yaka mamook."

"Here is the cat.
That killed the rat,
That ate the malt,
That lay in the house
That Jack built."

Jennifer was furious and she crossed her arms. What was she doing following a singing raven down the railway tracks at night? This had been a week of wonders for sure, but right now it was turning into a nightmare. She wondered if the raven might just be malevolent, a creature like the *púca* perhaps or something worse? She felt a prickle of fear penetrating her anger and she considered turning back.

"*Tawk-Tawk!*" The raven landed a few meters before her. "You have stopped. Why?" It hopped closer and bobbed its head; she could barely make out its movement in the darkness. "Open mind, warm heart! *Ohk*. Close and be cold!"

"Where are you taking me?" Jennifer asked.

"Told you already. To the *Pulkwutsang!*"

"Where is that," Jennifer insisted.

The raven was furious as it hopped and squawked. "It is near the lake you call Thetis! Delays! No more delays! Keep walking!" the raven screamed as it leapt into the air.

Jennifer resumed walking but not at a quick pace. She was not happy with the turn of events and she didn't feel particularly safe. There was something of the *púca* in this raven and she wondered what its presence portended. She mused on the name, *Pulkwutsang*, there was something vaguely familiar about it. She wracked her mind for several minutes and then finally the connection was made. Thetis Lake had several creeks; one of the larger ones was called Craigflower Creek, but at one time, it was known as Deadman's Creek. Could that be The Place of the Ghost? She wondered. Why they were going there was a mystery, and the raven was again flying high in the night sky beyond the distance of questioning. Jennifer plodded on.

The tracks crossed the Old Island Highway and Jennifer found herself walking briefly along the still black waters of Portage Inlet. The highway on the other side was punctuated with racing headlights, and the invasive sounds of traffic were surprisingly loud over the quiet waters. Jennifer only saw the deep inlet briefly, for the narrow cove soon disappeared and she left the tracks to walk along the noisome mud flats leading to the creek now exposed at low tide. It was dark here with little light and she felt a new trepidation as she approached the entrance to Craigflower Creek in View Royal Park.

"*Crooaak!* The *Pulkwutsang!* We are here!"

Jennifer found herself in thick brush as she walked along the creek. It was even darker and she had to pick her way slowly. It took an hour, and it was 11 p.m. before she nervously emerged from the brush, muddy and damp, to climb up to the highway, cross its empty lanes, and end up on a trunk road running alongside the highway. She could picture the area where she now stood, and following this road she would come to Highland Road and the eastern entrance to Thetis Lake Park.

Her pace was quicker now, and Jennifer pulled her hoodie over her head as a rain shower began. With her head bent, she moved with purpose while overhead the raven name Mlá squawked every so often to remind her that he was there. For thirty minutes she trudged through the showers, making her way north up Highland Road and then into the entrance of the park. Beneath the deep shadows of the rainforest, walking with caution through the mud and over the roots of trees, she followed a winding trail that eventually led her to the waters of the creek again.

As midnight approached, Jennifer scrambled along a twisted narrow trail in the darkness of Thetis Lake Park. Here, beneath the tall trees of the murky forest, she felt real fear. At one time she would have felt it an unreasonable fear, but the events of the past week had changed that. She had seen monsters and strange creatures, and she had a foreboding feeling that Thetis Lake was another such place to contain one.

"*Ohk*! Little legs are wet! Little legs must walk! The dog is waiting on the island in the lake!"

"What?" Jennifer searched the darkness for the raven, but she could see nothing.

"To the lake! *Ohk*!" The flap of wings resounded and Jennifer pushed through the brush and darkness until she found herself back on Highland Road.'

"*Cr-r-uck*! Cross the ridge! Cross the ridge! Tired little legs on the *stṁa*!"

Jennifer grumbled angrily as she paused on the path. She tried to visualize where she was, but couldn't. She pulled out her iPhone and tapped her Google Map app. The lake lay to the west with nearly six hundred meters of thick forest, bog, and hills in between. "I can't cross that at night?" she shouted to the darkness. "It's too dangerous!"

"Fall you might! *Tawk-Tawk*! Dog will be displeased! Fear must rule you!"

Jennifer gritted her teeth and tucked her phone away. She glanced at the sky and saw the cloud thinning. At least there wouldn't be more showers and likely the moon would even provide some light. Shouldering her pack, she left the trail and plunged uphill and into the forest, tripping and slipping as she climbed the steep mossy slopes amongst the majestic firs. It was very hard going as she picked her way over fallen trunks, sucking bogs, and thick brush made up of salal and ferns. She was soon soaked with water from the plants and sweat from the exertion, not to mention twice falling in small shallow puddles of mephitic mud. After an hour she reached the summit and began the slow and strenuous descent towards the darkness of the lake. The raven was her company and as frightening as that was, there was a part of Jennifer that thought she should feel safe, for if the raven was indeed leading her to Aeonghus, then it would ensure that she arrived safely.

Jennifer was exhausted when she finally reached the calm black waters of Thetis Lake. Nestled between the tall forested hills, the lake was an old haunt of hers that was both frightening and foreign in the darkest part of the night.

"*Ohk*! Time to swim. Time to swim! *Ohk*! *Stṁa* must kick little legs for the island!"

Jennifer dropped her pack. There were two islands on Thetis Lake, one larger with sheer sides, and the other low, with a handful of stunted trees and flat grass. She supposed she needed to swim to the smaller one which lay about one hundred and forty-five meters away. Could she do it though? Here there was real danger. Jennifer was a strong swimmer, but the waters were cold, she was tired, and she would be carrying a backpack full of clothing and food. She could easily drown, and no one would ever know. The utter darkness wrestled more unreasonable fears from her, for she recalled in the depths of her memory that the lake was reputed to have a monster in it.

"That's ridiculous," she said with chattering teeth. The infamous Thetis Lake monster from the 1970's had long been debunked as a tall tale told by teenagers who had reported a humanoid monster – a fantastic creature of the Black Lagoon type horror that frightened children and adults alike. It was preposterous a week ago, but not so much now. Maybe there was truth to it, and lurking in the shadowy depths was a creature waiting to pull her below the surface.

"*Crooaak*!" the raven dove at her. "Swim!"

> *"nqEti nayka tiqi whiskey*
> *pi alta nayka mash*
> *alta nayka mash*
> *whiskey hayas khEltEs*
> *pi alta nayka mash*
> *alta nayka mash."*

Jennifer was shivering as she stripped down to her underwear. She stuffed the clothing into her backpack and stepped gingerly into the chill water.

> *"I used to like whiskey*
> *but now I've given it up*
> *now I've given it up*
> *Whiskey's extremely no-good*
> *and now I've given it up*
> *now I've given it up."*

"Oh my God that's cold," she whispered as she waded in deep. She shrieked when the water rose to her midriff, and then gritting her teeth, she closed her eyes, held the backpack high, and plunged in. "Jesus, it's cold!" she roared as she flipped onto her back and kicked out towards the island. The water was a frigid blanket wrapping her as she stared at the star spackled darkness above. It was a considerable effort to fight the pervading fear of the depths below her.

Jennifer found herself gasping and her movements becoming sluggish. She gripped the backpack and rolled over to see her progress; she was aiming for the shadowy island. She was cold and tired, yet only halfway to her destination. Panic rose in her as the fear of drowning loomed her mind – a vision of death as the cold waters closed over her head. She gritted her teeth, dug deep for strength, and continued to kick while all too aware of her ebbing strength. What if she died here? She wondered as her breathing increased, a shallow gasping that would have been heard across the lake if someone were walking the trail. But no one would even know to look here, her mind screamed.

"Hayaleha, Hayaleha, Hayaleha,
Spos maika nanitch naika telhum,
Wēk saia naila memalos alta,
Kōpa Kunspa eli. Yaya!"

Her face dipped below the surface, and new panic and a surge of adrenaline coursed through Jennifer.

"Hayaleha, Hayaleha, Hayaleha,
If you see my friends,
Say that I had almost died,
In New Westminster. Yaya!"

She kicked harder, screamed in fear, and paused to roll over again to review her progress. The island was close; she could be there in a couple more minutes. On her back, she kicked with new strength, but she knew it would ebb fast. She had little energy left in her and the cold had sapped her endurance. She closed her eyes to the night sky and opened them again when she bumped her head on a rock.

"Ow," she muttered as she rubbed her dripping hair. She rose to her feet, rivulets of cold water running down her body as she puffed and crawled with heavy, frozen limbs up onto the rocky shore where she stood shivering. Icy tendrils of water ran down her chilled body as she stood on legs of rubber and fumbled with the zipper of her bag. Finally, as she cursed at her hands that were barely functioning from the cold, she wrapped herself in a hoodie and pulled on a pair of pants. Glancing at the darkness of the lake, she muttered, "I'm an idiot."

"*Cr-r-uck*! You did not drown! Little legs are strong!" The raven settled onto the branch of a scrubby Douglas fir above her. "*Ohk*! Time to meet the dog!"

"Aeonghus," she whispered through chattering teeth. She didn't bother with shoes; the luxuriant grass was soft with few rocks. The raven dropped from the tree limb and was almost indistinguishable in the darkness as it flew a few meters to another branch.

"*Ohk, ohk, ohk!*" it shrieked. Jennifer followed for a few steps until she heard a nearby 'zing' and a faint 'plop'. There was a pause and then the buzzing sound of a ratchet and gears.

It sounded like someone was fishing.

Jennifer took a few more steps, easing through brush and past the thin trunks of stunted firs. In the darkness, as the brush opened, she saw a figure sitting on the rocky edge of the island, a fishing rod in its hands. The figure was hooded and slight, but human size which puzzled her. It was much larger than Aeonghus.

"Aeonghus?" she whispered.

The figure finished reeling in the plastic bobber and placed the rod on the grass beside it. It twisted to look upon her, and as Jennifer felt a thrill of fear and stepped back against a tree, it brought shadowy hands up to the cowl of the hood that covered its head and pulled it back.

In the pale moonlight that danced across the wavelets of the water, Jennifer looked upon the head of a wolf.

"Hello, Mlá," the wolf said in a mild and kindly voice, "who's your friend?"

Part Twelve

The Tighearna

The Lord

Jennifer looked upon the human shaped vision with the wolf's head and gulped in terror. The creature allowed a small toothy smile and then looked at the raven. "Well, Mlá?"

"*Ohk!*" the raven shrilled as it flapped its wings. "*Stma!*"

"That is hardly polite, Mlá," the creature remonstrated, his sharp teeth bared in a hideous smile. "She hardly looks like a cow. More like a little girl, or a rather wet little girl, I suppose." He rose with ease, standing just above Jennifer in height. His slim human body was covered in fur and his tail was bushy. It was his curiously handsome wolf's head, however, that arrested her attention – regal yet feral. The creature was cloaked in what appeared to be a thick, knee-length plaid blanket tied at his waist with a leather cord. "What is your name, girl that does not look like a cow?" he asked graciously as he glanced at the raven on the branch above.

"Jennifer," was her whispered and fearful reply. "Are you going to hurt me?" she asked as she took a step away from the tree she had backed into.

"Hurt you?" he asked in surprise. "Now that's silly. Why would I wish to hurt a little girl out for a swim?" The voice sounded as if the face was grinning, yet all Jennifer could see was the horrific visage of teeth, bare in the moonlight, and the yellow piercing eyes. "No, I would never hurt you. Do you fish?"

"No," Jennifer stuttered. The creature took a step forward and leaned down towards her. The teeth were bared again, a hideous smile that made her want to scream.

"Not even once?" he asked.

"No," Jennifer repeated in an undertone, "not even once."

"Well that's unfortunate," the creature replied as he stood straight. "Yes, that is quite unfortunate. Fishing is not only a wonderful way to get food, but it is a most relaxing and enjoyable pursuit."

"I'm sure it is," Jennifer stammered. She was unsure what the creature was that stood before her, though she reasoned quickly as she swallowed and fought to control her breathing, that he was a talking wolf that looked rather human, but seemed friendly enough and not ready to pounce on her and tear her apart. That had to count for something. "You're not Aeonghus," she added after a few moments.

"Aeonghus?" the beast said as he cocked his head in confusion. "I would think not." He glanced at the raven that fluttered its wings and paced back and forth on the tree limb. His yellow eyes narrowed in suspicion. "Mlá, what exactly is this girl doing on my island?"

"*Cr-r-ruck!* See the dog, she is! See the dog! *Ohk!*"

"Is Aeonghus here in the park?" he asked as he raised his head. "Be truthful for once, Mlá."

"*Tawk-tawk!* The dog said bring her to the dog!"

"I'm not a dog, Mlá," he replied tersely, crossing his arms. "I doubt she finds it very funny that you made her swim across the lake to my island in the middle of the night in cold water."

"After coming up Craigflower Creek," Jennifer said with an angry pout as she shivered.

"Well, that was definitely not very funny," he tut-tutted. "Did you bring her up the entire creek?"

"*Ohk! Ohk!*" the raven flapped its wings. It was clearly enjoying the joke.

"Mlá believes himself to be rather funny. It's why the Salish people think he's the trickster. I find he's simply a bit rude."

"What are you?" Jennifer blurted out as she rubbed her arms.

"What am I?" the creature repeated with an air of surprise. "Well," he mused with a fearsome grin, "I suppose that is a good question. I must assume Mlá said nothing of me to continue his bad joke." This was said as the creature stared at the raven and shook his head. "My name is Machonna, and I am a wulver."

"What's a wulver?"

Machonna brightened. "Why, a wulver is me, my dear; a werewolf you might think me though I don't turn into a human or a wolf. I'm rather in between," Machonna said as he beamed with pride.

"Oh my," Jennifer said as she suddenly felt faint. She dropped to one knee to fight the waves of dizziness that sought to pitch her on her side.

Machonna stepped forward and knelt beside her. "You should breathe deeply. I wish I had a paper bag," he yelped as he glanced around the darkened grass and wrung his paws. "Normally there is always a bit of trash here; teenagers and picnickers can be rather untidy. Of course the one time I need it, there's nothing to be found."

"*Crooaak!*" the raven shrieked in delight.

"Oh hush, Mlá," Machonna snapped. "Now, Jennifer, place your head low and breathe normally. There now, how does that feel?" He patted her back with a large hairy hand. "Are you feeling better?"

Jennifer nodded, well aware that a werewolf, or something very close to it, was patting her back and asking her how she felt. It was utter madness.

"Where is Aeonghus?" she gasped.

"I'm not sure," Machonna said with growing worry. He glanced at the raven. "I assume he asked you to bring the girl to him? Why?"

"*Obk!* See the *Tighearna!*"

"Ah," Machonna said with a knowing smile. "Yes, He is here. I saw Him this very morning. So Aeonghus is going to present you? Now that's a rare honour."

"Present me to who?" Jennifer breathed. Now she felt sick and it was taking a lot of effort not to throw up.

"Why to the *Tighearna*, of course."

"Who is he? Or what is he, it seems better to ask?"

"Well," Machonna said as he sat back on his haunches, "if Aeonghus hasn't told you much, then maybe I should leave it to him."

Jennifer looked into the face of Machonna. The fur was mostly brown with a suggestion of grey at the tips making the head handsome in its lupine way and a little larger than a normal wolf head with not much of a neck. She didn't even know they had wolves around here, let alone werewolves. What a silly thought, she chastised. "Where are you from?" she gasped as she placed her head between her knees.

"Originally?" Machonna asked as he beamed in pleasure. "Why, the Shetland Islands. I'm not a local in case you're wondering," Machonna added with a wink.

"You have no accent?" Jennifer replied. Machonna laughed, a short deep barking that made Jennifer recoil in fear.

"I do. I'm just rather good at hiding it. I know Aeonghus still has a bit of his brogue. Would it be better if I brought my accent back for you?"

Jennifer shook her head.

"So," Machonna continued as he again stared at the raven, "Mlá, where is Aeonghus?"

"*Crooaak*! On the hill!"

Machonna frowned. "Come now, Mlá that is quite unhelpful." He turned to Jennifer and said as an aside, "Huginn and Muninn are generally much more obliging than Mlá, though they do have their moments. I suspect it has something to do with the breed."

"Huginn and Muninn?" Jennifer puzzled as she rubbed her temples.

"My apologies," Machonna said with a nod, "Odin's ravens. They are generally easier to deal with, while they wait for their tasks from Odin."

Jennifer found herself sitting on the damp grass, her legs tucked in and her arms wrapped around her. It seemed she was spending far more time in confused awe than not this past week as she puzzled over the incredible events that were gripping her life. The wulver named Machonna sat down before her.

"I must admit, it's been some time since a human was brought into the fold, as it were; many, many years in fact. With Aeonghus, it's well over a hundred. With myself, it's been about forty or so years."

"Were you the monster that attacked the teenagers? The Thetis Lake monster?"

"Monster is a rather hurtful term," Machonna replied with a pained look upon his face. "When I heard that, I was most distressed."

"It was you though?" Jennifer persisted as her eyes widened in surprise.

"Oh yes," Machonna said as he suddenly brightened. "They were swimming when they spotted me diving underwater. I was rather careless that day as I swam from the underwater cave I live in. I should have stayed the day, as I normally do, but I simply felt like stretching my legs. They saw me and panicked. They hurt themselves in their frenzy to get away and they blamed it on me."

"But they recanted that later," Jennifer replied.

"Did they?" Machonna seemed pleased. "So I'm not seen as a monster anymore?"

"No."

"Just as well," Machonna said as he stood. "I was not fond of the moniker." He looked down upon Jennifer who was still shivering in the cold. "I've been here for many years, many decades actually," he corrected. The wulver looked across the darkness of the lake. He was silent for several moments before he glanced at Jennifer and smiled.

"I came here when my own home was destroyed to make a new road many, many years ago, not far from the town of Aith. A road," he repeated as he shook his wolfish head in disbelief. "Would you believe that?" he sighed. "It was a beautiful little pond and a very lovely cave, and the fishing was wonderful." He paused and seemed to be considering his story. "I came here in the cargo hold of a steamer," he resumed after several more moments. "I snuck on with the baggage and was nearly caught when I tried to sneak off," he added with a wink of a yellow eye. "It was quite a long voyage to get here. I was fortunate to come with the mail."

Jennifer opened her mouth to ask a question but Machonna raised his hand to stop her. "It seems Aeonghus has plans for you if you are to meet *Tighearna*," he said to change the subject.

"Why won't you tell me who that is?" Jennifer groused as she rose stiffly to her feet.

"That is not my place, my dear. If Aeonghus is presenting you to Him, he must have an important reason.

It made no sense, Jennifer mused, but then what did? She was talking to a wulver after being guided here by a talking Salish raven, and was now wondering when a *ghille dubh* was going to present her to yet another mysterious creature. She placed her face in her hands and sighed.

Machonna gazed upon her with some amusement. "I can only imagine how difficult this all must be," he said as he gently patted her arm, a friendly and soothing touch at odds with the vision of the savage creature giving it. "I'm not sure why Aeonghus has befriended you, but it must have been important. He was sorely hurt by his last human friend."

"Who was that?" Jennifer asked.

Machonna was thoughtful for a moment. "It's possible I shouldn't say; however, it may help for you to understand him. The last human he befriended was a very young boy named Charlie. He died when the streetcar he was on fell into the water when the Selkirk Bridge collapsed."

"Oh no," Jennifer mouthed.

"Aeonghus has been in hiding ever since, and I thought he would remain that way, so hurt was he by the loss of his friend. For him to befriend you, well," the wulver said with a slow toothy grin, "you must be something special."

"He saved my life," Jennifer admitted while looking away in shame.

Machonna nodded and seemed to understand. "That is good. Yes, I think that is very good. So he will present you to the *Tighearna*, which I find odd, by the way," he added as an aside, "but that is his business, not mine. It seems that my business now is to get you there since I suspect Aeonghus is nearby. Mlá," he barked as he glanced at the raven in disapproval, "you could render a service and help curb my annoyance somewhat if you would find Aeonghus for me and have him meet us on the north shore."

"*Ohk*! Find the dog for the dog!" Mlá cackled as it took off.

"My apologies," Machonna said, "we'll find Aeonghus soon enough. You won't need to swim," he added when he noted the sudden look of fear and concern on her face, "I have a boat."

"A boat?" Jennifer repeated as she shivered beneath her hoodie. "Where do you hide it?"

Machonna tossed his head for her to follow as he pushed through the brush towards the shore of the island. Tucked beneath the overhanging branches of a sea spray bush was a small aluminum rowboat.

"As much as I enjoy a swim, I also rather enjoy rowing," Machonna said as he crawled into the back of the boat. "I hide it very well in the brush during the day near my cave, covered with branches and such. I use it only at night."

"I see," Jennifer said as she dressed and then took a seat in the stern.

Machonna rowed, powerful silent strokes that pulled the boat into the darkness of the lake. Jennifer glanced skywards, noted the brilliant moon and haze of stars in the ochre lights of the city to the southeast, and felt a profound peacefulness in the silence. It was pleasantly broken when Machonna began to sing softly in a strange dialect.

"Hear du da saft nots o Horeb whisper
Lullin wis tae a sleepin soond,
Facin mist an uncan waaters
Let wis come noo an lay wis doon."

Jennifer found the words difficult to follow. However, the honeyed tenor of the wulver proved soothing as the boat moved over the dark, silky waters.

"An dere sho stood
Da prood masts high.
Nae man wis watchin
Dis faersome moder-dy;
Nae man wis lippenin
Dis storm athin da calm;
Black wis da skerry as
Broadside sho'd faan."

The words, as foreign as they were, invoked such imagery in Jennifer's mind: the wind-whipped Shetland Islands, the tall masts of the fishing boats and their flapping sails, the sailors in heavy wool sweaters fighting the nets brimming with fish.

"Runnin doon ower da banks tae see dem
Families cam fae aboot da doors,

Hearin voices yall oot fur freedom,

Uncan voices on uncan shores."

Jennifer closed her eyes and smiled.

"What do you think?" Machonna said as he guided the rowboat towards a small shallow beach to the north.

"It was lovely," Jennifer replied as she glanced back at the wulver.

"Most kind. I haven't had an appreciative audience in many years. Aeonghus doesn't come around much now and the others are nearly all gone. There are so very few of us left. I must admit," he added as he paused in his rowing and rested for a moment on the crossed oars, "I'm rather enjoying your company tonight."

Jennifer felt a flush but hid her smile. A wolfman enjoying her company, how insane was that? She thought.

The rowboat touched the shallow, rocky bottom and Machonna hopped out to pull the bow up onto the shore. He glanced at the sky in the east now hidden by the forest and asked, "What time is it?"

"Nearly five o'clock," Jennifer replied as she fought a yawn.

"Hmmm, well if Aeonghus wants to present you we'll need to find Him before dawn. The *Tighearna* is usually active at night."

Machonna led Jennifer along the lake trail and then abruptly cut into the darkened forest. It was rough scrambling through salal, Oregon grape, and ferns; over fallen logs and in between towering firs and cedars; up rocky hills and cliffs; and through sucking bogs reeking of rot. It was exhausting, but as the sky began to lighten in the east they crossed Highland Road and thrust back into the forest.

"I believe we are almost there," he said. "Yes, here we are."

Puffing and sweaty, Jennifer found herself atop a low mound of mossy rock, and there waiting on the top stood Aeonghus, his pipe thrust in his mouth and a thin tendril of smoke rising past his angry eyes.

"Och, now what are you doing with the lass, Machonna? I sent the damned raven to get her and now she's almost too late."

"Not her fault, Aeonghus," Machonna returned with a wave of his hand. "Have words with Mlá if you need to."

"I should have guessed," Aeonghus grumped as he glanced at Jennifer; his anger softened. "You alright, lass?"

Jennifer nodded. "Just tired," she replied as she dropped her pack.

"I need to leave, Aeonghus," Machonna said. He gave a slight bow to Jennifer. "It was a pleasure to meet you, Jennifer."

"Me too," she replied after a clumsy curtsy.

The wulver disappeared into the darkness leaving Jennifer and Aeonghus alone.

"Where have you been?" Jennifer asked as she sat on the grass and rubbed her tired legs. "I've missed you all week."

Aeonghus nodded as he too took a seat. His movements were slow and deliberate, and he pulled the pipe from beneath his massive moustache before answering. "I've been out tae find the *Tighearna*. He's no' the easiest tae find these days. He doesn't spend tae much time around here now," Aeonghus added as he looked around the darkness. "Too many people."

"Who is he?" Jennifer pleaded. Her curiosity increased each time the mysterious creature was mentioned. She couldn't imagine what they were talking about as the last two weeks had included a *ghille dubh*, a *púca*, a *selchidh*, a talking raven and now, a wulver, of all things. She massaged her temples as a massive headache threatened to form.

"He is as I said He is," Aeonghus replied, his tone and words evasive. "He is the Lord of the Forest."

"Which is?" Jennifer persisted with some annoyance. She would not allow the *ghille dubh* to get off that easy.

"You'll see when ye meet Him," Aeonghus said as he glanced at the brightening sky. "Come, lass, dawn will be the best time."

Aeonghus rose, stiff and slow. Leaning on his staff, he moved through the brush to the trail that led back towards Highland Road. The trail was narrow and muddy after the showers of the night, and slick tree roots crisscrossed its length while ferns and salal lined its edges like a fence. The high canopy of trees obscured most of the light, keeping the forest in deep darkness that would have terrified Jennifer had it not been for Aeonghus' silent company.

They walked for a few minutes at a slow ambling pace, over humps of rock and around trees and brush, before they came to a sudden halt. He closed his eyes, whispered soundless words, and then shook his head in apparent sadness.

"What?" Jennifer wondered as she knelt beside him. "What's wrong?"

"He's here," Aeonghus replied, his voice cracking. He cleared his throat. "He's here," he repeated as he moved deliberately towards the road. Just before the last few meters, he paused, knelt, and looked between the branches of an Oregon grape. "Come, lass," he whispered as he patted the ground beside him. "See the *Tighearna.*"

Jennifer knelt beside Aeonghus and peered into the gloom. She could make out the unlit road in the muted light and as she did so, she spotted a pair of dim figures on the side of the road. It took a few moments of pondering before their forms materialized but when they did she cupped her hands to her mouth in horror.

A doe was lying on its side in a widening pool of blood, her chest rising and dropping slowly as a fawn stood over her nudging her nose.

"Oh no," Jennifer said brokenly as tears balled in her eyes.

"Aye," Aeonghus replied heavily.

The fawn squealed, a wailing cry that sounded like a small crying child, and then walked around the barely breathing body of its mother. It nudged the doe's body and squealed again. It was horrible to witness, and Jennifer felt a flush of anguish at the pathos of the scene and the gripping sorrowful emotions of the young deer.

It seemed as if it were crying.

Tears rolled down Jennifer's face and she wiped them away quickly. When she glanced over at Aeonghus, the *ghille dubh* was gone, replaced by the massive wolfhound that leaned against her to offer comfort.

Jennifer turned back to the heartbreaking vision before her. She wanted to rush out, to hold and offer comfort to the animal that was experiencing what she had – the loss of a parent. She was poised to move when Aeonghus leaned harder against her. "No," he whispered. "Wait."

There was movement in the shadows beyond the road, and Jennifer felt a thrill as a figure emerged from the brush and trees. It was a towering man, hooded beneath a cloak that fell to his knees. He appeared to be wearing something on his head, a crown of branches perhaps? Jennifer wondered. No, she thought, it was far too big to be a crown. The man walked towards the fawn, which showed no fear, and slowly knelt beside it while reaching out a huge hand to touch it lightly on its chin.

"*Tighearna*," Aeonghus muttered.

The man, whose head was deeply shadowed, lifted his hands to the notched cowl of the hood and pulled it back. Jennifer fell back onto her bottom gasping in shock as she gazed upon the creature.

The huge man had the head and antlers of a powerful stag.

"He was called Herne at one time," Aeonghus whispered as Jennifer scrambled back to a crouch, "and many other names before that."

Herne reached out and softly placed a hand on the doe's side. He closed his eyes and Jennifer saw that his lips were moving.

"Can he save her?" she asked. Her lip quivered and new tears rose in her eyes.

Aeonghus shook his head. "He could, but he will not."

The doe tried to raise her head from the bloody pool, but she could not. The fawn squealed and Herne placed a gentle hand over the deer's heart until she lay still. As the fawn cried out in renewed misery, Herne gathered it into his muscular arms and brought it to his chest. Dwarfed, the tiny fawn was still, and Herne lowered his mighty antlered head to whisper in its ear. They were still for a moment and then Herne stood tall and strode across the road, all the while caressing the head of the fawn and whispering in its ear.

Jennifer was wide-eyed as the towering creature walked past her and then down the trail. Aeonghus rose to follow and beckoned Jennifer do the same with the toss of his head. So many emotions tore at her as she stumbled in the gloom – fear of the magnificent and beastly creature whose mere presence emanated a very ancient power and wisdom, sorrow for the tiny fawn still crying out in despair, and deep curiosity at why she seemed destined to witness this terrible event.

They followed in silence for several minutes, losing sight of the imposing Herne, until they rounded a bushy corner and found themselves in a small clearing. The fawn stood trembling on the trail while Herne knelt on one knee before it. He was still touching the fawn's cheek and petting it behind the ears when Aeonghus and

Jennifer appeared. He turned and looked at Jennifer, holding her eyes with his own dark mahogany orbs.

Jennifer felt like she was suffocating as the creature stared at her. The eyes were deep and soulful within the massive stag's head, and she sensed very great age in them. This creature, she thought, has been on this Earth for a very, very long time and has seen much in its long existence. The antlers on its head were powerful and burnished, spread wide and with many points. Though they were scarred and old, they emanated a feeling of latent strength; she could imagine the creature charging her in a bestial rage. Herne's body was covered in hair, short and brown like that of a stag; it wore loose trousers of plaid – green and brown – beneath the thick sorrel coloured woolen cloak; and his broad chest was bare of adornment.

Herne rose with dignity until he stood tall beneath the darkened canopy. The fawn skipped towards Jennifer and paused at her feet. Jennifer dropped to one knee and slowly put out her hand. The fawn nuzzled it, its damp nose cold in the cool air. Jennifer, wiping her nose and eyes, found herself smiling at the fawn's affection. Her attention was so riveted that she did not notice Herne move until he towered over her and she looked up with eyes widening in fear as he knelt before her. Even on one knee he was so much taller than she was. Reaching out, he gently grasped her hand – his own was soft and warm – and held it as he placed it upon the head of the fawn.

* * * * *

The imagery was fast and confusing – a blur of leaves and ferns in the deep gloom of morning beneath the shadows of the forest. A small moth, its course aimless as it rose and fell beneath the branches or wavered between the ferns. She was following it, skipping for joy in the simple chase, jumping with a foolish glee each time the moth rose, and dodging in the ecstasy of childhood pleasure at the discovery of the smallest of things. The moth fluttered through a sea spray bush heavy with dew and disappeared.

Jennifer pushed her way through, heard the warning grunt of the doe behind her along with the sounds of pursuit, but ignored them in the thrilling focus of immature diversion. Before her lay the road and she could hear the sound of tiny hooves skipping across the hard dark pavement as she crossed it. Brilliant LED headlights intruded upon her periphery and then she heard the squeal of skidding tires. As the SUV paused for only a moment, she heard muted cursing over the beat of some nameless pop music, and then the vehicle disappeared into the darkness, its scarlet tail lights, like angry eyes, fading into the distance.

Jennifer looked back upon the doe now lying on the road, blood pooling beneath her head. The doe had been pursuing her, warning her against the danger of the road.

Now the doe lay dying.

* * * * *

Jennifer was gasping as she found herself staring into the abyssal eyes of Herne. Hot tears rolled down her cheeks as she glanced down at the fawn nuzzling against her. She found herself holding it, petting its head as she brushed her hand over her cheeks and eyes.

"It was an accident," Herne said in a deep, resonating voice that seemed to emanate from the very ground around her. He reached out and placed a gentle hand upon the fawn's head. "It was not her fault."

As Jennifer petted the fawn, Herne moved his hand and placed it on her cheek. "It was not her fault," he repeated as he gazed deep into Jennifer's eyes.

"It was not your fault."

A sudden and horrible realization washed over Jennifer, and she tried to pull her face away. "No," she mouthed as fresh tears rolled down her cheeks. "Please, no," she repeated brokenly, her voice collapsing in emotion. She closed her eyes. "Please, no!"

* * * * *

"Catch!" said her brother, Alex, as he tossed a red rubber ball at her. Jennifer was sitting on the right side of the second set of seats in the minivan playing Angry Birds on her iPod and she only had one bird left to knock down the glass house and kill the piggies.

"Alex," she snapped, "knock it off already!" She glanced past and out the side window of the mini-van beyond Alex, at the steady stream of lights and traffic in the rain, as they crested the summit of the Malahat highway.

"Come on," Alex repeated as he struggled in his booster seat to grasp the ball. "Catch!"

"Kids," said Jennifer's father as he squinted through the glare and rain, "we're only halfway there. Could you hold off the fighting until we hit the three quarter mark?"

"Yeah, Jenny!" Alex said as he stuck out his tongue. "Be nice!" Alex threw the ball and it bounced off Jennifer's head. Her last bird missed and she failed the level.

"Alex!" she snapped as she grabbed the ball and threw it at her brother.

Alex giggled as he batted the ball away with his hand. It bounced off the roof and hit the rear view mirror before landing in the front seat.

"Come on, you two," Jennifer's father said as he reached up to adjust the mirror back to normal. He held it for a moment, and Jennifer could see his eyes as they stared at her. "Jennifer, I'm trusting you to keep the peace back there."

The lights of the semi-truck were brilliant as the minivan crossed the centreline. Jennifer heard the deep roar of the truck's air horn and then felt the powerful jarring crash as the minivan was sideswiped and became a tumbling, shrieking world of rending metal and shattering glass as it rolled down the highway.

Darkness closed over her for what felt like an age.

Jennifer opened her eyes in the dripping gloom. The windows were smashed and the van lay crushed on its driver's side. As she hung in her seatbelt, she could see little of her brother in the mangled side of the van, and only the shoulder and arm of her father emerged from the collapsed roof and windshield. Water dripped around her, faint voices seemed to come from far away and then her father's hand moved. It lifted, a thin line of blood rolling down the finger as it reached towards her.

"Are you alright?" Her father's voice was muffled and slow. She knew he was dying.

"Yes."

"That's good. I love you."

"I love you too, Daddy. I'm sorry."

There was a long pause as the voices outside grew louder.

"Not your fault, Jennifer. Not your fault."

Then there was silence.

* * * * *

Herne pulled his hand away from Jennifer's cheek. She was stunned for a moment before new tears began to roll down her cheeks. She dissolved into great weeping, and Herne gathered her in his powerful arms, held her close, and gently patted her back.

"It was not your fault," he said, his deep voice low and soothing. "It was an accident."

Jennifer cried and buried her face in his chest. As Herne patted her back, he glanced at Aeonghus who sat on his haunches with his head low. "Yes," he said as he peered hard at the wolfhound. "It was not your fault either."

Part Thirteen

'S Rioghal mo Dhream

My Race is Royal

Jennifer sat cross legged on the forest floor, her hands resting on the moist, verdant carpet of moss while beams of sunlight burned through the tall forest canopy above. The silence of the night had faded as birdsong, indistinct yet pervasive as it filled the forest around her, announced yet another glorious October morning. Across from her sat Herne, powerful and statuesque, his eyes closed and thin vapour emanating from his nostrils in the cool morning as he breathed slow and deep. Jennifer was able to study him in great detail especially the polished antlers and the handsome stag's head with glistening nose, twitching ears, and bull neck. He was certainly no deer she recognized locally. On Vancouver Island, the blacktail deer were small, lithe, creatures – pale cousins to the larger deer of the interior of British Columbia. Herne's head, however, was of a breed she didn't recognize – larger, older, and more fearsome. He was an otherworldly creature, ancient in age and wisdom. His body was muscular beneath the fur, well defined and powerful. The threadbare trousers and homespun cloak seemed fitting, and his large bare feet with thickened soles were black with grime.

For perhaps an hour she sat before him, watching him in his somnolence, or perhaps it was meditation, she wasn't sure. Not a word and no movement from him save for the odd twitch of his ears or his nose. He seemed oblivious to the world around him, or perhaps, Jennifer wondered, he was fully immersed in it. The fawn still sat in his lap, sleeping after the horrors of the morning and Aeonghus slept respectfully beside him, his long legs twitching in dog dreams; a sight that made Jennifer smile.

"It is good to see you smile," Herne observed as he opened his eyes. The voice reverberated softly in the trees around her. He tipped his stately head forward. His words were deep and sonorous with a slow, thoughtful cadence. "I believe it has been a long time since that was common."

Jennifer bowed in confusion. Beyond her wondrous awe for the creature, she did not know what to make of him. All of the feelings inspired by him, were vague and unfulfilling. She perceived that he was a creature of ancient knowledge and primeval power, but she had no concept of what that power might be. Perhaps his mere existence was enough; in a world of electric cars, the International Space Station, and Google, the simple presence of such a wondrous creature was sufficient to suggest there was so much more to him than what met the eye. Then again, the presence of so many wondrous creatures suggested that there was much more to this world than was known.

Steeling herself to ask the question that had been on her mind since she had first heard about him, Jennifer glanced first at Aeonghus who now sat beside him, back in the grizzled form of the *ghille dubh*. His features were blank as he pulled out his pipe and began to smoke it; there was no warning on his face, nor was there assurance. Jennifer had to make of the meeting what she could.

"Who are you?" she finally asked and then bit her lip in fear of the answer.

Herne began to pet the tiny fawn. "I am the forest," he replied. Jennifer found the answer evasive and mysterious but she would not be put off.

"What does that mean?"

Aeonghus glanced at Herne, an eyebrow raised.

Herne continued to pet the sleeping fawn. "It means I am the forest personified. I am the ancient existence of trees, the fury of the bear, the cunning of the wolf, the permanence of stone, and," he said as he glanced down at the fawn in his lap, "the innocence of the fawn."

It was one of those non-answer answers, a deflection and deferral that hinted at truth buried deeply if one wished to probe. Looking upon the bestial creature before her, Jennifer wasn't particularly tempted to do that. And yet, parsing through that answer, Jennifer understood enough to feel that Herne was at least confirming her one suspicion – he was very old indeed.

"You are not satisfied with my answer," Herne said in a deep grumble. "You wonder what I am and where I am from. You wonder why I am here," he looked at the trees surrounding them, "in a park on Vancouver Island in your year, 2015. I am a curiosity and more. I am a monster but less."

Jennifer rubbed her nose. She wanted to look away, but Herne's eyes held her. "Yes," she finally replied.

Herne glanced at Aeonghus. "Some have stories they wish to tell." He glanced at the fawn, now yawning in his lap. "Some have stories they cannot tell." His gaze returned to Jennifer. "Some have stories they do not wish to tell."

Jennifer avoided Herne's penetrating gaze.

"My story is simple; I exist where the forest exists, nothing more."

"Why here?" Jennifer dared. "Of all places, why on Vancouver Island in British Columbia?"

Herne snorted; the stag's nostrils flared. "There is still very old forest here and very old memories." He looked at the thick boughs above. "I am still strong in this world when I am amongst these trees. Here, there is great age." He paused, closed his eyes and took a deep breath. "So many memories here."

"This world?" Jennifer asked.

"Yes," Herne replied as the fawn stood. He ran his fingers along its back. "This true world where we all exist, where you and I may sit and face each other and talk," he added with a knowing look. "We can come here to this world but you cannot stay in mine."

Confusion and curiosity ate at Jennifer. "What is your world?"

Herne watched as the fawn hopped off his lap. It sniffed at Aeonghus, reeled from the fragrant pipe smoke, and then began nipping at ferns. Herne's eyes remained on the tiny creature as he spoke. "There are many human names for it in our ancient lands: *Mag Mell*[29], *Emain Ablach*[30], and *Tir nan Og*[31], to name a few. There are many other names though, some much older, and most lost in time. I prefer the last though – *Tir nan Og*, the Land of Youth. Yes," he nodded his majestic head, "the Land of Youth is most fitting. It is where we shall all go eventually."

"You said I couldn't stay in your world," Jennifer interjected. Herne nodded.

"You cannot, at least, not while you inhabit yours."

---

[29] Mag Mell – pronounced 'Mak-mel'

[30] Emain Ablach – pronounced 'ehmaeen ablachk'

[31] Tir nan Og – pronounced 'Cheer nan Ok'

"Do you mean after I die?" Jennifer asked.

Herne gave her a knowing look. "Yes, we all go there in the end; a few like Aeonghus and I may travel back and forth if we desire."

"What's it like?"

Herne rubbed his jaw. "It is much like this place," he said at length, "but more peaceful." He sighed and closed his eyes. Jennifer wondered if she saw a smile, or what would pass for one on a stag's face. "There it is always spring; there we have all of our kith and kin."

"It sounds nice," Jennifer replied with a sigh. "Is it Heaven?" she asked after a pause.

Herne shook his mighty head. "No, not in the way you would imagine it, at least."

"Oh," Jennifer was disappointed.

"For you, however," Herne added thoughtfully as he gazed upon her, "it is where the *Griogaraich*[32] dwell."

"The who?"

"Your people, the *Griogaraich*, the MacGregors," Herne said. "All peoples find a place to dwell within their version of *Tir nan Og*. There is a place within it where the MacGregors have dwelt from their beginning." He searched her face for a moment and then reached out and lifted her chin. "Do you wish to see it?"

A flush a fear ran through Jennifer. "I'm not staying, right?"

Herne shook his head as he rose to his feet. "You cannot. But you may look upon it if you wish."

Jennifer stood up, her stomach suddenly in knots. "How do we get there?"

"Through a *sìth*," Herne said. "A mound." He glanced down at Aeonghus who was now a wolfhound again. "Will you come, Aeonghus?"

"Aye, I will."

Aeonghus gazed upon Jennifer who stood in sudden irresolution. "There's no' a thing tae be scared of," he said as he nudged her with his great grizzled head. "We'll be together."

---

[32] Griogaraich – pronounced 'Greeoh-gar-aaechk'

Herne led them through the brush. It was slow progress for her as she pushed through fern and salal though the mighty creature before her passed with ease. The morning was warming up and Jennifer had broken a sweat by the time they came upon a rocky mound dotted with arbutus and twisted Garry oaks.

"Here is one, a *sith*[33]," said Herne. The mound of loose rock, the size of a house, was covered in a thick layer of moss and dead leaves and topped with a tall fir; it looked like an ancient pile of stone left behind by a retreating glacier.

"How does a gateway get to be named after something in Ireland or Scotland?" Jennifer whispered as she gazed upon the mound. "Did it exist before you got here? What did the Salish call it?"

"They have been here for an age before our arrival and they go by many names, old and new. It was felt by some of the first peoples who lived here that you could find *Dokibatl*, the Changer in them. Others believed they were the homes of the Sasquatch. They are many things, but they have always been the entrance to the otherworld."

He reached down and offered his hand. "Come."

Jennifer grasped his hand with reluctance and then marvelled at the warmth and the peace that enfolded her.

"Close your eyes," Herne said as he led her forward.

"Don't be afraid," Aeonghus said at her side.

Jennifer kept her eyes closed and her breathing came in nervous gasps. She walked deliberately, each foot placed after the other with careful concentration. For a moment she felt herself ascending the rocky, uneven hill, and then suddenly her next step dropped and she began to descend. The sun no longer burned through her eyelids and the warmth vanished. Cold and dark was this world, though only for a few moments. Again she began to ascend and warm light again fell on her face.

"We are here," Herne murmured.

---

[33] Sith – pronounced 'She'

Jennifer opened her eyes and saw that nothing had really changed. The forest was the same, even the mound was there. Aeonghus stood panting beside her and Herne still held her hand.

"It is time for you to meet the *Griogaraich*," Herne said as he led her forward. Jennifer noted a path before her, wide and flat and lined with tall ranks of firs and cedars on either side. As they walked down the path, she began to notice movement in the shadows; figures flitting through the gloom began to emerge from the forest and walk towards the path.

"They come," Aeonghus said.

Jennifer gripped Herne's hand much tighter as the first figures came to the edge of the path. They were dressed in plaids, some plain, others of varying hues and complexity. They wore light blue bonnets of wool, jackets and jerkins of wool or leather, crossbelts, and vests. Most were bearded and filthy; some were mere children, others elderly, but most were of middling age. Their faces were scarred and weathered though their eyes were young and they twinkled as they smiled in welcome upon her. Some held broadswords and Lochaber axes, other scythes and shovels. All lined the path on both sides and beamed benevolently as she walked by.

Jennifer heard shuffling behind her and felt a thrill as the MacGregors fell in behind them. They walked quietly, chattering softly amongst themselves in Gaelic; she didn't understand a word of it but they seemed pleasant enough. When she brought her attention back to the path, there were more figures coming from the forest – men in scarlet coats and tartan, with muskets and wearing tricorn hats, shakos, or feathered bonnets. They were soldiers mostly; British and some American, dressed in a dozen different uniforms and a variety of civilian trousers, vests, and coats. They nodded in welcome, and some squatted beside the path to touch her arm as she walked by.

Herne said nothing as he held her hand and guided her forward, and Aeonghus ambled along the path as if he knew it well. Jennifer was wide-eyed and incredulous as the crowd of MacGregors gathered.

"Where are all of the women?" Jennifer asked.

"They're coming," Herne replied. "It is the warriors and soldiers who wished to greet you first though, the men and the boys."

More soldiers walked up to the path. They wore blue and grey, butternut and scarlet, with kepis and slouch hats and shakos. Others were dressed in scarlet tunics and kilts topped with cork pith helmets; their grinning faces were filthy with dust and grime, and blackened from muskets. Some looked like cavalry from the American west; others looked like soldiers she'd seen in a history book about the British in Africa. They smiled and nodded in welcome, and the Americans in their civil war uniforms from both sides of the conflict elbowed each other in grinning chumminess.

"Why are they here on Vancouver Island?" she asked as she gazed upon the rainforest around her.

"This is the world you recognize within *Tir nan Og*," Herne replied. "Each will see the world that they most loved in life. These people," he added with a wave at the jostling crowd on either side, "see the world they most desired. The glens of Alba, the Sand Hills of Nebraska, the river valleys of Ohio, or," he added with a squeeze of her hand, "the rain forests of Vancouver Island."

The trail wound on, and the people changed. Uniforms turned khaki, and British and American helmets appeared. There were pilots, sailors, bomber crews in fur trimmed jackets and leather flying helmets, and mud spattered boys in olive drab with peace symbols on their helmets with wisps of beard on their faces and cigarettes in their mouths as they winked and joked. They all fell in behind the growing host of the MacGregors.

Before her, the crowd thickened until the path vanished beneath them. There were new uniforms of desert camouflage, and these men were covered in armour, webbing, and backpacks. They wore sunglasses and *Shemagh* scarves, and they waved to her in welcome. Herne came to a halt before them, as did Aeonghus, and Jennifer was at a loss as to what to make of it all.

"The *Griogaraich*," Herne rumbled. "'*S rioghal mo dhream*," he added. "My race is royal."

The crowd moved closer, and Jennifer noted the smiles and welcoming words, so at odds with the grimy clothes and weapons. One man stepped out, a towering black man with a MacGregor nametag; he was dusty in his American desert camouflage, his hands were thick with grim, and he appeared somewhat confused.

"Hello," he said as he squatted before her and extended his hand. Jennifer took it; it was warm to the touch. "My name is Evan MacGregor," he said with a lopsided smile. He looked around and whispered, "I'm new here, like you."

Jennifer glanced down shyly. "I'm just visiting," she replied.

"Didn't know you could," Evan chatted as his smile grew. "This morning I was on a patrol in Afghanistan, outside Combat Outpost Jelawur. It was hot and man, I was thirsty and tired. There was a flash, a lot of dust and noise, and now I'm here," he said as he held her hand. "Only, I don't really know where here is," he breathed as he looked at the faces around him. "I think I died," he finished. "The people here are nice though," he remarked as he turned his attention back to Jennifer. "I've met a lot of nice people here, lots of them. Real friendly people. One of them I met said he was waiting for you."

Evan rose and moved out of Jennifer's way and looked behind him towards the crowd. Jennifer followed his gaze, and in between the grinning soldiers stepped another man; he was tall with short brown hair greying at the tips, a few days of beard on his face, and flashing brown eyes and a wide smile.

"Daddy," Jennifer mouthed as her eyes widened. She brought her hands to her mouth. "Daddy," she repeated as she ran the short distance and threw herself into his arms.

"Hello, pumpkin," her father said softly as he dropped to one knee. "It's been a while."

Jennifer felt the tears rolling down her cheeks as she held her father tightly. "I've missed you," she said, her voice wracked with sobs.

"I know, sweetie," her father said as he patted her on the back. "It's good to see you."

Jennifer felt a tug at her sleeve and she turned to see her brother, Alex, an impish grin on his face, standing beside her.

"Hey, sis," he chuckled as he hugged her.

"Alex," Jennifer cried as she drew him into the embrace with her father. "I'm dreaming," she mouthed in a broken voice.

"Kind of," her father said as he released himself to look at her. He brushed her curls back and gently wiped away the tears. He shook his head and smiled wildly. "You are beautiful," he whispered.

Jennifer's face crumpled as she wept.

"Listen to me now," her father instructed. "Your mother needs you; she needs your help."

"I don't think she wants my help," Jennifer wept.

Her father smiled. "She does; she has just forgotten. She loves you, just like I love you. She needs to know that I will see her again. That will help her."

"Okay," Jennifer returned between sobs.

"I need you to tell your mother something for me," he said.

"I'll try," Jennifer sobbed.

"Tell her this," her father murmured as he leaned forward to whisper soft words in her ear. "Remember now," he added as he stood and took Alex's hand. "We'll see you again. I love you." He stepped back and faded into the jostling grinning crowd.

"Daddy!" Jennifer called out as she made to follow. The world disappeared into darkness and cold, and suddenly the path was gone; the luxuriant shadows of the forest intruded as she stood atop the low grassy mound.

"Daddy!" Jennifer shrieked. She turned back and Aeonghus was panting while Herne stood motionless beneath an arbutus.

"Where did he go?" Jennifer shrieked as she brushed tears from her eyes.

"We brought you back," Herne replied. He stepped forward and knelt before Jennifer. "I told you that you could not stay."

Jennifer brushed away more tears. She was sobbing now and asked brokenly, "Will I see him again?"

"Yes," Herne hushed as he laid a massive hand on her shoulder. "Come, I will show you something else."

* * * * *

"I don't understand. What was that place? It felt like Heaven," Jennifer sighed as she stepped over a fallen log and pushed through the crisp vertical leaves of a deer fern.

162

"Some might call it that," Herne replied after a thoughtful pause. He stopped and turned to look at her. "Those people that you saw, most of them are memories that exist there – a part of all of the stories of this world. Some are not; some are souls waiting for their next life." He knelt before her and grasped her hand while his deep eyes looked into hers. "They will come back, live, die, become part of the story, and be born again. There are many such stories that exist in that world, more than you can count. Some are small; many are large and long. They revolve around families, places, events. Sometimes," he whispered as he squeezed her hand, "they enter this world, the memories that is. You call them ghosts."

"Ghosts?" Jennifer fiddled with the fern leaves. "I've never seen a ghost."

Herne released her hand and stood. "They are the memories that have slipped through. I don't know why they have, though. Sometimes even the souls can enter – another type of ghost, sometimes a far more dangerous one."

Jennifer plodded along behind as Herne resumed his hike through the brush. She was feeling emotionally drained and tired after the long, laborious night and her brief encounter with the *Griogaraich*. The image of her father came to her and tears welled in her eyes again. It caused her surprise that it was not grief that bought forth the tears, but a general feeling of happiness and relief. The guilt that had been wracking her was gone, replaced now with regret at the loss of both her father and brother, but also at the loss of the past seven months of her life. Her father and brother were not gone, well, not gone gone, she corrected herself. They had simply moved on. Perhaps it was another dimension, she tried to reason as she stepped through a noisome bog. She'd heard of that before – scientists talking about the theoretical existence of other dimensions, perhaps many of them. Maybe Heaven, or this *Tir nan Og*, was simply another dimension that the consciousness moved to after death. It was hopelessly perplexing, and Jennifer was quickly becoming overwhelmed by the possibilities. She decided to banish the racing thoughts and emotions, and focus instead on the broad back of Herne as he led her and Aeonghus out of the thick forest and towards a hill.

"Why do you come here?" Jennifer asked as she came to a halt. Puffing, she brushed sweat from her eyes. "That is such a beautiful place. Why would you come here instead?"

Herne halted for a moment and then turned and sat down on a fallen log. Aeonghus sat down as well, panting and yawning.

"Why indeed," Herne pondered as he rubbed his chin. "*Tir nan Og* is the land of youth, but it is not the world we are born into." He glanced at Aeonghus and reached out to pat the wolfhound's head. "It is an odd thing in this long life of ours, this connection that we have. We are born of this world, Jennifer MacGregor; it is here in the ancient darkness that we awoke. We may dwell in *Tir nan Og* for an age, but we are still drawn back. We cannot linger there forever or one day we will simply fade away."

"Why?" Jennifer asked.

"No one knows," Herne replied as he placed his hands on his knees and leaned forward. "I have been here for many ages and yet I do not know all that there is to know. I do know that there are many who chose to sleep again in this world, deep in the cold and darkness from which they awoke, until the world changes and they awaken again. I have no easy answers," he rumbled. "All I know is that it is here that I will dwell. I will follow the forest as it moves. Aeonghus," he added as he rested his hand on the wolfhound's broad back, "will protect and befriend the children. That is what we are," he finished simply. Herne stood and resumed his climb.

Jennifer trudged behind him, her thoughts jumbled as she mused on what Herne had said. He really had said so very little, but did she really need more? Did she have to understand the intricacies and the minutia of his existence or should the mere actuality of his existence prove answer enough; there were things beyond the understanding of humans, beyond their science. She had proof; maybe she didn't need the science behind the proof.

"Isn't this the hill with the cairn on it?" Jennifer asked as she glanced around the rising hillside. There should have been people about – dog walkers, joggers, and hikers – all out to enjoy a beautiful morning in the park.

"It is," Herne replied softly.

"Won't they see us?"

"They will not," Herne replied without looking at her.

They crossed a narrow trail that ran the length of a forested gully. Jennifer still fully expected to see people, but there were none. She was unsure how this was possible, but one look at the imposing creature before her as he ascended the rocky hill told her that he was likely exercising some mysterious power that ensured they remained alone. The forest was thinning as they climbed – more arbutus and Garry oaks and far less Douglas firs and cedars – and the underbrush of salal and ferns gave way to luxurious grass and moss. The space between the trees was wider, the canopy much thinner, and warm sunlight beamed down upon them. Herne paused to allow Jennifer to catch up and he reached out his hand. Jennifer was still apprehensive of him, and she grasped his hand with a shyness that brought an amused flick of the ears from him.

"I am the forest," he said, his voice a low growl that seemed to echo around her. He led her up the last of the hill until its summit, and the small stone cairn at the top, appeared. Here he released her hand and continued alone while Aeonghus stopped beside her.

"What's he doing?" she whispered as Herne strode past the cairn. Beyond lay the wide vista of Thetis Lake and its surrounding forests, and further, the mountains of Mill Hill and Mount Finlayson. To the south rose the Olympic Mountains of Washington – snow-capped and majestic against the brilliant azure of the morning sky. From here, Jennifer could hear the noises of vehicles and she could see the distant buildings in Langford – an intrusive Costco blotted the landscape with its boxy building.

"A very rare thing these days," replied Aeonghus as he sat. "I believe he's going tae make 'The Call'."

"What's that?" Jennifer unshouldered her backpack and dropped it on the grass. A sudden feeling of restlessness, almost of electricity in the air, came over her as she watched Herne stand still on a hump of rock near the edge of the cliff that rolled steeply through the forest down towards the lake.

"You'll see," replied Aeonghus as he stood up and panted. He was clearly restless as well, Jennifer thought.

Herne was still, his eyes closed, his lips moving as soft words were uttered into the morning breeze.

"Nuair dhubhas dorch m'an domhain stoirm,

Le torrunn bòrb is dealan beur

Seallaidh tu nad àill o'n toirm,

'S fiamh gàire 'm thruaillean mòr nan spèur.

Ach dhomhsa tha do sholus faoin

'S nach fhaic mo shùil a chaoidh do ghnùis,

A sgaoileadh cùl as òr-bhuidh' ciabh

Air aghaidh nial 's a mhadainn òr."

He inhaled, his broad chest expanding; his booming voice deepened and rose in volume:

"When darkness grows about the stormy world

With fierce thunder and lightning,

Thou gazest lovely through the rack

And smiling in the big violent sky.

But to me your light is useless

As my eye will never see your face

When you spread the back of your bright gold tresses

On top of clouds on a golden morning."

Aeonghus was pacing, an agitated gait that was distracting for Jennifer. She noted he was wholly focused on the figure of Herne.

"A sgaoileadh cùl as òr-bhuidh' ciabh

Air aghaidh liath nan nial 's an ear

No nuair a chritheas tu 's an iar

Aig do dhorsaibh ciar air lear.

Ma dh'fheudte gu bheil thu 's mi fein

An àm gu treun 's gun fheum an àm,

Ar bliadhnaibh teàrnadh sios o'n speur

Là chèile siubhal chum an ceann."

Herne spread his arms wide and raised his face to the sky.

"When spreading the back of your bright-gold tresses

On top of grey clouds in the east

Or when you tremble in the west

At your dark doors over the seas."

Movement caught Jennifer's eye. She turned to see a pair of does and a buck exit the forest. They stood on the periphery, their deep eyes focused on Herne. In the air came birds: starlings, chickadees, robins, nuthatches, bushtits, and thrushes. Higher, she could see the sable silhouettes of turkey vultures, ospreys, ravens, herons, geese, and bald eagles while near the trees glided owls, falcons, merlins, and hawks.

"Biodh aoibhneas ort-fèin, a Ghrian,

A thriath 'ad òige neartmhor tha!

Oir 's dorch' mi-thaitneach tha an aois

Mar sholus faoin an rè gun child.

Bho neòil a sealltuinn air an raon,

'S an liath-cheò faoin air thaobh nan càrn

An osag fhuar o thuath air rèidh,

Fear siubhail dol fo bheud 's e mall."

More movement caught Jennifer's attention – more deer, at least a dozen now, and small brown rabbits, grey and red squirrels, racoons and martins. Mice darted by her feet, and the grass before Herne was suddenly a living carpet of attentive animals staring into the sky. Jennifer's breath was coming in gasps as a smile crossed her lips. The air was electric with a tingling surge and she was suddenly and keenly aware of the world around her – the colour of the grass, the wind in the branches, the smell of the deer. Her smile widened as a joy she had not felt for some time overcame her. Herne's voice, booming and deep and resonating throughout the bowl of the hills holding Thetis Lake, grew even louder as he chanted.

"Rejoice, O Sun, in this thy prime;

Rejoice, chief, in youthful might.

Be happy yourself, O Sun,

O lord, in your powerful youth.

From clouds showing on an upland way,

And the lonely grey mist beside the cairn

Cold gusts from the north on a plain

A traveler goes slowly in the gloom!"

Jennifer heard the crack of a twig, and she nearly tripped over her feet in fright as a black bear ambled beside her. It spared her a cursory glance and an unnerving nod before it moved to stand near Herne. Jennifer's smile, already wide, grew even wider. The feelings in her were so powerful, so compelling, such an intoxicating brew of euphoria, that she could no longer focus on the minutia. The whole world was calling to her, flowing through her very soul; hers was a rapture too deep to contemplate. She looked at Herne, at the birds beginning to swarm around him and in the sky above.

"Oh my," she said as she closed her eyes as she drowned in her growing ecstasy.

"I am the forest!" Herne thundered. He braced his powerful legs, clenched his fists, and facing the far hills he opened his mouth; the roar that came was powerful, a concussive cry that shook the trees, flattened the grass, and scattered the birds above.

Jennifer was pushed back by the shockwave and landed on her bottom. She looked to Aeonghus who was howling, his back arched and eyes closed. The bear stood on his hind legs, his growl deep and piercing. The deer squealed, the racoons squawked, the squirrels chattered, and the birds, swirling in a thickening cloud above Herne, shrieked.

Pushing herself to her feet, Jennifer could not take her eyes off the swelling cloud of birds above. Darkening the skies in a spinning swarm that towered above her, it was like standing beneath a screaming tornado.

"Oh my God," she breathed in joy, "oh my God!"

Jennifer stepped forward, closed her eyes, and added her voice to the Call.

The noise enveloped her, held her tight, and rose in a resonating crescendo that shook the very ground beneath her feet. She screamed until her breath was gone, inhaled deeply and screamed again. She joined with the animals around her, heard their thoughts and felt their emotions. Fear, joy, sorrow, and love – primal drivers that were within herself – there was a bond she had never felt before and could not imagine feeling again. The trees and stone, the holders of memories new and ancient, embraced her. A thousand sunrises and a thousand sunsets, towering glaciers and blowing snow, fiery maelstroms ripping through the forest, drenching downpours, and winter winds. The memories rolled over Jennifer like a rising tide, engulfing her, but a powerful hand suddenly gripped hers – warm with soft fur.

Herne was beside her.

The noise faded, soft echoes reverberating off the hills and mountains, and then silence. The animals faded into the forest; the birds dissipated like fog before wind.

Suddenly all was quiet.

Jennifer found herself sitting, her head in her hands, and feeling terribly dizzy.

Herne knelt before her and touched her arm. He gazed upon her for several long moments, his puffing chest slowing to normal. He placed a hand on her shoulder and Jennifer felt faint.

"Remember," he whispered as she closed her eyes to the waves of dizziness. "It is time to live again."

Jennifer opened her eyes and looked around the hilltop. Only Aeonghus remained. The wolfhound panted as he sat beside her, and then he rose to his feet.

"Time tae go home."

Part Fourteen

Is Maol Guala gun Bhràthair

Bare is the Shoulder Without a Brother

Mrs. Fletcher finished scribbling a final note on a notepad before placing it and the pen on her desk. She sat back in her chair, ignored the soft creak, crossed her legs, and placed her hands upon her lap. Jennifer sat opposite, a wad of damp tissue on the table beside her, and her eyes reddened by tears. Mrs. Fletcher was speechless for a few moments as she digested the story that Jennifer had told her; the family trip with her father and brother to see a friend in Duncan was well known to her, but the details of the events leading to the accident, the horrific moments of the crash, and most importantly, the words from her dying father in the minutes after, were the important details she had been anticipating for seven months. She hadn't truly expected to get them. She had expected a suicide attempt in the coming months as Jennifer seemed to slide further away and she found Jennifer's unanticipated revelations almost unnerving.

"Jennifer," Mrs. Fletcher said as she handed the girl another tissue, "last week there was no change, no new memories; this week, everything has come back. What happened to change that?"

Jennifer was looking at her feet, her fingers intertwined and her thumbs wrestling against each other. She paused for several moments, as if unsure how to answer. Mrs. Fletcher was about to repeat the question when Jennifer murmured, "I had a dream."

"A dream?" Mrs. Fletcher cocked an eyebrow and picked up her pen. "What kind of dream did you have?"

Looking up, Jennifer's eyes were bright and clear. Her jaw tensed with determination and she said, "A deer took me to see my father. He told me that it wasn't my fault. It was an accident."

"A deer?" The pen was scribbling. Mrs. Fletcher smiled. "A deer took you there?"

"Yes."

"What else?"

Jennifer shook her head. "Nothing else. When I woke up, I remembered everything. I remembered him saying it wasn't my fault while we were in the car." She reached for the tissue on the table as new tears welled in her eyes. "In the dream he said he missed me."

Mrs. Fletcher reached out and patted her hand. "This is a remarkable day, Jenny," she said. "This is the breakthrough we've been waiting for." Her own eyes seemed to mist over and she blinked rapidly. "Yes, this is wonderful progress."

* * * * *

Jennifer walked into class feeling a confidence that she had not felt in months. As much as she was still drained by the raw emotion from the events of the weekend, they were overshadowed by new feelings of happiness. There was joy in her heart, and when she mused on the images of her father and brother, it was not sadness that brought tears to her eyes, but happiness and hope. They were not gone; she would see them again.

"Come on in Jenny," Ms. Burbank said as Jennifer entered the classroom. "Take your seat, please. We're working in our science books; photosynthesis is the topic of the day."

Jennifer nodded and took a seat at her desk. A few of the students stared at her, and a couple made wry faces or whispered and snickered, but Jennifer pointedly ignored them. Who cares what they think, she mused as she pulled out her science book and opened it to the topic. I know and have seen so much more.

Brian Howard glanced slyly at Jennifer, and then at the back of Ms. Burbank as she wrote on the whiteboard, before throwing the ball of paper. It missed Jennifer's nose by a few centimetres and hit a girl sitting beside her. Jennifer didn't look up as she said, "You should read in your science book about how your fat falls into the laws of motion. Betcha that throws your aim off."

Brian's eyes widened in anger. "What?"

"I said," Jennifer repeated, running her finger along the text, "your fat body throws your aim off – Newton's laws of motion and all." She spared him a withering glance. "You should go for a run, fat boy."

"You little bitch," Brian hissed, "you wouldn't dare say that again."

Jennifer glanced at Ms. Burbank who was still facing the whiteboard and talking about carbohydrate molecules before saying. "I would, you tub of lard. Bullies like you are cowards at heart. Your name should be Brian Coward."

There was an aggressiveness to Jennifer's voice that was not lost on Brian. He clenched his fists and growled, "You wouldn't say that to me again outside of class. You wouldn't dare. I'd kick your ass."

"No," Jennifer whispered, "you wouldn't." Seven long months of abuse were coming back to her and she was feeling a rare rage. For some time, she had been the victim of this boy, a boy who had taunted and tortured her, who had used an unspeakable tragedy to hurt her. This was a boy of appalling moral depravity who took a delicious desire in hurting those who could not fight back. She had seen it with herself and had seen it with others. She glanced again at Ms. Burbank who was now drawing a picture of a tree leaf and chlorophyll pigments. Jennifer felt her rage boil over and she turned towards Brian and leaned forward, her brown eyes narrowed and focused on him. "You name any time and any place and I'll meet you. I'm not afraid of a fat bully like you. I know you are such a coward that you would only target those who you think are weaker than you, but I'm not weaker. I'm a hell of a lot stronger than you will ever be. 'S rioghal mo dhream," she added as she stuck out her chin in pride. "My race is royal."

Brian Howard's eyes were wide in shock and in fury. Jennifer knew no one had ever stood up to him like that and it surprised him greatly. His face paled and his fists clenched tighter. "You can meet me at the cairn tonight at midnight, you little bitch," he hissed. "Then we'll see who's the fucking coward."

"Is there a problem back there?" Ms. Burbank said as she paused in her drawing. All eyes were on Jennifer and Brian as they glared at each other. Jennifer sat back in her chair and smiled.

"No, Ms. Burbank. No problem at all."

Ms. Burbank looked at both, noted the sour look on Brain's face and the beatific look on Jennifer's and said, "Uh, okay then. Please pay attention. Now, let's talk about organelles and chloroplasts."

"Jennifer," called a girl named Jordan as she jogged to catch up with her as she started to walk home. "Are you actually going to meet Brian Howard at the cairn tonight?"

Nodding, Jennifer replied, "Yes. I'm not going to take any more crap from him."

Two more girls joined them, as did a boy named Michael.

"He'll beat you up," Jordan warned. "He has no problem beating up girls."

"I know," Jennifer admitted. Her confidence was unmoved by their concern, for deep down she knew that she had an ally on High Rock who would ensure Brian Howard never touched her again.

"Aren't you afraid?" asked one of the girls, a small redhead named Julie.

Jennifer shook her head. An image of the highlanders she had seen in *Tir nan Og* suddenly came to her mind. Theirs was a strength she could feel running within her, as if they were a wall around her. It was fleeting and it disappeared in a heartbeat, but she knew it was there. "I am not afraid," she boasted as she turned and walked away.

The others did not follow as she made her way to High Rock. It gave her the solitude to muse upon her actions of the day. Something in her had snapped, and although she didn't really regret her actions, calling Brian Howard out and agreeing to meet him tonight at the cairn was not one of her wisest moves. Yes, Aeonghus would be there and he would not allow anything happen to her; still, there was no surety of his presence, and there was every possibility she might be there alone. It was an unlikely scenario that she hadn't thought about in her flash of anger, but now she felt the first pangs of fear. Brian Howard would indeed have no problem beating her up, though at least everyone knew where and when they were going to meet. She had committed herself, however, and irrespective of the outcome, it was time she took a stand.

It was time for change.

Jennifer ambled along the narrow paths of High Rock, her eyes open for the wolfhound or perhaps the fleeting movement of a tiny creature that would suggest the presence of Aeonghus. Nothing stood out, and she eventually found a hump of rock to sit on and wait. She closed her eyes, placed her palms upon the warm scarred stone, and slowed her breathing. Random images flashed through her – the poor drawings of the chloroplasts, algebra equations, and the past tense of *travallier* in French – all mundane imaginings of the day. She rubbed the stone slowly, feeling the warmth seep from its rocky flesh, feeling the pocks and scars and the distress of its great age. The memories of the day faded and she felt suddenly cold. Rain came down in sheets, blown sideways by the wind. Trees were tall and rocking in the powerful south-westerlies battering the island. Dark clouds scudded above her, whipping past at a terrific pace. Near one lofty fir sheltered a bear, powerful and black as it sulked in the shadow of the tree while water beaded on its coat and dripped down its nose. The creature looked miserable and slowly turned its attention to her. It seemed to see her, for its head rose in curiosity for a few moments before it puffed in annoyance and resumed glowering at its damp feet.

Jennifer opened her eyes and looked at the shadow to her left. Aeonghus sat there unmoving, his gaze on the brush and trees.

"I was hoping to find you," Jennifer remarked as she wiggled over to give the wolfhound more room. "I said some things today that I might regret." She had a nervous smile as she tried to make light of the subject she was about to raise. "I challenged Brian Howard to a fight."

Aeonghus turned to look upon her. "A fight?" he asked with surprise. "Why would you do such a daft thing?"

The nervous grinned remained and Jennifer looked at her toes. "I had to stand up to him; he's been bullying me for way too long and," she added with a sheepish smile, "I hoped you'd be here to help."

The wolfhound looked at her for nearly a minute – a time of silent contemplation that wiped the smile from Jennifer's face and filled her with a gnawing fear. Finally, he turned to stare ahead.

"I cannot do that."

Jennifer's eyes widened. "You can't?" She exclaimed. "Why? Why can't you help me? Brian is a huge bully who wants to beat me up. All you need to do is scare him as a dog! You did it before?"

"That was no' me," Aeonghus said as he stood. He was anxious, clearly anxious, for he began to pace while his voice, normally deep and grave, rose in pitch to near panic. "You cannot ask me tae do that! Even as a wolfhound, he will call the police. People will be up tae search for me. They will hunt for me; they will always look for me then – the big wolfhound on the hill – and they may even find me." Aeonghus looked around as he panted. "I cannot do that! They will know I am here!"

Jennifer had never sensed fear before in the creature. The ancient wisdom and serenity was gone, replaced by a feral dread that seemed nearly beyond his control. It horrified her.

"You won't be caught," she said as she rose to her feet. "I need your help, Aeonghus."

"You should have asked me first!" Aeonghus shot back. The hair on his back rose in anger and he bared his teeth. "You have no right tae ask o' me such a thing! You have no right!" he repeated. "They will hunt me down!" The panic was growing.

Jennifer felt tears in her eyes. She had never for a moment suspected that he would abandon her in this hour of need, yet it was clear now – Aeonghus would not help her. She was again on her own.

Her jaw tightened in anger and Jennifer clenched her fists. So be it, she thought. She didn't need him anyway. Yet the fickleness and fear from this creature of power were perplexing. This creature could switch between itself and a wolfhound at will, exert influence over the animals around it, could move between existences, and yet the notion of getting caught terrified him. As angry as she was as she stood there with her arms crossed and her eyes narrowed, a small part of her felt pity for the creature who was in so much distress.

"Alright, Aeonghus," Jennifer said with a flat finality that stopped the wolfhound from pacing. "I won't ask this of you. I don't need you. I will stand and fight on my own. That's what you been trying to teach me apparently, that I'm strong and that I'm not on my own, even if that really has been the case all along."

Jennifer picked up her backpack as the wolfhound remained unmoved and then she turned and walked away.

* * * * *

Aeonghus sat on the rotting log of a fallen oak in a tiny meadow deep in the urban forest surrounding the *Beinn nam Fiadh*. He looked wretched; his wizened head bowed in sorrow, his skeletal fingers intertwined and shaking, his face a mask of untold misery. Tears gathered in his eyes and then rolled down the scarred crags of his cheeks before collecting in his beard to become translucent gems of grief. His shoulders shuddered as his open weeping grew and he pulled his woven hat down to his nose in child-like embarrassment.

It had happened again, like it always happened. The fear had settled upon him, not a slow emerging like a seedling in the spring sunshine, but a vicious, horrific attack full of violence and malice. It was unreasonable, unimaginable, and illogical. A fight, Jennifer had said, she had merely challenged a boy to an after-school fight. Of course he could help; his mere presence as a wolfhound would end it by terrifying the fat brute. Of course he could help; even if he did nothing more than the first time he had helped Jennifer, by willing another dog to intervene. The risks, however, were magnified by his fear, or perhaps his fear was magnified by the risks. It was paralyzing, ridiculously so. New tears fell down his cheeks and he clasped his hands tighter. It was indeed absurd, the depths that his fear was taking him, and all due to a simple request from a girl to protect her from a bully.

"You've pledged yourself," he told himself as the sorrow wrenched a small wail from him. "You've sworn your protection o' her until she becomes a woman. It was a calculated risk you took and now that risk had come tae fruition," he blubbered. "The *Geis* will be broken if you no' help her," he muttered as he rocked back and forth, "you will break the *Geis*, again." Aeonghus buried his face in his hands.

"Why?" He whispered brokenly. "Why must this happen again?"

Aeonghus brushed his hand over his eyes. All of his anxieties about befriending Jennifer returned. His heart would be soon broken and now, when she needed his protection – his physical intervention for her protection – he would fail her because his old fears had renewed their tenacious grip upon him.

He pulled his hat off and placed it on the log beside him. The desire to help and protect was instinctive in him, Aeonghus knew, it was what drove his existence. It was as natural to him as eating or breathing; he might be able to banish that need for a period of time, to drive it beyond his consciousness, but it was always there lurking on the periphery of his knowledge. It was always threatening to intrude upon him with renewed demands for obedience. The joy of abandoning himself to that desire, to befriend a child, to protect them until they reached adulthood, gave him happiness beyond reckoning, only to be replaced by sadness beyond calculation when the child moved on. It was made so much worse if the child died, like poor Mollach so very long ago or young Charlie more recently.

"Or Catriona," Aeonghus added as his lip quivered and new tears formed. "Like Catriona."

Aeonghus closed his eyes and remembered.

* * * * *

The musket shots in the glen, a distant popping that echoed off of the snow covered peaks, wrenched Aeonghus from his sleep. A single cry followed, then more, and shouting; fearful and angry outbursts echoed in the darkness of early morning. More musket shots and the long agonizing scream of a woman.

Aeonghus rushed to the narrow opening of his cave. He could see little of the buildings below – a few chinks of light behind shutters closed against the cold, a lantern running across a darkened yard, the flash of muskets. He could hear though – screams of terror, shouts of anger, and cries of agony.

"The Campbells are killing them," he mouthed in horror.

Aeonghus had seen the soldiers come two weeks before, dressed in the red coats of the King and the dark plaids of the Campbells of the Earl of Argyle's regiment. They were billeted on the MacDonalds, he was told by Catriona, and specifically, old MacIain their chief. He had listened to the fearful voices that were unsure of the portent of their arrival, though in the days after, as peace and quiet prevailed, those fearful voices had grown quieter. The Campbells had no love for old MacIain and his MacDonalds, but they were guests and MacIain had pledged his allegiance to King William in January, even if he was late for the January 1st deadline. There should have been nothing to fear from the King's soldiers, Aeonghus had heard whispered as he lurked in the shadows; they were only there to collect the Cess Tax of the Scottish parliament.

More musket shots and screams in the darkness.

"Catriona," he murmured as he grabbed his targe and sword, and exited his cave to flit down the hillside towards the village of Invercoe.

Women and children straggled past in the gloom, fleeing to the heights for safety from the murderous intentions of the King's soldiers.

"They're killing the men," one woman wailed as she hiked her skirts with one hand while carrying a squalling baby in the other.

"They killed my Da!" shrieked a child as he was dragged up the snowy slopes by his sister.

Aeonghus ducked behind the stone slabs of a house and peered into the early morning gloom. A light snow was caught in the breeze which fanned the flames of several burning cottages. He saw more flashes from the soldier's muskets, heard more screams as men were cut down and women and children fled in panic. Across the snow Aeonghus sprinted, racing for the small house of dry stone and a thatch roof that Catriona lived in. He could see flames inside, and as he approached, a soldier in a scarlet coat with a flickering torch exited the door.

"It burns," he cried as flames erupted from the roof.

"Where away the wee bairns and the hen?" cried a second soldier.

"Down to the river running like deer!" said the first as he tossed his torch on the roof.

"Then let's go and find them!"

The pair of soldiers jogged through the blowing snow and down towards the sluggish black waters of the Coe. Aeonghus followed, darting from tree to house to fence post in the gloom of dawn. As the river appeared through the leafless branches of the oaks and the blowing snow, the screams and shouts from behind him began to fade; the menfolk were dead and the women and children had fled into the growing blizzard.

"Catriona," Aeonghus breathed as he hid behind a fallen oak. He could see a few figures running along the slush and ice of the Coe, women and children from Invercoe trying to make their quiet way to safety.

There were sudden screams as the two soldiers appeared. The women attacked but were beaten back with the butts of the muskets while the soldiers laughed.

Aeonghus saw Catriona kneeling beside one of the fallen women; her mother, Aeonghus saw beneath the blood on her battered face.

"Come along, little girl," one of the soldiers said as he grabbed her by the arm, "time to go."

Catriona shrieked and cried out while she struggled against the soldier's iron grip. Aeonghus leapt over the fallen log and pulled out his sword and rested it on top of the targe as he prepared to attack.

"Come on, lass," the soldier said again, his pockmarked face split into a hideous grin. "Proper hell cat she is," he said with a chuckle.

"Let her go," Aeonghus whispered from the shadows as he took a step forward. Fear was upon him, a cold dreadful fear that gripped his heart and slowed his legs. "Let her go," he repeated in a breaking voice.

Catriona swung a closed fist and hit the soldier in the groin. He let her go as he grunted and fell to his knees. Catriona also fell, but she was up in a heartbeat, slipping and screaming in the snow. The second solider took a single step and struck her on the back with the butt of his musket.

"Catriona," Aeonghus sobbed as he took another step. The sword and targe felt like lead and he couldn't keep them up. His legs felt heavy and slow, as if he were walking through thick mud. The fear was growing, choking him, suffocating him, and making him deaf and blind.

"Little girl is a real hellcat," the first solider groaned as he staggered over and grabbed her by the hair. Still clutching his groan, he dragged her forward to the slushy waters of the Coe. "You'll think twice before striking one of the King's soldiers, hen," he said as he dragged her into the frigid waters.

"Catriona," Aeonghus choked as he dropped the sword and targe from nerveless fingers. He fell to his hands and knees and crawled forward a few more feet. He held out his open hand as tears fell down his cheeks.

"Aeonghus!" Catriona cried as she glanced at the shore. The soldiers looked about but saw no one, and resumed their sport.

"Have a drink, hen," the first solider said as he thrust Catriona's head under the water. The girl struggled, punching and splashing, while the soldiers chuckled. He pulled her head out and she screamed in terror.

"Aeonghus!"

"Back you go," the soldier said through gritted teeth.

Aeonghus lay on the snow, motionless and weeping, and paralyzed by terror and helpless rage as he watched Catriona's struggling body. The soldiers joked as they held her down until her desperate jerking movements ceased.

"No wee bairns will come from this MacDonald," the first soldier said as he rubbed his groin.

"Did you enjoy the love tap she gave you," guffawed the second. Both soldiers disappeared down the shore in pursuit of the women and children.

Aeonghus lay in the snow, his face buried in the slush as he sobbed with a despair unheard in the glen for a thousand years.

* * * * *

The sun was inching its way westward towards the low green mountains in the municipalities of Metchosin and Colwood. The towering Olympic Mountains to the south, bathed in an alabaster grandeur that complemented their godly domain, were brilliant in the azure sky, yet the slightest tinges of coral could be discerned as late afternoon changed to evening. Birdsong carried in the cool breeze coming through the distant bank of fog over the Salish Sea, and a pair of grey squirrels, their abundant tails thickening for the long winter, chased each other amongst the crooked hoary branches of the Garry oaks of the grove while a pair of black-tailed deer munched in blissful satisfaction on the grass.

In that small meadow, Aeonghus sat weeping in despair, unhidden from and uncaring of the world around him. His filthy woven Salish hat was on a tree trunk beside him as was his staff with the single hawk feather. The plaid blanket belted around his waist hung loosely upon his heaving shoulders and his worn boots had slipped off of his feet.

Truly, he was the picture of misery.

He cupped his face in his hands, felt the tears gather in his beard and in the crevasses of his closed fingers, and keened as if Jennifer were dead and not merely angry at him.

It was like she was dead, he mused as he snuffled and brushed his eyes. He had abandoned her in her hour of need and she had walked away. Yes, it was over such a simple thing, a fight between children, as common as a dog fight or a winter cold, but he had refused to help when that was his sole burden, his sole joy. He had chosen to be her friend and protector, a solemn pledge that meant he should fight and die for her, but as had happened so many centuries before, he failed. The fear that lay within him, usually so well bottled up, had escaped in its most dreadful way. Aeonghus buried his face in his hands again. The sorrow, shame, and guilt were overwhelming.

"Yours is a broken heart, *Ghille dubh*," said a deep grumbling voice that seemed to come from the ground around him.

A shadow fell on Aeonghus, and when he looked up in surprise, he beheld the stately figure of Herne standing over him. For several moments he could say nothing; he could only mouth the sorrow and shame that was gripping him. Finally, in a voice broken and barely audible, he said, "I've failed her."

Herne took a slow deliberate seat before Aeonghus; even sitting he was so much taller than the *ghille dubh*. His dark mahogany eyes were unreadable, though his ears flicked in thought and he cocked his massive antlered head. "How have you failed the girl?" Herne asked. His bass voice was slow and resonated through the log that Aeonghus was sitting on. "What have you done to cause yourself such grief?"

Aeonghus brushed his eyes, blew his beaky nose in a dirty scrap of cloth, and answer, "I said I would no' help her in her fight against the bully named Howard."

Looking up into the azure sky, Herne nodded. "I see," he said after a time. "It is a dangerous thing she does and now your fear has returned."

"Aye," Aeonghus' head sank in shame.

"Like it did before," Herne added with a thoughtful glance at the wizened creature.

Aeonghus nodded but said nothing.

"We spoke of it once," Herne continued as his hand reached out to touch the moss on an exposed stone. "Her name was Catriona."

"Aye." Fresh tears fell down Aeonghus' cheeks.

"You could have helped her, but you did not," Herne said in a flat, emotionless drone as he continued to run a finger over the deep, luxuriant carpet. "Your fear stopped you and she was killed. You broke the *Geis* placed upon you so long ago by Fionn."

Aeonghus looked away from Herne's penetrating gaze.

"The fear of death in this world is powerful, for you will not be able to return to *Tir nan Og* should you die in this mortal land. It is why you have shied away from danger, even at the cost of those whom you love."

Aeonghus bowed his head and looked wretched.

"It is true, to die here is to truly die. There is nothing that can get you to the otherworld, and yet," Herne puzzled, "so many have taken that chance. Braonán and her folk for one," Herne rumbled as he looked to the distant waters that held the *selchidhean*.

Brushing his eyes, Aeonghus nodded.

"They took their chances for love."

Aeonghus bowed in misery.

"And now," Herne murmured without judgement or sentiment, "you are old, withering slowly as the years march by. You have run away from love these many ages and all of your happiness has slipped away. Your eternal youth left you long ago and now, slowly, you are dying; the curse of the broken *Geis* is upon you, *ghille dubh*. The fear has cost you deeply. It is a terrible position you are in – crippled by the fear of dying in this world and yet unable to live in ours because you need to protect the children of this one. Yours is a consuming desire," Herne concluded with a deep sigh, "a desire that is fought by an equally consuming fear. What shall be the outcome of it all, this terrible battle within you?"

His shoulders shaking, Aeonghus bowed his head lower.

"I wonder at what this portends," Herne said as he crossed his legs and placed his hands upon his knees. "You have pledged yourself?" Aeonghus nodded and Herne continued as he closed his eyes, "Then you would break the *Geis* again. I do not know what would happen."

"Would I die?" Aeonghus asked, his hands wringing in fear.

"I believe you will," Herne returned.

"I don't want tae die," Aeonghus whispered.

182

"No one does," Herne returned.

"There will be nothing," Aeonghus interjected with a whisper. "There will be the eternal darkness that I once heard o' so long ago."

Herne nodded. "Yes. We, of all creatures, know that there are many lands around us. We travel between the *Tir nan Og* and this world." He glanced at Aeonghus. "We give that up if we die in this world and yet we cannot fully exist in the other."

"I know," Aeonghus replied with a deep heaving sigh. "So many of our folk are gone now," he added.

"They are," Herne agreed. "Some have long since returned to the depths of the earth and the oceans to sleep as we all once did. Most have died, killed off as the humans expanded into the wilds. Some, like ourselves moved on, finding a life amongst the humans in what was once a world we shared. Now we are mere guests."

"If they found me, would they kill me?"

Herne looked away, closed his eyes to the setting sun, and after a long silence replied, "You may die anyway, *ghille dubh*; you have broken the *Geis*. Your death may be coming." Herne looked down upon him. "You may not be able to save yourself, but you can save her. You must find your courage." Stretching his legs before him, Herne pushed himself to his feet. He again looked south as the sun moved towards the distant mountains in the west. He gave the *ghille dubh* a final, thoughtful look before turning away and striding into the brush. Aeonghus watched him until he disappeared.

Part Fifteen

Is Aithne Do'n Chù a Cliòre fhein

A Dog Knows his Own Fault

Jennifer sat in the cold, wooden lawn chair, her fingers playing with the peeling paint as she held the empty cup of tea resting on the chair arm. Her eyes were red, for the disappointment she felt at being abandoned by Aeonghus was a terrible wound, an emotional blow that was staggering. She had finally found trust and friendship, in the most unlikely of places, and in a heartbeat it was gone when she most needed it. She felt anger as well, but it was moderated by gratitude. She was thankful, mostly for having been able to see her father again, but also for the knowledge that she was not truly alone, no matter how much she thought she was. Even now, as she mentally prepared herself to meet Brian Howard tonight on High Rock and for the terrible beating and the pain that would accompany such an encounter, she knew that she would not be alone, at least in spirit. The *Griogaraich* would be there and she would fall back on their support throughout the pummeling and perhaps even the death that she was going to endure.

The sun was approaching the mountains in the west and the light was fading from the brilliance of the afternoon to a comfortable beaming that brought warmth and contentedness without the glare of midday or the cooling gloom of the evening; it was the perfect time to relax in the yard. Jennifer glanced into the oak tree above, saw the tiny grey birds flitting from branch to branch — bushtits most likely, she thought — and then closed her eyes and breathed in the scents of the new leaves and fresh cut grass. It was a wonderful fragrance that brought back memories of playing in the backyard with her father and brother; tag or some such game was the usual favourite.

"Are you done with your cup?" Helene said as she stood beside the chair for a moment. It was the first time she had spoken to Jennifer that day.

"Sure," Jennifer said as she handed her mother the empty cup. Helene turned to leave and Jennifer reached out, her hand impetuous and insistent as she touched the sleeve of her mother's shirt, "Why don't you sit down for a minute."

Helene paused and stared at her daughter. She looked at the grass and then back towards the open door. "I have things to do," she replied.

"Please," Jennifer insisted, "for a minute."

Tight lipped and shrugging, Helene placed the empty cup on the chair arm and took a seat in the other lawn chair beside Jennifer. They looked upon the darkening sky in the east, the distant hills and mountains blotted by the houses and trees. The silence was tense and anything but companionable, and Jennifer, her stomach flip-flopping and her hands fidgeting, looked at the dour façade of her mother for a moment before returning to look ahead. She took a deep breath, let it out slowly, and then said with a voice soft and shaking, "I have a message to pass on to you."

Helene looked at her nails, picked away an invisible bit of grit, and said, "A message, eh? From who?"

"From Daddy," Jennifer whispered.

Helene froze and then fixed a gorgon's glare upon her daughter. "That is not funny, Jennifer!" She hissed. Her hands gripped the chair arms and her face paled. "That is not funny at all!"

"It's true though," Jennifer persisted." She cleared her throat, looked away from the furious look on her mother's face, and finding the courage to continue she said, "He gave me a message to pass onto you."

Thrusting herself to her feet, Helene's face twisted into a rage that made Jennifer blanch. "How could you do this? You are a horrible little bitch! Why would you try to hurt me so badly?" Her Greek accent thickened in her rage. "I hate you so much!"

Jennifer closed her eyes to the waves of fury rolling over her and then blurted out, "Daddy said he misses you!" Helene stopped, her eyes wide and ferocious. "He said he will see you again."

"What did you say?" Helene whispered as her fists clenched. "Why are you doing this?" she added as tears of anger balled in her eyes.

"Daddy said he'd see you again," Jennifer replied as her own tears formed. "He gave me a message especially for you."

"What message?!" Helene raged.

"He said he will always see the wildflowers in your hair."

Helene froze, her eyes were wide in shock and her face went deathly pale. She sank to her knees and her hands gripped the chair arm as she fought against a wave of dizziness. A brittle silence followed for nearly a minute allowing birdsong to intrude, a light tittering as chickadees chased each other through the branches above.

"How could you know that?" Helene whispered as she looked upon Jennifer. She looked away, as if seeking the answers from the very world itself and then she shook her head in disbelief. "How could you know he said those words?"

"He told me," Jennifer snuffled.

Helene MacGregor sat back in the chair, her face heavy with bewilderment. She glanced at Jennifer as her daughter brushed tears from her eyes, and then she looked away in silent contemplation of the message. For nearly a minute she said nothing but when she spoke, the astonishment in her voice could not be mistaken. "Your father and I had a small honeymoon in Tofino and we took a boat out to the hot springs north of the town," she said in a slow voice. "We were there all day, and when the last of the tourists left to walk the long boardwalk back to the jetty, we had a short time alone together. He made me a crown of wildflowers that I wore in my hair as we made love in one of the hot spring pools." She glanced at Jennifer. "We believed that was when you were conceived because I was pregnant eight weeks later."

Jennifer smiled and wiped away the tears again.

"Afterwards, when we were sitting in the water," Helene continued, her voice growing husky as it began to break," he looked at me and said, "I will always see the wildflowers in your hair." She looked at Jennifer. "I know that your father never told you that story and neither did I; it was our one true secret from the world. How did you find it out?" she demanded.

"Daddy told me," Jennifer said as she looked down at her folded hands. "He knew you wouldn't believe me if I said I had talked to him. He said that message would be his proof. He told me."

Helene MacGregor began to weep, a wracking series of sobs, as she reached out to hold the hand of her daughter.

* * * * *

Aeonghus sat on the rotting log, his legs crossed, his head bowed, and his hands grasped loosely before him. He mused silently as he considered the passage of his long life and the many children he had cared for and said goodbye to once they had become adults. In fact, all but two had either moved on to adulthood or had died beyond his protection. Poor Charlie had been the most recent, he recalled with a sigh. Young Molloch had been out of his protection as well, though not completely. He could have gone down at the first sign of fighting, when the *Lochlannach* had first come in their longships, but the fear had come over Aeonghus, and he had hidden in his cave until the fighting was underway and it was too late to save the boy. With Catriona though, it had been much different. He had watched her die; he had gazed helplessly as the soldiers drowned her only a few dozen feet from where he stood. He had been paralyzed by fear and the greatest punishment had not been the curse of the *Geis* which was now aging him as no creature like him aged, but the memories that came upon him every day as he relived her murder.

He heaved another sigh, a deep cleansing sigh that should have shaken the melancholy from him, a sigh that should have banished the misery that was gripping him so tightly.

It did nothing of the kind.

Aeonghus kept his eyes closed as he meditated on the terrible fears that gripped him, the fears that controlled his very being, and he wondered what it was that would allow him to change not his destiny, but possibly the destiny of Jennifer. His doom was at hand, sooner now if his fear retained its domination and he once again broke the *Geis*. Yet there had to be some inner strength that he could summon. He wondered, as he had wondered so many times before, what it was about mortality that was so terrifying. He understood that the unknown was perhaps the biggest reason, but certainly the potential finality of it had an equal part – the end of all things he had ever known. Jealousy rose in him, as he considered the short, sometimes brutish life of humans who at the very least would eventually have another chance at existence when they left *Tir nan Og* and re-entered this world.

For Aeonghus and his kind, there was no such chance.

It was a terrifying thought for a creature that had enjoyed such a long existence.

"Hello, Aeonghus."

That voice! Aeonghus gasped. He recognized the musical lilt of the light Gaelic voice from so long ago; the melodic utterance was a song of joy to his ears! A sudden ambiance of childlike happiness washed over him like a fast rising tide, lifting his soul in a writhing maelstrom of ecstasy that brought an oh so rare smile to his wizened face. He breathed in again, and when he sighed with that smile, he whispered, "Catriona."

Aeonghus opened his eyes, and she was sitting on the grass before him, dressed in homespun wool and that lovely plaid *arisaid* of blue and purple that he remembered. Her copper ringlets fell down her cheeks, and her brilliant blue eyes, in a childlike face aged beyond her years, nearly disappeared as she smiled.

"I've missed you, Aeonghus. I've missed you very much."

Aeonghus raised his shaking hands to his face and covered his mouth. Tears welled and rolled down the deep crags of his cheeks as he gazed upon the friend he had missed the most.

"Och," he whispered, his voice breaking, "my dear, I've missed you too."

Catriona reached out and touched his knee. "It's been a long time," she said in her sweet sounding voice, "so very long."

"My dear," Aeonghus croaked as he buried his face in shame. "Oh my dear, I'm so, so very sorry tae have failed you."

Touching his knee again, Catriona nodded. "It is okay, Aeonghus. You were frightened. I forgive you."

"I so wanted tae help," he continued as the tears flowed and his voice gave out. He choked and cleared his voice then began to blubber. "I wanted tae help you."

"I understand, Aeonghus," Catriona said. "I'm sorry it has cost you so much," she added as she looked upon the frowzy, aged creature before her so unlike the young *ghille dubh* of three hundred years before.

Aeonghus' shoulders were heaving as he sobbed; shame and guilt had not weighed so heavily upon him since the morning of Catriona's death.

"I have waited for you for a very long time, Aeonghus," Catriona said as she looked away into the late afternoon sky. "I wanted to come back before, but it never seemed the right time." She turned her face towards him. "I wanted to move on as well, but I never seemed ready. I stayed in *Tir nan Og*, but you never came to find me."

Aeonghus hung his head. "I could not bring myself tae come find you," he muttered. He wiped his nose with the back of his hand. "I had failed you, my dear."

"I wish you had come," Catriona returned as the air of happiness around her faded. "I wish you had found me and I would have told you long ago that I had forgiven you. Your years of guilt and shame have been wasted, Aeonghus."

Looking into her eyes, Aeonghus said, "I would no' have forgiven myself. I cannot forgive myself. There is nothing I can do, ever, tae forgive myself for failing you, lass."

"Aeonghus," Catriona said, her voice soft and soothing as she placed her fingers on his shoulder, "I forgive you; I truly do. I want you to forgive yourself." She saw Aeonghus look away and her lips tightened in determination. "If you cannot forgive yourself, Aeonghus, then I will lay a task upon you as payment for your failing me in my hour of need."

Aeonghus looked up, his face a mixture of fear and hope. "Aye, that is fair," he said as he pulled out a filthy hanky to blow his nose. "Yes, that is fair." A feeling of subtle disappointment penetrated Aeonghus; what should have been the most joyful meeting in his life was becoming the trial he most feared and deserved. Nothing would ever erase the guilt or the debt he owed Catriona, and as much as he demanded that she name the repayment, there was a small hurt in his heart that she would actually do so. "Yes," he said again as he nodded and stuffed the hanky under his belted blanket, "I will do as you desire, lass. Upon my oath, I will do it."

"You have a friend in need," Catriona said after a long thoughtful pause, "in a greater need than you may ever think. She is in great danger, and you must fulfill your promise and protect her."

"I want tae," Aeonghus sputtered after a moment, his hands wringing in fear.

"You must, Aeonghus," Catriona said, her smile returning. "You must," she repeated. "You have strength in you, Aeonghus, if only you can find it."

Aeonghus looked upon her, felt the joy of seeing her again slowly push aside the horrible guilt and shame. Catriona's smile widened and she closed her eyes and slowly bent forward to give Aeonghus the tiniest kiss on the beak of his nose. He closed his eyes and felt the surge of her love flow through him, that child-like adoration he remembered from so long ago. When Aeonghus opened his eyes he beheld a young doe standing before him, a small beautiful doe whose lustrous coat shone in the late afternoon sun.

"Catriona," he sighed.

"You must help your friend, Aeonghus," Catriona said as her ears flickered.

Aeonghus nodded as fresh tears began to form. "I will," he said. "No matter the cost," he affirmed through clenched teeth.

The fawn's ears flicked and her small black tail swished. As the beams of sunlight backlit the creature through the branches of the forest, she raised her head high and closed her eyes. "You will find your strength, Aeonghus," she said as he began to sob again, "and you will not be alone."

The words caught Aeonghus' attention, and as he brushed his eyes, he looked upon the doe who was staring into the distance behind him.

"You were never alone," she said.

Rising to his feet, Aeonghus turned, his starched legs and arms making his movements slow and stiff. His eyes widened and he gripped his staff tightly in both hands.

"Oh my," he whispered.

On a low mound of moss covered stone, there were animals, a line of animals that looked upon him intently and with deep respect. There were deer, a dozen or more bucks and smaller does; racoons, mink, and martens that stood between the taller animals; neighbourhood dogs that had answered the call with lolling tongues and wagging tails; cats sitting attentive and subtly malevolent; and grey squirrels and Norwegian rats. Aeonghus looked up as the branches of a fir filled with ravens, barred owls, Cooper's hawks, a bald eagle, Steller's jays, northern flickers, and a dozen other chattering birds. He felt their combined goodwill and their desire to help. Against humans it was difficult to see what they could do, but as Aeonghus looked upon them, he felt he had an army at his back.

Aeonghus wiped his eyes with his hand. "Thank you, lass," he murmured.

"We all must be saved at some point in our lives," she said as she nuzzled him with her small wet nose.

* * * * *

As Jennifer was walking past Serious Coffee in Esquimalt's Plaza, she paused, foolishly she knew, to see if the young woman named Braonán was in there drinking coffee and pouring over Facebook on her phone. She was not, of course, and Jennifer walked on with a certain degree of disappointment; the young *selchidhean* was gone, perhaps for a long while. The empty coffee shop was yet another blow, and it helped fuel her growing fear as evening approached. The sun was moving towards its setting, the light was fading, though it was still warm, and a light breeze was blowing from the west. She paused near the coffee shop, sat on a cement bench while avoiding a wad of chewing gum, held her shaking hands together, and fought the nervous waves washing over her. Aeonghus was gone, Braonán was gone, and she did not believe it likely that she would ever see Herne again. This brief moment of her life where she was exposed to the *sidhe*, seeing the other world of *Tir nan Og* and talking with one of the elder creatures in the form of Herne, was passing; she was returning to the life she had known before a *ghille dubh* had saved her from death only weeks before. She was not the same Jennifer MacGregor, however; the *Fey* and *Tir nan Og* had ensured that. Jennifer knew she was stronger; she knew she was happier in the knowledge that she would one day see her father and brother again; and she knew that she had been given the most remarkable of gifts – the knowledge of what was coming. It was not faith, Jennifer concluded as a smile touched her lips; it was fact. She would live on after her death, taking a path to begin what was just another path on a very long journey. Those she loved were not gone; they were simply waiting to meet up before they all moved on to try it all again. That knowledge had power for her, such a power that she had never conceived. The fears that had so plagued her were gone; the worries and anxieties were finished. Jennifer had assured knowledge and she felt the weight of the world lifted from her shoulders.

Jennifer was no longer afraid.

There were teens exiting Serious Coffee, and they spied Jennifer sitting on the concrete bench. Jennifer recognized them from school and found their surprised looks and excited chattering amusing. One of them, Brittany Fox, came over with an iced latte in her hand.

"Is it true that you're going to meet Brian Howard tonight on High Rock?" The other girls were looking furtively around them while Brittany, over painted in makeup and chewing a wad of bubblegum seemed overly trashy.

"Yes," Jennifer replied.

"You know he's not coming alone, right?" Brittany asked. She looked at the three other girls behind her. "We've all heard he's bringing others."

"Who?"

"Some gang he's trying to join or something. He's going to use beating the shit out of you as his initiation to get in. Like that fat idiot wannabe gangsta is ever going to be accepted by the E-town Gang."

"How many?" Jennifer found herself asking. Brittany shrugged.

"Don't know. Not that I like you or anything, but maybe you shouldn't go. That gang has a lot of older punks in it. You might get hurt."

"Thanks for the thought," Jennifer returned, "but I'm not afraid. I'll meet him tonight."

"Suit yourself," Brittany replied after blowing a massive coral bubble. "Don't count on anyone else being there to watch or help. Brian made it pretty clear that anyone showing up to watch will get the shit kicked out of them by the gang."

"That's okay, I'm not afraid."

"Then you're crazy," Brittany hissed as she walked away with the other girls in tow.

Jennifer watched them go and allowed the anxieties that had begun to build up melt away. Even if it was true, it didn't matter. She would not be alone this night on High Rock and even if she were killed, she knew what was waiting. There was no fear in Jennifer's eyes as she rose and stared towards the hill obscured by trees and apartment buildings, only a steely determination.

She would never be afraid again.

* * * * *

Aeonghus sat on a creaking wooden box before a rickety pine table that had come from a doll's house nearly a century before. His woven Salish hat sat before him on the flaking table top while his staff leaned against a damp, stone wall in the narrow cave on the summit of High Rock. In the murk of the cave, lit obliquely by light coming from a short narrow tunnel and a slender crack beneath a massive moss covered erratic boulder, he stared upon a small oak chest in the corner, covered deeply in accumulated dust and dirt and beneath a myriad of old trinkets he had collected during his many decades in Esquimalt. He had been staring at it for several minutes, a silent musing over the box's contents and the courage he needed to open it. It was the courage that could have saved Catriona three hundred years ago. A courage he had never found before and he was wondering how he was going to find it now.

It should have been easy, Aeonghus mused as he pulled out his pipe, his eyes still fixed on the chest, so easy to make such a simple decision. Defend Jennifer, scare off the bully, and live longer. How could any sane creature not leap at that? His fear though, was deep set, and even such a simple decision would require a great effort.

Aeonghus' kept his eyes upon the chest.

"*There were others,*" Fionn had said of his divination so many centuries before. "*Other creatures and great danger. Perhaps a great battle on a hill top as well.*"

"A great battle," Aeonghus sighed. "There will be a great battle. It has come," he grunted, "his vision and perhaps my end has finally come."

He had found the chest not long after his arrival in Esquimalt, set aside by a sailor on *HMS Thetis* in 1852. He had spirited it away, disappointingly empty as it was, when the sailor turned his back, and he had used it ever since to store his most precious belongings.

It had remained closed for one-hundred and sixty-three years.

Aeonghus lowered his pipe to the tabletop. He closed his eyes, breathed deeply, and placing his hands upon the table, he pushed himself up. He moved stiffly to the chest and looked upon the clutter of dusty curios that covered its lid. His withered hand picked up a button; the green patina on the brass did nothing to cover the fouled anchor of the Royal Navy. He placed it on the table and picked up a weathered pewter kilt pin, a copper ring, a chipped emerald, a mangled lead soldier from the Royal Horse Artillery, and a rusted Kokanee beer bottle cap. All these he placed upon the table until the lid of the trunk was clear.

For nearly a minute Aeonghus stood silently before the trunk, his lips moving as he read the faint lettering that spelled out *HMS Thetis* in faded black ink. His hands were wringing and his breathing was in short soft gasps of anxiousness; blinking away tears, he strode forward and lifted the creaking lid of the trunk. Within the shadow of the trunk lay packing tissue, wrinkled from so many decades in the moist darkness. Aeonghus brushed it aside and beheld the small round targe – its lustrous leather faded and smelling of mould and its steel knobs, dull. He lifted it, marvelled still at the workmanship, and noted the weight and solidity before he placed it on ground leaning against the trunk. Beneath the targe was a blue bonnet of heavy wool that smelled musty as he lifted it to his nose. It was in remarkable shape and he placed it on the table behind him.

For a moment, Aeonghus paused, and then gritting his teeth he reached into the trunk and pulled out the folds of plaid that lay there. They were still soft to the touch, musty and aromatic as he brought the folds to his face. He closed his eyes and breathed in deeply allowing the subtle smells of mildew and earth to fall away leaving the clean perfume of the spring air of the Highlands of Scotland. He sniffed again, sighed and longed for the crisp air that could be drunk like water, the snow covered peaks that rose in benevolent magnificence, the green glens of lowing cattle, the icy streams, and the colourful heather. He began to wrap its length around him, his eyes closed and a smile playing across his thin lips.

* * * * *

"You look very fine in that," Catriona said as she tittered at Aeonghus as he swung his sword. She sat on the grass, wrapped tightly in her *arisaid* as she plucked heather bells from a sprig. Aeonghus smiled, pulled his bonnet low over his eyes and then raised his targe. "How will you fight, friend Aeonghus?" she asked as she clapped her hands in joy.

"I will listen to the wind upon the hill till the waters abate," Aeonghus replied as he stabbed with his sword.

"That is very good," Catriona replied.

* * * * *

Aeonghus lay the plaid upon the table and again reached into the trunk. He pulled out a thick tooled belt and laid it aside before he pulled out a long package of wrapped burlap tied with aged string that came apart in his hands. From the noisome cloth he pulled the sword, brilliant even in the gloom of the cave.

"*MacMeanmna*," he muttered; his words were soft and filled with emotion, "Son of the Spirit." He held the blade with both hands and rested his forehead against it. "Courage."

* * * * *

"What will happen when I grow up?" Catriona asked as they sat together, feet in the shallows of the River Coe while the sun blinked in and out of the shadows as a breeze wrestled with the limbs and leaves of the oaks around them. "Will I still see you?"

Aeonghus said nothing as he wiggled his toes in the cool clear water. He glanced at the seated girl now musing over the turgid waters flowing around the green tinged rocks. She was afraid, he realized; she knew what would happen when she became a woman. "You will not," he said.

"Could I not come to see you?"

"You cannot come to *Elphame*, lass. You know that."

"Not even to visit?" she asked as tears came to her eyes.

Aeonghus shook his head. "No."

Catriona rested her chin on her hands and allowed the misery to flow over her. Aeonghus glanced at her and then looked away. His heart was already breaking. Their time together was drawing to an end.

* * * * *

Aeonghus let his hand touch the stalks of lush grass beside the path while in the other he held his walking staff. He paused at an Oregon grape bush, touching the spiked leaves. Stepping back, he allowed a hummingbird to pass and he smiled as it moved off to a snowberry bush.

"*Gluais faicilleach le cupan làn*, friend," he said with a snigger. "Move carefully with the full cup."

The hummingbird buzzed to a dahpne plant, heedless of the friendly warning. Aeonghus watched it fondly and then turned back towards the hidden cairn on the summit of High Rock. He plodded along the path, his stiffened joints creaking and his breath coming in gasps. The growing autumn grass held his attention for a moment, luxurious and a deep green in the dying light of the day, and then his eyes caught the quivering nose of a rabbit that had emerged from beneath a snowberry bush. Overhead robins flew from branch to branch while a barred owl, silent and intense in the shadows of an arbutus, watched him with keen interest and no little anticipation.

The cairn appeared, absent of humans and their dogs, and Aeonghus ambled towards its rocky base. He glanced to the west, noted the sun was near the distant hilltops in a brilliant cloudless sky, and proceeded to mount the cairn. It was hard going; his old bones felt weaker than they had ever before. His muscles were failing and his heart was beating fit to burst. Panting with the effort, he pulled himself onto the dull brass disk on the top of the cairn, his hands and face resting on the warm metal. He pushed himself upright with his staff, breathed in deeply, and turned to face the sunset.

"*Mol an latha math mu oidhche*," Aeonghus murmured as he closed his eyes. "Praise the good day when it is night."

For a moment, as the sun dropped below the distant ridges and hilltops, it took on a brilliance unparalleled and Aeonghus felt a beatific warmth flood his tired body.

"I will fulfill my pledge," he said. "I will fight and I will die for you, Jennifer MacGregor."

196

The weakness shrank away as his bones thickened and his muscles strengthen. His labouring heart was emboldened; his breath became slower and deeper. The wizened stilted body stood tall, filled out, and grew strong.

The light faded and the sun set.

Aeonghus pulled out his sword and stared into its burnished length. Gone was the

white hair and beard, and the aged countenance of many centuries; a youthful mien framed by red locks and a thick russet beard stared back from the blade.

"*Aithnichear an leomhan air scriob de iongann!*" he murmured as he held the sword high. "A lion will be known by the scratch of its claws!"

Part Sixteen

Bithidh an Osnaich Dheireannach Cràidhteach

"My, that is a big doggie," the elderly woman mused as she gazed upon the wolfhound seated with impressive majesty on top of the cairn. She looked around the summit of High Rock, as her Pomeranian stared in mute astonishment at the wolfhound, but saw no one in the gathering darkness. Her gaze fell again upon the brutish animal, a colossal creature that elicited both fear and awe as it sat statuesque and looking down upon the rock before the cairn. As much as she was overtly curious about the massive wolfhound, she felt a certain reserve as well that went beyond the mere physical dominance of the animal. That grand and stately animal, still as an oak and staring at the rock unnerved her and she would come no closer.

"Here, doggie," she said as she reached into a small rhinestone studded bag for a doggie treat; it was ludicrously small as she held it out. "Are you hungry?"

The wolfhound made no movement and the Pomeranian looked anxiously between the wolfhound and the doggie bone. The woman looked at her own dog and then back at the strange wolfhound. "Something's not quite right, Maggie," she said to her nervous dog now pulling away from her. "That big doggie has to belong to someone." She looked around again in the deepening dusk. "Hello!" she called out, "Anyone missing their big dog?"

There was no answer and she stepped back. "Very strange, Maggie," she said as she handed the treat to her dog; the Pomeranian, its eyes still fixed on the wolfhound, ignored the gesture.

The wolfhound turned its head with a slow deliberate movement to stare at the Pomeranian; the tiny dog fell to its belly, lowered its head onto its paws, and began to whine.

"What's the matter, Maggie?" the woman asked as she crouched to pick up her dog. She looked again at the wolfhound, blanched at being stared at by the powerful animal, and slowly stepped back. "Maybe you're not a very friendly doggie," she said as she stepped back a few more feet.

Aeonghus returned his gaze to the rock before him and closed his eyes.

* * * * *

A frigid slurry of snow and ice covered the river Coe beneath deep, glowering skies threatening a renewal of the storm. Aeonghus stepped through the fresh fallen snow dragging his sword behind him while tears rolled down his face. He could see the feet on the river bank, the small body bobbing in the icy waters, the copper ringlets straightened by the current. He paused before the body of Catriona, his sobs filling the air, and then he dropped the sword and sat down in terrible misery and cried as he had never cried before.

Aeonghus sat in the snow for hours meditating on his misery; the sky was fading as a new veil of snow approached.

The body of Catriona had drifted away.

He tried to stand, to go and find his friend, but Aeonghus found himself terribly weak. His legs were shaking and rubbery, and the grip of his hand on his sword was feeble. He moved with unsteady steps to the lapping waters of the Coe and looked at the dull reflective surface.

Gone was the red beard and hair, the rosy cheeks, and stout body; an old creature looked back from the water.

"The *Geis*," he whispered as he sank to his knees. The white hair and beard, cadaverous limbs and hands, and the dull look in his eyes – these were the signs of the curse of Fionn.

"I'm dying," he said as he closed his eyes in shame.

* * * * *

The wolfhound's eyes opened and the elderly woman, still petting her anxious dog, caught a fleeting glimpse of feral rage in the deep brown eyes. "Doggie, there is nothing to be so mad about," she said as she wagged a wrinkled finger. "You should come off that cairn and go home to your owner," she added with a stern, scolding look.

"*Is ioma mùthadh a thig air an oidhche fhada Gheamhraidh,*" Aeonghus growled. The woman grew fish-eyed in shock and took another step back. He turned to look upon her. "Many a change comes in the long winter night. You must leave this place."

The wolfhound exploded into a baying leap, throwing itself off of the cairn and onto the stone. His paws caught the scars and gouges, and he pushed himself down the hill in a raging, roaring frenzy. Moss and dirt flew about him as he tore the ground with a ferocity unseen in centuries. Down the hill he ran, his mouth open with teeth bared and tongue lolling, until his paws hit the sidewalk and then the street. A pair of walking children stopped, their eyes agog and their jaws dropping, as the massive animal tore down the centre of the street. Around corners, past cars and pedestrians who paused in shock and wonder as they gazed upon the enormous wolfhound running through their midst.

The wolfhound crossed Colville Road and entered the ball field that lay before the low forested rise of the *Beinn nam Fiadh*. There were a few children tossing balls and they froze as the baying wolfhound ran amongst them. They watched as it exited the field and entered the forest where its barks and howls quickly faded in the growing shadow.

"Wow," said one young boy as he tossed a ball into the air and caught it, "you sure don't see that every day."

* * * * *

Jennifer climbed the stairs that entered High Rock from the western entrance. The sun was hours past its setting and the night had settled beneath a vault of darkness. The shadows beneath the trees were heavy and she had to pick her way through the growing darkness as she made her way towards the cairn. For a moment she paused, a keen understanding of the present danger growing within her. A gang was involved, Brittany had said. Jennifer mused as she leaned against the coarse bark of a Douglas fir. That could really mean anything, she reasoned. The E-town gang, Brittany had also mentioned. It didn't mean much to Jennifer beyond the general knowledge that they were a group of self-appointed toughs and punks. Dangerous? Sure, Jennifer thought, but how much so? Would they hurt her, like *really* hurt her?

Pushing her around, maybe a punch or kick or two, was one thing; but would they really hurt her?

Would she become another Reena Virk – murdered and cast aside by callous teens?

Jennifer gritted her teeth and clenched her fists. "'*S'rioghal mo dhream*," she whispered. "My blood is royal." She again stepped forward, walking carefully between trees and brush until she exited the forest and found herself approaching the cairn. The city lights were all around the hill with the only darkness coming from the low rise of the *Beinn nam Fiadh* across Colville Road. She looked around the summit and saw nothing except the stars above, the growing city lights, and the fading traffic noise; it was yet another beautiful, cool evening on High Rock in the township of Esquimalt.

"I didn't think you'd actually come," Brian Howard said as he stepped from behind a gnarled oak. "I thought you'd be a little bitch about this and chicken out."

Jennifer swallowed, took a deep breath and said, "You don't scare me, Brian."

Brian Howard ambled forward, his hands buried deep in the pockets of his hoodie. A sardonic smile crossed his face. "You may not be scared of me," he said with a malevolent snicker, "but I betcha you'll be scared of my friends."

From the forest came a number of figures, a dozen at least, Jennifer noted with sudden alarm. They were older teens mostly, probably seventeen or eighteen, and none of them looked friendly. She took a step back as they slowly surrounded her and she found herself standing beside the cairn.

"This your friend?" chuckled a tall swaggering punk in a hoodie and backwards ball cap. Jennifer recognized the face behind the lit cigarette as a twenty-year-old named Derek Fry, a somewhat notorious gangbanger wannabe and Esquimalt tough guy. He had a backpack slung over one shoulder as he pulled his cigarette out of his mouth and flicked it at Jennifer; the burning end struck her on the cheek and she cried out in pain.

The teens and Brian laughed.

"Scared ya?" Derek asked as he dropped his bag on the ground. "Brian here says you're a real little bitch to him in school; like to hit him and then hide behind the teachers." He smiled. "Are you a tough little bitch?"

"Tougher than Brian," Jennifer replied as she rubbed the burn on her cheek and cast a withering look on Brian. He blanched and stepped back.

"Yeah," Derek remarked as he pulled out another cigarette, "I'll bet you're real tough." He lit the cigarette and put away his lighter. "Tonight, we're gonna find out just how tough a bitch you are."

Jennifer found her eyes moving to the nodding, smiling faces around her.

"Only," Derek said as an evil smile grew, "you ain't gonna have a teacher to hide behind, right Brian?"

Brian Howard looked distinctly uncomfortable, as if he was privy to a very frightening piece of knowledge. "Uh, right, Derek."

"Right," Derek said as he cracked his knuckle. "So let's begin"

* * * * *

"Sith co nem.

Nem co doman.

Doman fo nim,

nert hi cach, an forlann,

lan do mil, mid co saith.

Sam hi ngam, gai for sciath,

sciath for durnd."

Aeonghus knelt before an oak, his head bowed and the hilt of the up-turned sword held tightly in his hands.

"Peace to the sky.

Sky to the earth.

Earth under sky,

strength in us all, a cup so full,

full of honey, mead in plenty.

Summer in winter, spear over shield,

shield strong in hand."

The sky was dark, haloed by branches of dried oak leaves and pine boughs that moved and rattled in the soft, cool breeze. Stars covered the sky like freckles, giving it a cheery mien that belied the grim urgency of the night. He had been feeling it – a growing unease as the darkness grew and the animals gathered. Behind him were dozens of shadows: deer, dogs, cats, racoons, rats, and squirrels while above owls, eagles, and hawks filled the tree branches; they were gathered and waiting for the signal that Aeonghus would lead them.

Aeonghus once again lowered his head.

"A mhic mo mhic's e thubhairt an rìgh,

Oscair, a rìgh nan òg fhlath,

Chunnaic mi dealradh do lainne's b'e m'uaill

'Bhi 'g amharc do bhuaidh 's a chath."

His lips moved and he whispered,

"Son of my son," said the king,

Oscar, king of young nobles,

I saw your shining blade and I was proud

to see your valour in battle."

Aeonghus took a deep breath and slowly released it. "Now is the time."

The wolfhound stood before the gathered animals, a powerful creature radiating a primal fury that had not been seen for an age. The mouth opened, baring the teeth and tongue.

"Lean gu dlù ri cliù do shinnsireachd 's na dìbir a bhi mar iadsan," he said as he gazed upon the assembled host. "Follow closely the ways of your ancestors and behave like them." The wolfhound turned and trotted down a narrow beaten trail through the brush and blackberry canes, well aware of the soft commotion of cracking branches that announced that the animals were following him. He glanced up and saw the shadows of a hundred raptors, owls, crows, and ravens leave the branches of the firs above to soar silently in the cool breeze, flapping to gain altitude in the night sky.

The line of animals entered a widened trail that led over a few acres of Garry oak meadow on military property. Glancing behind him, Aeonghus could see the growing line of animals led by the deer and dogs while the smaller creatures in the back fought to keep up. On his left and beyond the grassy field lay the military housing, and from there came four more dogs: a German shepherd, a pair of smaller mixed breeds, and a lumbering Saint Bernard. Another cat, two more racoons, and a score of rats joined the growing line as Aeonghus led them down the trail. The silence was intimidating, and he could feel their growing anger at his back. He could not recall the last time the animals had made a stand, certainly not in this new world; it would have been many centuries before in the old lands. And even then, he could barely remember it.

"*Us mairidh an iomradh 's an dàn air chuimhn' aig na baird an déigh so,*" Aeonghus growled from deep within his chest. "And their fame and fate will endure in the memory of the poets forever after."

The line of animals grew: proud bucks and determined does, a pack of growling dogs now numbering over a dozen, skittering racoons and cats, rats and squirrels, and now, a deeper shadow lurking through the tall lush grass. Aeonghus ignored the new arrival as he led them down the path towards the military soccer pitch on Colville Road. Above it was a small open field bordered by oaks and chestnut trees; here he paused to allow the ranks of his allies to gather. They formed a long silent line radiating rage, and the birds circled above as Aeonghus spied the lanky, shadowy shape lurking behind the deer which were nervously aware of its presence.

A stately form emerged from the shadows, and Aeonghus offered a bow to Quelatikan. "It is good tae see the *ty-ee* of the Esquimalt *tillicum* o' the *mow-itsh* this night."

Quelatikan looked upon his deer, now nearly twenty in strength, before grunting and taking his rightful place at their head. Aeonghus looked at the ranks of eager animals, friends and allies, and some, like the lithe animal that growled and entered the dim ochre street lighting, strangers that had answered the call. Aeonghus bowed to the cougar that sat on the moist grass beside the anxious deer with its tail flicking. "Greeting, *hyass puss puss*," Aeonghus said in Chinook Jargon, for this was an animal he had had no dealings with before. "*Kahta maika?*" The cougar yawned, ignored the question, and began cleaning its paw. Its yellowish eyes, however, never left Aeonghus.

Silence intruded. The dogs sat quietly, their tongues lolling; the deer fidgeted and flicked their ears; and the raccoons, squirrels, rats and cats stood expectantly. For a moment, Aeonghus could say nothing. Then, remembering the Irish words that had been floating in his mind, he roared, "*Na aobhar shininn mo làmh, le fàilte rachainn 'na choinnimh! 'Us gheibheadh e fasgadh 'us càirdeas, fo sgàil dhrithlinneach mo loinne!'*

He breathed in deeply and bellowed, "In his cause I would stretch out my hand, with a welcome I would go to meet him, and he would find shelter and friendship beneath the glittering shade of my sword!"

Aeonghus began a deep soulful baying that the other animals took up, a clamorous wailing howl that echoed off of the buildings around them. Above, ravens croaked, eagles screeched, owls hooted, and crows cawed. Then the swirling cloud of birds above straightened and headed for the nearby High Rock. Aeonghus watched them before his howling renewed and he led the line of animals to the entrance of the military hospital and down towards Colville Road.

"Cross the road!" he roared as he loped out onto the street and stopped as the headlights of a car fell upon him.

Tires screeched and the car came to a halt meters before the line of crossing animals. The door opened, and a gruff incredulous voice asked, "What the hell is going on?"

The bucks and does skipped across the road followed by the barking dogs, and then the cats, racoons, and smaller animals skittered into the light. The owner of the car stood astounded and wide-eyed as he watched the procession, but always his fearful face came back to the powerful wolfhound that stood staring at him, its hackles raised and its teeth bared.

"Holy shit, man," the driver said as he got back into his car.

The last of the animals had crossed to the sidewalk and were now moving with great purpose towards High Rock. Aeonghus led them with singular determination, ignoring the cats and dogs that ran to join the growing ranks of animals. He turned right onto Intervale Road and then made a swift left onto a bike trail that ran beside the E&N Railway tracks. Here it was dark, a lightless path with little chance of a random encounter. The animals crowded behind him as he led them east to Hutchison Road, another road that crossed their path. Here he paused and the animals surrounded him in a huffing mass. The road led south, rising swiftly over the lower reaches of High Rock. Houses lined the narrow road and the streetlights gave it a warm welcoming glow so much at odds with the simmering rage of the animals.

"There's a wee trail up and tae the left," Aeonghus growled as he stared towards the darkened summit of High Rock. He looked at the German shepherd who lowered its head in deference. "You'll take most o' the dogs and go up the street and stairs and intae the back entrance. Do not attack unless I give the word. Understood?"

The German shepherd again lowered its head.

Aeonghus looked at the deer with proud Quelatikan at their head. The cougar was sitting beside him and the tension between the two was palpable. Tonight they were allies, however, and Aeonghus would take them up the northern slope to the cairn.

"It will not take long for the policece to come," growled a voice from the darkness.

The deer were startled and they backed away from the voice. The dogs whined, the cougar hissed, and Aeonghus soon found himself alone before a deeper shadow in the night.

"Fachtna," he said in a flat toneless voice, "you've come."

From the darkness the deeper shadow moved until the small goat-headed *púca* was backlit by the dim light of a streetlamp. The animals were terrified of the unnatural vision and they crowded away further. Fachtna nodded towards the animals. "What will you do with that?" he asked. "There isss so much fear."

"Only of you," Aeonghus observed as he sat on his haunches. "It's no' often they see the *púca* away from the shadows of Macaulay," he retorted. "And what is it that brings you here?" He glanced up towards the hidden cairn. "Speak quickly."

Fachtna stepped forward, a silken, black finger outstretched and his golden goat eyes burning as he gazed upon Aeonghus. The curled burnished horns tilted as he cocked his head. "You are different, Aeonghusss," he whispered. He took another step forward so that his finger rested on the chest of the powerful wolfhound. "The *Geis* has been lifted."

"Aye, for now," Aeonghus replied.

Fachtna's eyes narrowed and a small smile crossed his muzzle. "The policccce," he repeated, "they will come and you will be caught. There may be fighting, shooting, maybe dying."

"Aye," Aeonghus replied with a nod and he caught his breath as the fear fought to return. "That may be." He glanced up to High Rock. "I'm running out o' time, Fachtna. What do you want?"

The *púca* stepped back and clasped his hands together while looking down. The massive horns and oversized goat's head on the small shrunken body was a nightmare vision, but to Aeonghus, there was a flash of the old childlike creature he had known so very long ago.

"I will buy you time," Fachtna said.

"Why?" Aeonghus replied, his voice sharp and suspicious.

Fachtna would not raise his head nor look Aeonghus in the eye. "Your friend," he hissed, "wasss very niccce to me. She wasss very niccce, Aeonghusss." He looked upon the wolfhound. "She isss like Muirne from so long ago."

"Aye," Aeonghus said after a long thoughtful pause. The distrust in his eyes softened. "She is." He looked upon the shrivelled *púca* now crumpled in miserable remembrance. "There is good in you, Fachtna. Muirne would be proud."

Fachtna did not look up.

Aeonghus looked once again at High Rock. "Whatever your idea is, Fachtna, you need tae do it now. I'm out o' time."

The *púca* fixed his gaze upon Aeonghus; his eyes grew in scorching brilliance. "You will have your time," he replied. "Do not fail, Aeonghusss. You must save her."

"I will no' fail, Fachtna. I will save her, whatever the cost."

Aeonghus watched the *púca* step back into the shadows and disappear. He glanced over to Quelatikan who moved up beside him. "I've no' a clue what he's about tae do, but I doubt we'll have a problem with the police for the next hour or so."

Quelatikan grunted and huffed through his nose.

"Aye," Aeonghus said. "Time tae go."

* * * * *

Fachtna ran as swiftly as his short legs would take him, ducking through the shadows and darkness as he raced back down the darkened bike trail towards Intervale Street. He came to the road, turned left and followed it as he ran up the middle of the rising street, heedless of the barking dog that had seen him, and the shriek of a woman getting out of her car. As he ascended the road to the top of the low hill, he ducked to the right and onto a darkened narrow trail meandering through a miniscule Garry oak meadow. This he followed until he exited onto another street, a narrow darkened dead-end road that ran south towards Esquimalt's Memorial Park.

"There isss good in me," he whispered.

The clatter of hooves suddenly echoed off of the rock walls and houses.

"Is that a freakin' horse?" a bewildered teenager on a smartphone asked his girlfriend as her thumbs were tapping out a text on hers.

The jet black horse with yellow eyes burning brilliantly in the night trotted down the centre of the road towards Memorial Park.

"There isss good in me," Fachtna repeated as he picked up the pace to a canter.

"That is a horse," the girlfriend, wide-eyed in surprise, said as the phone slipped from her hands.

The boy quickly entered 911 into his phone as he watched the powerful animal trot towards the park. "Hey," he said to the police dispatcher, "there's a freakin' horse in Memorial Park in Esquimalt, a big black one!"

Fachtna maintained a canter as he crossed the road and entered the small park. There were a handful of other people in the park on this pleasant October night; they were walking dogs, smoking in the bushes, or sitting at picnic tables and enjoying each other's company. All stopped to watch as the commanding obsidian horse cantered through the middle of the park with its eyes shimmering in the darkness.

"That's a horse!" cried one human as he stood up from a picnic table.

"There's a horse loose!" yelled another as he tried to snap a picture with his smartphone.

Fachtna came to a halt at the park entrance that faced Esquimalt Road. Traffic was light and the night air cool. He glanced to his right and saw the police car ambling down the road, its searchlight a penetrating beam that scanned the parking lots and darkened park.

Fachtna trotted out onto the street and turned left towards downtown Victoria.

* * * * *

"There it is," the police officer said as she placed the spotlight beam on the horse. "It is a horse too!" she said with a smile. "How the hell did that get out and where the hell did it come from?"

Her partner shrugged as he keyed his mike and reported it. "Dunno, but follow it, only not so close that you scare it."

"Thanks, John Wayne," she said as she rolled her eyes, "glad you're here to tell me that."

"Just sayin'," her partner replied. "Don't want you to have to explain why the car is beat up because you ran over a horse on Esquimalt Road."

"Smart ass."

"He's picking up the pace," the male police officer said as he pointed to the horse that was now cantering down the road.

"Doing twenty clicks now. Not bad speed." She eased down on the accelerator to keep up. "Wonder where he's going?"

"Don't know. Harry is blocking off Head Street. See if we can coral it."

"Cowboy," she chuckled.

"Don't lose the horse, Tex," he replied in a terrible southern drawl.

"Another great night in E-town," she laughed.

* * * * *

Fachtna knew the police car was following closely. He glanced back and saw the flashing red and blue lights at a respectful distance that was meant not to frighten him. Fachtna felt a smile cross his muzzle as he faced the road before him and breathed in deeply.

"Many the ragged colt became a noble horssse." The shimmering eyes burst in brilliance like a pair of radiant suns reflecting a pent-up eon of anger and regret.

"For the little girl named Jennifer," he sighed.

The jet black horse exploded into a gallop that sent sparks flying from its iron shoes.

"There isss good in me!"

* * * * *

"Holy shit!" the driver said. "That thing's doing eighty!"

"Keep up!" her partner responded as he grabbed the mike. "CD this, you're not going to believe this," he began. "I think we have an 11-30."

"Injured animal?" the driver asked as she sped towards Lampson Street with lights flashing and now, siren wailing.

"What the hell else do you call it? Besides, he will be when he gets up to Harry."

* * * * *

The lights and blaring siren were a distraction, but barely so. Fachtna's deep rhythmic breathing, the pounding hooves with waves of sparks dancing from them like fireflies, the billowing mane of coal black hair, and the burning eyes showed only a deep and extraordinary focus. He came around a bend, passed a slow moving pick-up so close that he ripped off the driver's side mirror, and then saw the intersection of Head Street and Esquimalt Road. A police cruiser was parked in the middle of it, lights flashing, and with a lone police officer standing by the opened door. Fachtna's eyes burned brighter as he dug deep into his strength, and his gallop increased. The mouth of the officer by the car dropped in shock, his hand moved to his pistol, and he screamed into a radio. Fachtna bore down upon him like a missile, and at the last moment, the officer dove into the front seat of his cruiser while Fachtna leapt easily over the hood of the car to continue on down Esquimalt Road towards Victoria.

* * * * *

Aeonghus stood at the base of High Rock, his ear cocked to the fading sirens. There were several, and he thought for a moment that he heard more in the distance. He fixed a questioning look on Quelatikan as he muttered, "It seems Fachtna has done his part." He looked at the deer and dogs as they stood in the darkness at the foot of High Rock. The slopes rose before him, tumbling folds of etched rock and thick grass. A cool breeze came from the west, one that held the raptors, ravens, owls, and crows aloft against the heavenly backdrop of stars. The other dogs, led by the German shepherd, would have ascended the forty-three steps of the western entrance of the park, Aeonghus surmised as he imagined their progress and the terrain. They would be in a position to attack when needed.

Quelatikan and the deer gathered around Aeonghus, silent and attentive, as the *ghille dubh* stared up at the darkened summit. He was motionless, a miniature statue staring intently, the targe hanging limply in one hand, the sword in a sheath on his back. Aeonghus breathed deeply and closed his eyes.

"*I see a great rage; the forest will fight back.*" Fionn had said.

"Aye, we will," Aeonghus murmured.

* * * * *

Jennifer was facedown over the cairn, a trickle of blood running down her lip after a slap by Derek. The teen pulled his ball cap off and made a gang sign as one of the older girls used her phone to snap a picture of him.

"I be like smackin' down the bitches," he said with a wide grin as he kicked Jennifer in the leg. She cried out, lost her balance, and then found herself lifted back to be face down on the cairn again. It had been this way for fifteen minutes now. A light beating, Derek called it – punches, kicks, slaps – nothing really hard yet, but terrifying all the same. It was escalating though, and the older teens were laughing and swearing, throwing a slap of their own or pushing her to the dirt while they chugged beer and smoked cigarettes. There was something in the mood that was growing altogether much more malevolent and Jennifer was thoroughly regretting the bravado that had brought her there. She glanced at Brian Howard who stood a few steps back from the cairn; he was pale and frightened, looking more like a terrified child than a bullying teen.

That frightened Jennifer even more.

Derek put his ball cap back on, swung it backwards as he stalked over to face Jennifer. He leaned down so that his foetid breath fanned her face. "Ma homey, Brian," he said in a gangsta speak that would have been laughable in another situation, "he be like, the bitch is always getting' me in trouble!" Derek slapped her face. "Is that true, bitch? Really, is that true?" The teens giggled as Derek lit a cigarette. "I mean, really now, what's Brian ever done to you." He glanced back at the boy who stood silent and horrified. "Whatever did you do to her?"

"Nothing," Brian whispered.

"Nothin'," Derek repeated as he faced Jennifer. He clenched his fist and punched her in the face, much harder this time. Jennifer shrieked as blood ran down from her split lip. "Now, it's in yo' best interest, bitch, that you be real quiet now, or it gets to be a lot more painful." The voice was malicious, a cold calculating evil, as he stood and walked to Jennifer's side. "Hold the bitch," he snapped.

Two teens grabbed her hands and held her down against the cairn. Derek clenched his fist and punched her in the side. Again he punched her, and again, as Jennifer grunted and muffled her shrieks, until he felt the ribs crack.

"Ow, man," he laughed and danced as Jennifer gasped and cried, "man, I bet that hurts!"

Jennifer sobbed from the pain in her side, a burning piercing agony that nearly made her faint.

"What do you think of that, Brian?" Derek asked as he took a drag off of his cigarette. "Think she'll hit you and nark on you?"

Brian said nothing but shook his head.

"No, I don't think so either." Derek moved to stand behind Jennifer as she lay bent over the cairn. "No, I think we can make sure she keeps real quiet." He eased a lock blade knife from his jeans and flicked it open. He moved closer until he was rubbing against Jennifer's legs and backside. Slowly, Derek slipped his hand beneath the waistband of her leggings as he bent over to whisper in her ear. "You'll have to be very quiet now," he hissed as he gripped the waistband and pulled it down a few centimetres. He placed the knife beneath her throat. "Be real quiet, now." He glanced up at Brian who was staring horrified at Jennifer. She was beseeching him and when he did nothing, she gritted her teeth and looked down.

"Yea, bitch," Derek said as he stared at the expectant faces of the teens around him and pulled the leggings down a few more centimetres, exposing her underwear, "now the party is really about to begin."

Jennifer closed her eyes. "I'll see you soon, Daddy," she whispered brokenly.

* * * * *

A feeling of intense revulsion fell upon Aeonghus and his eyes snapped open. It was a horrible fleeting image of Jennifer, bent over, in pain, and resigned to cruel

212

agony and death. Tears balled in his eyes and he choked back the grief and fear that throttled his breath. The revulsion was quickly replaced, however, by a white, hot rage that enveloped him. He hands shook as he climbed upon the back of Quelatikan and pulled out the sword given to him by Fionn so many centuries before. His friend was in mortal danger and he would save her, at whatever cost.

"Whatever the cost," he said out loud. Through eyes blurred by tears he looked skyward and said, "Now!"

Like a hailstorm, the heavens opened and unleashed a physical fury upon the summit of High Rock. In their hundreds, birds streaked from the sky: starlings, robins, chickadees, towhees and more. They fell upon the teens – shrieking, pecking, clawing, and batting with their wings. The teens cried out in pain and panic as they tried to flee, and Derek stood up in shock and released Jennifer's leggings.

"What the fuck!" he said as he raised the knife. From the darkness came a whipping shadow, and Derek's knife skittered across the rock and he was flung beneath the weight of a screeching bald eagle. Brian Howard threw himself to the stone while Jennifer, released by her tormentors, rolled off the cairn to curl up in agony by its side.

The birds dove, and then soared and attacked again. The teens' cries grew louder as the cuts and pecks drew blood, while the birds herded them each time they tried to break and run. Derek, enraged and terrified, grabbed a bat lying beside his backpack and swung at an owl flapping in front of one of the girls.

The bird fell to the ground dead.

"Come on you stupid fucking birds!" he shrieked as he swung at a Canada goose. The goose flapped and struck his arm with one of its wings. Derek cried out, swung the bat again, and broke the goose's neck. "Fuck you, bird!"

The throng of birds began to thin, leaving the teens bloodied and shocked. Derek was panting with blood running down his cheek and the bat spattered red when he saw the cats. "What?" he cried out as cats, racoons, and rats flooded around their feet. The cats clawed at legs, the racoons bit and chattered, and the rats ran up and over the teens' bodies. Derek kicked and danced and swung his bat, and all of the teens cried out with new pain and rage.

Barking came from below the lip of High Rock, and suddenly a half dozen dogs were jumping amongst them. Jennifer, crouched and holding her side, watched as a St. Bernard pounced on one of the female teens, and then barked and bayed while the girl punched it. A golden retriever ran at Derek, but he kicked it in the face and then struck it with the bat until it fell on its side. The summit was a living carpet of animals and struggling teens with two of their number already lying unconscious.

"Help me, Aeonghus," she cried as she gripped her side.

* * * * *

"Now!" Aeonghus touched the powerful haunches of Quelatikan and held on with his legs as the deer exploded up the hill with his *tillicum* at its heels. He leapt over the rolls of stone and between the brush and tall grass. Aeonghus raised his sword and cried out in rage as the buck ascended the hill; he could not remember when he had felt so terrified yet so alive. It was intoxicating.

Quelatikan topped the summit of High Rock and came to a skidding halt before Derek; the rest of the deer fanned out, kicking and pouncing on the struggling teens. Derek spied Aeonghus on the back of Quelatikan and his eyes widened.

"What the fuck are you?" he shrieked as he raised his bat. Quelatikan lowered his antlered head and charged. Derek swung; his timing was perfect and he hit the buck squarely on the head shattering one of its antlers to pieces.

Aeonghus threw himself off of the collapsing buck, rolled and came to a halt on his feet. He spared the deer a brief glance and then turned his rage on Derek.

"Now's the time you deal wi' me, boy!" he roared. Derek was still wide-eyed and in shock.

"What the fuck are you?" he shrieked as he raised his bat and stepped back.

Aeonghus raised the targe and laid the flat of his sword on its top edge. He inhaled deeply and then let it out. "Fear is worse than fighting!" He cried as he lunged forward.

Derek cried out and swung his bat, missing Aeonghus by centimetres as the *ghille dubh* ducked between his legs. A back swing from Aeonghus caught Derek on the calf, cutting through his jeans and slicing his flesh. As Derek hopped around in pain, he aimed a clumsy swing, missing widely as Aeonghus rolled beneath the

214

waving bat. Derek swung again and Aeonghus ducked each blow, stepping out of range or leaping aside until he ascended the cairn. Derek followed, a bestial look on his face as he aimed each clumsy swing.

Aeonghus parried a blow on his targe, ducked a second, stepped back from a third, and then as Derek screamed and swung his hardest, Aeonghus swung his sword and sliced the bat in half in an explosion of splinters. Derek held the shattered stump, gave Aeonghus a shocked and frightened look, and then dropped it and fled into the darkness.

The melee around Jennifer reached its peak as the animals pummelled the teens into silence. She was hugging her ribs and watching the terrible fury – as if two hundred years of pent up rage was being released. One girl lay unconscious on the ground, blood running from a slash on her brow. A boy in a jean jacket and holding a knife was staggering with blood running down his cheek, slashing at anything around him that moved. A buck bounced by, kicked him in the stomach, and as the boy dropped the knife and staggered, it spun and punched into him with its antlers.

Brian Howard was still cowering near the cairn. Cautiously he stood, owl-eyed in terror, looking around him for a way to escape. The animals had him surrounded, and as he pivoted in panic, a slinking shadow suddenly leapt and threw itself onto the petrified boy and crushing him to the ground. Brian shrieked and cried as the cougar placed its teeth over the boy's neck and bit down, softly without breaking the skin, and held him there.

"*Hyas puss puss*," Aeonghus said as he raised his hand, "you've made your point."

The cougar released Brian who was in a dead faint, and disappeared back into the darkness.

Slowly, the battle subsided until all of the teens had either fled or lay on the ground, battered and bleeding. Jennifer wiped the tears from her eyes as she looked upon the animals that lay dead and dying: a dog, two deer, a cat and a racoon, and a number of birds. Some were limping or whining in agony; the outcome of the brief battle had been horrific.

"Are you okay?" Aeonghus asked as he placed a small gentle hand on Jennifer's cheek. She shook her head and looked at her ribs. "Aye," he said as he touched them. She winced and he nodded. "Broken, but you'll live."

"You saved me," Jennifer whispered in between her short sharp breaths. "You saved my life."

"You are my friend," Aeonghus replied with a smile and a pat on her arm. "I would do anything to protect my friend."

"Even die?" Jennifer replied as she lay on her side and closed her eyes.

"Even die," Aeonghus agreed.

* * * * *

Derek wiped blood from his temple as he picked himself up after tripping over a fallen branch. In the darkness the bushes, tree roots, and rocks were grasping at his stumbling feet as if they were alive in their efforts to slow him down. He pushed through the brush, ascended a low mound of rock, and in the faint light saw a snarling German shepherd blocking access to the western exit of the park. He swore, dropped down off the rock, and pushed his way east towards the trails that eventually led to Lampson. His breath was puffing and his arm hurt where the eagle had hit it. He stumbled and fell, bashing his knee on a root.

"Fuck!" he shrieked as he stood. He spied a St. Bernard sitting on the trail a few meters in front of him, blocking the exit with a deep rumbling growl. He turned north, his faltering steps slowing as he climbed the rolling rock, and wriggled through Oregon grape and Indian plum. He was scratched and bloody, and there were growling dogs to the left and right of him, but nothing before him. "Fine!" he rasped as he found a trail and followed it. In his panic he lost his bearings, left the trail, found a new one, and ascended a small hill.

Derek found himself once again standing on the summit before the cairn.

"Shit!" he swore as he looked around the bloody chaos. Spotting his backpack nearby, he ran to it, ripped the zipper open, and pulled out a 9mm pistol. He cocked it and looked around in abating fear. "Who the hell wants some if this?" he yelled at the darkness. He saw Jennifer lying beside the cairn and the small figure of Aeonghus hovering over her. "You!" he roared with spittle running down his lips. "I'll fucking kill you!" He aimed the pistol at Jennifer.

Aeonghus stepped forward, braced himself on the pock-marked stone, raised his targe and placed the flat of the sword to rest on its lip aimed at Derek.

"No," he growled, his voice deep and grumbling from the rock, "no you will not. No' without going through me." He moved another step forward and Derek lowered the pistol to aim it at him.

"You suit yourself, whatever the fuck you are!" he aimed the pistol as the vision of the creature vanished to be replaced by a massive wolfhound. As the animal leapt at him, he pulled the trigger; the pistol jumped in his hand, and Aeonghus was bowled over by the bullet.

Jennifer, lying on her side and sobbing, reached out to touch the wolfhound. "Aeonghus," she mouthed through her tears.

"You're next," Derek said as he aimed the pistol at Jennifer. She closed her eyes, waiting for the crack of the weapon and the burning pain.

None came.

From the darkness came the animals – a circle of boiling fury that surrounded Derek and Jennifer and the cairn – deer, dogs and cats, raccoons, and rats. Derek stepped back, raised the pistol to aim at the various animals, swinging the weapon around in growing panic as they closed on him.

"Stay back!" he shouted as he aimed the pistol at Quelatikan, and then pointed it at the skulking cougar. He swung it towards the German shepherd and then back to Jennifer. "Stay back!"

The animals advanced; their silence was menacing as they approached with slow measured steps. There was a lethal anger in their eyes and Derek's hand shook. "Stay back or I shoot her!" The animals approached, slower, more cautious, but they still came on.

"I warned you!" Derek said as he waved the gun and aimed it again at Jennifer. "She dies!"

"No!"

The voice was deep and powerful, and emanated from the forest. There was a cracking of brush being pushed aside and the snapping of branches between heavy footsteps. Derek turned to look behind him and into the darkness. The noise increased as the footsteps grew louder, and he saw a shadow moving amongst the trees. It was a massive figure, striding purposefully as its powerful arms pushed its way through; its eyes burned with a fiery glow that was terrifying. It was the head, however, that terrified Derek as the starlight and the sliver of waning moon fell upon it.

It was a massive stag's head.

The pistol fell from Derek's fingers as he stared at the approaching creature. It towered above him, as broad as an ancient oak, and there was a malevolence in its eyes that nearly made him faint.

"What the hell?" he squeaked as the creature mounted the low stony rise of the cairn.

Herne reached out a massive hand and grasped the neck of Derek, lifting him off of his feet as if he weighed nothing. His pace did not slow as he walked towards the cairn with Derek struggling in his grasp, nor was it slowed as he mounted the stone cairn. With one foot on top, Herne raised the wriggling Derek high above him and slowly brought him towards his muzzle. Derek shrieked in horror as the magnificent stag's head melted away to reveal a hideous rotted skull with burning eyes and a fiery glow from the cavern of its mouth.

"I am the forest," Herne whispered as he brought Derek close. Suddenly both vanished.

Jennifer had watched as Herne and Derek disappeared but now she turned to the still figure of the wolfhound as it lay on its side. "Are you alright?" she asked, her voice faint.

"Aye," Aeonghus replied after a long pause. "Well, maybe not."

Her hand was pale in the starlight as it reached out to touch the bloody wound in Aeonghus' shoulder; it was gaping and raw. Jennifer fought new tears as she placed the flat of her hand on his chest.

The *ghille dubh* appeared lying on his back.

"Help me up," he said, his voice weak and thin.

Jennifer helped Aeonghus to sit and held him there as Quelatikan, limping and missing one of his glorious antlers, stepped up to them.

"Put me on his back, will you?" Aeonghus gasped.

Jennifer lifted the *ghille dubh*, feather light and faint, and placed him on Quelatikan's broad back. Aeonghus leaned against the deer's neck, unmoving and weak, as he stared at Jennifer.

"You're safe now," he whispered.

Fresh tears rolled down Jennifer's cheeks; she brushed them away on her sleeve. This was good-bye, she realized. "I'll miss you," she said her voice thickened by grief.

"I'll miss you too, lass."

Quelatikan gave a small toss of his noble head and stepped forward into the darkness of the forest.

Jennifer sank down to lean against the cairn. Her broken ribs were burning and there was dried blood on her face and arms. The summit had been cleared of the terrible detritus of the brief battle. The animals that had died had been spirited away, and the teens, beaten and bloodied, had come around and limped off. It was over – the adventure that had begun only three weeks before was over. The *ghille dubh* named Aeonghus, the mysterious little creature who had saved her life, who had led her into a new understanding of her existence where there were no absolutes, where mystery and answer existed, where hope was now a steady companion, was gone. The loss she felt was great, a piercing agony of grief. Yet, there was more. There was the hope that Aeonghus had given her; Jennifer MacGregor was no longer alone, had never been alone, and would never be alone. There would always be someone in the shadows watching.

It just wouldn't be Aeonghus.

As Jennifer wept at the loss of her friend, for the creature who had saved her life twice, a voice sounded as a beam of light played over her.

"I'm Constable Merrick, Victoria Police. Are you okay, miss?"

Jennifer hugged herself and cried.

Part Seventeen

Garbh-innse nan Ùirsgeulan

The Big Telling of Stories

Jennifer MacGregor-Lovette sat on a half-buried log that had likely been sitting on the beach below Dallas Road for fifty years. It would have washed ashore when she was a child, she mused, as her hand ran over its bleached surface. It was smooth, soft, almost mirror like after so many hot summers and pounding winters. A smile crossed her weathered face; there was such a simple pleasure in the touch of the wood. It could tell you a story if it felt so inclined. This one did not.

Clover Point stretched out on her left, packed now with tourists on the hot summer day. Kites flew in the cool south-westerly breeze blowing through the traditional summer fog bank on the Salish Sea that ran the length of the Straits of Juan de Fuca. It was altogether a pleasurable day where children played, young lovers clasped hands, and Jennifer MacGregor-Lovette knew she was about to die.

The meeting with her doctor had been sympathetic in its institutional tones – the therapies had not worked and the brain tumour was beyond medical help. She had weeks, perhaps a month.

Jennifer's husband was gone; he had left her at the diagnosis a year before. He was never strong nor, Jennifer decided, terribly committed to the relationship. They could have ended it any time, but twenty years of marriage had its own momentum, one that only a potentially terminal medical condition seemed to have any success at stopping. She hadn't been devastated to see him go; the awkwardness of trying to find common ground as their relationship crumbled was too much. Jennifer wished him well, helped him pack, and then never saw nor heard from him again.

Jennifer's mother was gone as well, dead many years before from her drinking. Their relationship had survived, prospered maybe. The revelation from her father – that one snippet of information – had saved them. Yet it had damned their relationship as well for Jennifer could never tell her mother the true source, and her mother never fully accepted that it had been a dream. Jennifer was happy with the outcome in the end, for it was so much more than she could have hoped for. She knew her father and mother were together now with her brother or at least she believed they were. The years had dulled the memories of those three weeks to mere whispers and there were times she wondered if any of it had ever happened.

The cool breeze died away as Jennifer recalled the doctor's words "I'm sorry, Jennifer, we've done all we can." They had done all they could, she thought, as tears rose in her eyes. Now, all she could do was wait for the death that was coming for her.

The tears rolled down her cheeks; she tried to remember the vague memories of her childhood, but they would not come. Maybe they were just illusions, she thought with growing dread. All her anxieties returned; the fears she had fought for so many years rolled around her like a rising tide. She brushed her hand over her eyes, blinked away the fresh tears, and looked across the waters to the majestic Olympic Mountains.

The rippled ocean dazzled her in the warm afternoon sun, forcing her to squint against the brilliant bursts of light as the ocean surged and danced as if in celebration of its simple joy of life. A kite boarder struggled in the gasping breeze while friends in the surf up to their knees egged her on with friendly jests; three children worked with studious focus on a sandcastle, gathering drift wood for the perimeter wall; and an elderly couple wearing matching sunhats sat on a pair of beach towels holding hands, enjoying the pleasure of being together on the beach in their old age. The world had proceeded past that dark October night so many years before, Jennifer mused with a wistful sigh, when the dream of the forest spirit had come to her.

Another tear rolled down Jennifer's cheek.

The heavy footsteps were surprisingly soft, barely noticeable on the gravel beach. As Jennifer wiped her tears and looked upon the distant bobbing head of a harbour seal that seemed oddly fixated on her, a shadow fell upon her, blocking out the beaming brilliance of the sun. The silhouette that stood beside her was massive and a sudden feeling of longing and joy came over Jennifer; one she had not felt in many years.

A hint of a smile came to her face as new tears fell down her cheeks, and Jennifer choked, "Hello, Aeonghus, I've missed you."

The wolfhound stepped closer, its towering head above her shoulder. He leaned his bulk against Jennifer in a sign of affection and lowered his head onto her shoulder.

"I've missed you too, lass," Aeonghus murmured.

Jennifer leaned back and sighed.

"Come, Jennifer, it's time tae come home."

The End

About the author:

Sean Pól MacÚisdin grew up in the Okanagan Valley, British Columbia, enjoying the outdoors and the simple life before choosing a career in the Canadian Navy. Although he saw many countries during his career, it is the fjords and bays of the coast of British Columbia that inspire him most with their rugged beauty and awesome sense of isolation. Although his writing career was slowed by his time at sea and raising a family, it has renewed itself in the world of the ebook.

Other books published by this author:

Europa Rising: The Divine Hammer

Jupiter Rising: The Columbus Protocols

The Scarlet Bastards – A Company Soldier

The Scarlet Bastards – The Cardinal of Gleann   Ceallach

Made in the USA
Charleston, SC
23 June 2016